So Much Joy

Linda Jewel

Writers Club Press
San Jose New York Lincoln Shanghai

So much joy

All Rights Reserved © 2000 by Linda Jewel

No part of this book may be reproduced or transmitted in any form or by any means, graphic, electronic, or mechanical, including photocopying, recording, taping, or by any information storage or retrieval system, without the permission in writing from the publisher.

Published by Writers Club Press
an imprint of iUniverse.com, Inc.

For information address:
iUniverse.com, Inc.
5220 S 16th, Ste. 200
Lincoln, NE 68512
www.iuniverse.com

This is a work of fiction. Names, characters, places and incidents are either the product of the author's imagination or used fictitiously to give the story a sense of reality and authenticity. Any resemblance to actual persons, living or dead, is entirely coincidental.

ISBN: 0-595-09854-1

Printed in the United States of America

Dedication

To Ingrid E.

Acknowledgements

I am totally grateful to everyone who encouraged and motivated me to write this book.

My friends, including Bigi and Jan, my strongest supporters, helped to make my job easy.

Kathleen, I love you for editing my book in no time. You have been so patient with me and you understand me like no other.

Mama and Daddy, you are at the top of my list, and so are you Aunt Jewel: I miss all of you.

1

Fall, 1993

The weather Saturday night in late October was no different from the temperature the night before. Frigid breezes slapped against walls of fresh stucco on the buildings outside, where busy parents, bundled like Eskimos, put up decorations for the Fall Festival planned for tomorrow. No one knew it would be that cold so early in the season but the Homeowner's Association voted unanimously for the annual event, for the children. The condominium complex was just a year old with the last unit completed only six months ago. My neighbors worked on the project like they had known each other for years. I did not want to participate. It was just too cold.

A very light, almost invisible blanket of cigarette smoke traveled toward a slightly open bedroom window, only to be sucked outside in the swift moving current. A blast of cold air caused the sheer curtain panel to drift upward, allowing more ventilation in my room.

I got up right away from the upholstered chair at the dressing table. I had been sitting there smoking my last cigarette, talking on the phone, trying to stay warm. What remained of the smoke in my bedroom seeped into the peach curtains and the comforter. Damn. I just washed this stuff. On my way to the window I pulled the silky robe I was wearing closer to my body and retied the belt to keep my legs warm. I had just shaven them. Why did I need to smoke that cigarette anyway?

Instead of going back to the dressing table I stood at the window and looked down, at neighbors who were setting up game booths, and draping them with cut out cardboard witches, spiders, and scary looking cats that crawled around jack-o-lanterns and scary skeletons. That would scare the brats. I saw swirling leaves picked up by wind that tossed them in the courtyard.

I turned around and looked at a copy of Vogue magazine on my bed, the last journal in the stack of magazines I forced myself to read that night. I sat on the edge of my bed and opened the magazine. I didn't think it made sense to subscribe to magazines if I wasn't going to read them. So, once a month I would spend a quiet evening reading Essence, Family Circle, Ebony and Vogue. Earlier that evening I had read an article in Ebony about healthy relationships and what a person needed to do in order to have and keep one. I was no closer to experiencing bliss with a man than I was before I read the damn article. The standards in that article were too high for the men I knew.

I put the magazine down, gently shook my head, and decided that like me, Pam didn't know what she was going to do with her men either. It was crazy at times for her, just like it was for me. I didn't have an answer for her, or for myself. I was no expert. "I love him, Sasha", Pam sighed on the phone, earlier. The man she sighed about was getting out of prison. Soon. I tried hard not to be judgmental about Pam and her love life, especially with my own life the way it was. Involvement without commitment was my safe reality, but with Pam, it was a little different. My relationships with men were very short lived. Always have been. Pam's relationships always seemed dragged out.

My first marriage was brief. No experience. And my second trip to the alter was a disaster when one day I realized I married a man I didn't even like. Both times I just did it. I didn't know either spouses very well beforehand. I did it and regretted it later. And after both divorces I swore I wouldn't do it again. I'm hoping my last divorce taught me never to kid myself about love again. I learned that it's important to take time to know the man first, if you plan to spend the rest of your life with him. I also learned the value of a healthy sense of humor. I dream of the day a man will come into my life and stick around long enough for me to watch his hair turn white. Mine remains the same natural color, of course. But with each passing day, that reality is more and more remote.

My two children insist that I keep my current style and modern look. The *bomb* mom of the nineties. My daughter, Eileen, lets me know when it's time to get my braids done. She suggests styles she thinks will continue to conceal my forty-something age. I like a style that curves braids gently under my chin in a pageboy. It creates a frame for my high cheekbones. I got the smooth skin and pecan eyes from my mother, features I thank her for. My black rimmed circular eyeglasses make me look studious, plus I need them so I can see. Occasionally I wear contact lenses, but it's less hassle to just put on the glasses. My son Teddy, likes to see me in my Gap jeans, My tapered legs fill them out politely. Eileen envies my bust line and hates having to wait on motherhood before she sees full development.

I thank the Lord for blessing me with my talents that always kept me occupied. I declared myself a Fashion Designer when I learned how to sew in junior high. I was good at it.. I realized it as my true passion after years of teaching school. As a kid, I could always grab a piece of fabric and a pattern, and get totally consumed. I would escape to the world of high fashion and make unbelievable costumes. My dolls were my models back then.

Now I prefer using my own body as a mannequin. The one I purchased is in the garage gathering dust. There wasn't enough space in the condo for it, so I dragged it out. I bumped into it one time too many. My body is much better anyway. I am a slave to my sewing machine. I don't mind because I know one day my hard work will pay off. I want to manufacture my designs. Love interests never keep me from designing. If it weren't for my craft, I would be a candidate for a mental hospital.

A long time ago, I thought I was cursed with an overactive libido. In retrospect, my desires turned out to be a blessing. I was gang raped by guys I knew, after a tutoring session, off the campus where I was going to school. I thought they were friends. The ultimate betrayal opened my eyes. It was impossible to comprehend why they did that to me. In order to survive the ordeal, I had to pretend it was a sick sex fantasy of mine.

I could hear the howling wind outside my window, gaining momentum and volume with every clock stroke. Teddy knocked two times on my bedroom door, then came in.

"Mom! Do you hear that wind outside?" He walked to the window and moved the curtain aside so he could look out. He looked down at the activity on the ground below. "What are they doing down there?"

"Yes I hear it. They are decorating for the Fall Festival tomorrow. They should be finished by now. But if they aren't, they're crazy."

I thought he knew about the decorating party. And since he hadn't mentioned it, I decided not to say anything, knowing he would want us to take part. He wasn't dragging me out of my warm condo to decorate for some party.

"Mom, why didn't *we* help?" Teddy asked me this in an irritated way.

I was too busy thinking about the conversation I had had earlier with Pam to answer him. Pamela Best, a registered nurse and my best friend, told me earlier I was being overly concerned about a picture I saw on the dresser of my lover. The picture was of his x-wife. "It's only a picture", Pam said, but I thought there was more to it than that.

"Mom..." Teddy was standing right in front of me, wondering what planet I was on. I looked up at him, "What did you say, honey?"

"Why didn't we go down to help decorate?"

"Baby, do you hear that wind?"

Teddy shrugged his shoulders and left the room leaving me to my thoughts. Thoughts about Pam.

I had listened to Pam say *'Over a picture? You're upset over a picture?'*, for the tenth time that weekend. I had heard enough. Why couldn't she understand why I was upset about the picture? She was the only person who really knew me. We'd been friends since kindergarten. She must have forgotten how possessive I am.

Earlier on the phone I gave in and admitted to her that my reaction to the displayed photograph was a bit much, but I made no apologies. I just kept asking myself why Pam badgered me that way. Making me feel guilty about being jealous. I wanted to hang up on her, and get back to my sketching. The daily phone call of support had an unfavorable result.

I love my tiny best friend, Pam, who, like me, has not changed much over the years. Pam likes dooky braids she wears up high in a pony tail. The style is cute on her. She's barely five feet tall with a mean streak as wide as the Santa Monica Freeway. We've been through a lot.

When we were teenagers, we left parties so wasted that Pam would refuse to drive her car down a simple hill, always asking me to drive. Like a fool, I would get behind the wheel of her huge Oldsmobile and drive it as straight as I could, down the hill. Our speed of travel always depended upon what we had at the party and how loaded we were after that. Everyone drove down a hill leaving View Park. During those times, we rubbed elbows with celebrities who lived in View Park. People who lived in the hills gave good parties. Especially those with money. After a party, all I knew was that I had to get both of us back to South Central in one piece. I always thought about my electric blanket waiting for me at home. I just concentrated on getting us there. Pam's mind was altered and she couldn't remember how I had saved her life, one more time. We had major problems back then.

As usual, talking about men had been our main topic of conversation on the phone. I did not fully trust my new friend, Rod, and Pam was not sure about her friend either.

"Now finish telling me about Rod," blurted Pam without a hello earlier that evening.

"Oh, we just got a few things straightened out," I replied. "We just need to remember to respect each other's viewpoint". I continued, "I let him know he was being insensitive about the picture. I told him I accept the fact he can't see my point about it. But everything is okay now. He's not upset or anything..."

"Oh, see, I told you...Girl, you sure tripped over a picture! A picture!" said Pam. I didn't think Pam was qualified to comment on this, because *her* man, Pookie, was in State Prison. Again. But I listened to her anyway. Pam didn't want the people she worked with at the hospital to know about him, that she was waiting for him to come home reformed, and get a real job, and love her forever. Unrealistic, okay? How many times had I heard this? Too many to count. I shook my head, really hard this time. I knew that tall, crazy Pookie could go off on Pam anytime and that made me uncomfortable. I understood Pam's disappointment with men. I've been there too. When a man gets out of the joint, there's no way to know how he'll adjust. But Pam was committed to making it work, no matter what. I wanted what was best for my friend, but I knew what Pam was up against.

At about midnight I heard faint sounds of music videos coming from Teddy's bedroom. I got up and went across the hallway to wish Teddy goodnight, only to find him sleeping soundly, snoring, like his father.

I turned his television off, and the pole lamp from the switch panel by the bedroom door. I checked to make sure all was safe, and quietly closed the door.

On the way down the dimly lit staircase leading into the living room, I caught a stabbing draft of cold air between my legs. I walked a little faster to the thermostat. The vertical blinds in the living room were still open like they had been all day. I thought about the good sense I had to get out of Los Angeles and looked at the amber lights on the desert floor that resembled a blanket of pavé diamonds. I smiled when I thought about the great deal I got when I purchased the condo, although it was much smaller than I would have liked. The two bedrooms were all I needed, since Eileen decided to move out. It was peaceful living in the north desert, away from Los Angeles. I found comfort in the dry land and Joshua trees, even though I knew it was hot as hell in the summertime. I knew there was little to distract me from sketching and sample making. A little discomfort from the heat would be worth it. No night clubs to speak of, unless I was interested in country western or jazz. The party scene was out for me anyway. I gave up alcohol. I gave up teaching too, deciding never again to allow someone else's child to abuse me in the classroom. I closed the blinds.

I looked for peace in my life I knew would come only from solitude and a commitment to satisfying myself. I learned to see humor in all things, no matter how bleak the situation was. That was a given. And the occasion to look on the bright side of things came often. I still struggled with unhappy childhood experiences that forced me to develop an aggressive subordinate personality, a personality that shielded me from predators in the neighborhoods of Los Angeles.

Physical and emotional pain chaperoned my growth and caused a protective person to develop inside of me. My basal ego developed around age sixteen. The result of exclusion and years of teasing by male classmates. I had no problem making friends with girls in school. They liked me. And I liked them. But if any of them lived in Nickerson Gardens, I was not allowed to visit or play with them. 'Nickerson had a reputation for breeding socially unacceptable types', Mama said. Some of the kids I knew from there *were* arduous, street wise, and ready for anything. For me, that was cool. The unspoken rule at home was never to mention Nickerson Gardens. So I didn't and grew up always wondering what it was like in the projects. The *Gardens.* I knew from experience with people I made friends with at school, that they *all* were not bad. Later on when difficult times challenged me at every turn, I relied on the outrageous tenacity of my east side nemesis, Shaquita. Shaquita was the personality that developed unconsciously when I knew those people I was going to school with. Shaquita didn't take *shit* from anyone and would curse you quick. When I started having problems, Shaquita took on a life of her own inside of me. It's funny when I think about it now.

In the years following high school, I knew some things I was doing were not always right. At age eighteen, Pam and I knew we had no business on 103rd and Grape Street past midnight, but at the time, we thought it was safe to go where the party was with our other friends. My parents never found out we crossed Figueroa and traveled to the

East side. Pam and I knew how to take care of ourselves and always got to safety if we had to. People from the East side knew their own and resented preppie-types in their neighborhood. We were Preppy types. That was reason not to stay in Watts very long.

By the time I realized my parents had been correct in assessing how different our family was from *those people*, my personality had acquired another side that would be known only to those who encountered me outside of my parents home and church. After dark, when a bad situation warranted a slick solution I would become Shaquita, who could talk her way out of any threatening situation. Shaquita would stoop to any level for revenge. The assimilation of Shaquita into my confused life was complete by my twenty-first birthday.

I simplify survival by allowing Shaquita to quietly reside inside me. I realized the self-made armor was necessary to protect me from the additional emotional pain and scars inevitable in life. When Shaquita struggled to come out, she was quickly halted by a new set of principles I imposed for myself. My own boundaries of control.

I walked to my work area near the dining room table. Earlier, I finished a blouse that took only days to complete. Using light from the illuminated curio in the living room, I picked up scraps of fabric and thread trimmed from the blouse that littered the carpet and table top. I thought about how my sewing machine had saved me so many times from mischief early in my life. When I was a young teen, I wanted to run with friends other than Pam, but later found out my other girlfriends were doing things with boys I was not ready for. I was always on the sewing machine and told my mother to tell my friends I was busy when they called. I realized it was best that I stayed at home and out of trouble. I didn't want to give them any reason to think I was ever naughty.

I was not yet ready to go upstairs, so I sat down at my work table to finish a sketch. I added features to the face on the sketch pad in front of me and saw a distinct resemblance to someone I had known years ago. I erased and made changes numerous times until I saw the face and body of a friend from design school, a perky southern blonde, named Cindy. In school twenty years ago, we were best friends.

She became a friend, looking like Leeza Gibbons. The friendship was too much for the black students in our class to handle but we didn't care about what they had to say. We each possessed what the other lacked in skill. Cindy and I quickly became friends and realized we had a lot in common. She was an inspiration to me when I was learning how to draw. She had a natural talent for sketching. For her, sketching was much easier than sewing. She made me comfortable with sketching. But the girl couldn't sew.

On the sketch pad, I began to draw a full length gown on the body of the sketch that had become Cindy. I painted the evening gown a deep royal blue, to match her eyes that carefully glanced downward at a sapphire tennis bracelet that loosely dangled from the wrist. I placed a few dabs of metallic paint in the penciled area of the shoe peeking from under the dress. There was no need to mix paint for the complexion tone. The sketch of Cindy was perfect the way it was. I was pleased.

While sitting there, I thought of my upbringing, which invaded the quiet moment I was having. I wished my father had bounced me on his knee when I was young. Instead, he whipped my ass on what seemed like a regular basis. In my family, my mother was the dictator, and my father was the enforcer. Had I been a quiet child, I would not have gotten so many whippings. I was outspoken and my frequent opinions guaranteed frequent punishment. My father would never discuss the transgression for the whippings. Instead he would reach for the belt buckle at his waist. The clanging sound of the metal prong that disengaged from the leather holding point lives with me to this day.

The leather strap flew through the belt loops with the speed of lightening and went directly to the bulls eye that was always somewhere on my ass. I felt lucky though, because he never hit me in the face or drew blood. The day after a beating he always acted like it never happened and was actually nice to me. This blew my young developing mind causing me to have a strange respect for my father. He would never discuss a whipping later, never.

The only way to be happy is not to be seriously involved with anyone. I turned all the lights out and went back upstairs to my bedroom. Instead of going to bed, I began reading another article in Ebony.

*   *   *

"If I could just get through one day without someone abusing me, I might be able to spend that million dollars I dream about every night." Pam mumbled to herself the next morning as she stormed out of the hospital room and down the empty hallway to the nurses station. She slammed the aluminum medical chart down on the counter and stood there boiling with her hands on her hips.

"Who does that bitch think she is?" she finally said.

Everyone at the nurses station knew who the *bitch* was. It was Needa Stream, the rich black lady from Dallas, who recently moved back to Southern California. She was difficult to deal with and incapable of showing kindness to anyone, not even her doctors. Needa acted like she was the only cardiac patient on the floor. She claimed no one was capable of taking care of her. In reality, she was in the best facility for cardiac care in the city and had the best doctors her money could buy. She demanded a private room, because she didn't want to spend money to have a roommate investigated. She trusted no one.

"She insisted I wash my hands before touching her IV! Then she wanted me to empty her fuckin' bedpan!" Pam made her comments to no one in particular. She was pissed off.

Pam had her own physical problems. Twenty years of nursing caused strain on her body and mind. The backaches had become a nagging problem. Before she became a RN, she was a private duty nurse, and cared for wealthy incapacitated patients who couldn't move an inch without her help. She always bent over backwards to please her patients, especially the ones who complained the most. Her tiny frame gave way after years of lifting and moving bodies twice her size which left her with chronic low back pain, eventually causing her to have other physical problems. She loved her profession but she knew that at some point she would walk away from it. She was getting tired of being mistaken for a nurses' assistant. The long hours and hard work she did in school for the degree was supposed to give her new status, but lately she wondered if it was worth all the effort. Some patients were downright mean to her and the last thing Pam wanted was a repeat of her childhood. Like me, her experience growing up at home was no fun even though she did her best to please her parents. Pam tried to overcompensate for the loss of her baby sister who, at age two, was run over by a car. Pam was four years old then.

Pam and her sister were outside in front of their house. They had moved dolls and toys to the curb where they sat with their feet dangling in the water that flowed down the street. Pam forgot to get a toy she left on the porch. When she got up to get it, the baby wandered out into the street, right into the path of a moving vehicle. The tragedy happened the day before Pam's fifth birthday, leaving a legacy of pain to follow on every birthday thereafter. The drunk driver had no idea the bump he felt under his wheels was a small child. Thinking nothing of it, the driver kept going. He was eventually apprehended and prosecuted, but Pam was left emotionally devastated long before justice was served.

"Pam, are you doing the meds?" Her train of thought was interrupted by the voice of a fellow nurse.

"It's been done. I'm going to lunch." Pam's response was one of total disgust.

With all the strength she could gather, she walked around the counter, grabbed her purse and disappeared into a waiting elevator nearby. All she could think about was getting out of the hospital. If she could have at least one hour a day off the hospital grounds, she could perform her duties with maximum results. In the elevator, Pam kept hearing Needa's whining voice and wanted to stay away from the hospital, for as long as she could. She decided to spend her lunch hour in the park across the street, where it was peaceful and quiet. In the park, however, she relived the distant echoes of her mother's voice in her head.

Pam's mother started drinking when her baby sister died. She was a nurse too and insisted upon a very organized, beautifully decorated, germ free home. Pam's weekend chores often resembled those of a slave, unreasonably confining her to the house until all work assigned had passed inspection. The kitchen was the hardest room to clean. The all white kitchen sparkled down to its white linoleum floor that had to scrubbed with Brillo pads, weekly. There were to be "No scuff marks, ever!" her mother would scream. Pam would remain on all fours until the task was done right. Nona, Pam's mother, drank because of the pain associated with the loss of her child. She told Pam she never held her responsible, although when the housework was assigned, it seemed like Pam was being tortured. Nona was incapable of making the connection between her drinking and the drunk driver who killed her child. She became the alcoholic she hated and continued to drink to find answers.

Pam lay on the grass in the warm sun thinking about Needa Stream and wondering why she and Nona, now deceased, were so much alike. Needa was particular about her surroundings like her mother. Needa's private hospital room was always decorated with pictures of dearly departed family members and every type of floral arrangement imaginable. Pam believed she sent the flowers to herself because no one could possibly like the self-centered sick woman that much. Needa had a small table brought in just to hold the flower overflow and her lotion and perfume collection. Eccentric Needa insisted upon using her own bed linen while in the hospital. She had the carefully laundered sheets and pillowcases brought in each morning and always gave instructions on how they should be put on her bed. The tramp.

Needa's episodes of dizziness and shortness of breath brought her to the hospital unexpectedly. This time, not giving her enough time to close a real estate deal, she was rushed off from her house under sirens and flashing lights. She was upset about the missed opportunity to make money and brought the bitterness with her to the hospital, as usual. The doctors told her of the necessity to stay calm in a crisis, but Needa refused to listen. Her irate state contributed to the clogged arteries and increased heart rate she had. She continued to defy the reality of her condition, not making it easy on herself or the hospital staff. The recent loss of yet another business deal because of her health made her angrier than ever.

Pam sat up on one elbow and glanced at her watch. The hour passed too quickly. She looked up at the tall antique healing factory across the street and took a deep breath. She questioned herself about how much longer she could allow herself to be tortured in the name of work. She shook her head when she stood up. A blast of warm air hit her in the face when she turned into the sun. She walked back across the street to rejoin the daily grind.

Pam crossed the street, and thought about Sasha, who had been treated there recently for a broken ankle. She was amazed at how well Sasha had gotten around with a cast on her leg, never slowing down long enough to complain about it. Sasha broke her ankle while playing with Teddy. They were in the desert close to their home when, in her youthful state of mind, she leaped over a wall, not knowing the ground was lower on the other side. She crushed her ankle on the impact.

Pam always admired Sasha's spunk. She knew she had little patience for people who did not fight to overcome obstacles. Right after the cast was put on her leg, she took two Tylenol-3 for pain and headed straight to a lover's house for comfort. The thought of her being sexy with a cast on her leg made Pam laugh out loud.

By the time the elevator doors opened to the cardiac care floor, Pam was feeling strangely rejuvenated. The fresh air had done her some good. For the remainder of her shift she decided to keep her distance from Needa. She was not the only patient on the floor.

As Pam walked down the hospital hallway she switched her thoughts to Pookie, whom she knew needed her the most. She was silently planning her next visit to see him, hoping that he would not be in lock-up again. She hated to waste an all day trip to the prison only to find out that he could not have any visitors because of his smartass mouth.

* * *

A few years ago Pam and I lived next door to each other in Culver City and drinking had been a problem for us. We were notorious for dressing up and going out. We were always flawless when we stepped out for a night on the town. We would leave our apartments arm in arm, ready to party. Savvy, we knew everyone, even the bouncers at all the clubs in Inglewood. The bouncers would usher us right in the clubs past the long lines of waiting customers, always going in through the VIP entrance.

We made our usual trek to the bar, claimed our stools for the evening, and the fun would begin. Two shots of cognac, always Remy Martin and, as we took our first sip we would decide if we needed to chase it with 7-Up, or not. By the time we finished our cognac, an unsuspecting gentleman would appear and offer to buy us more.

The men knew the rules. Two ladies were together and no matter who he wanted to talk to, both needed drinks. Long Island Iced Teas were the drinks we ordered because of the potency, and before long, one of us needed to pay a water bill. The action of getting to the restroom always established the depth of our intoxication. We performed balancing acts to get to the ladies room. It was truly an effort to weave through a crowded dance floor being held up only by the moving bodies of strangers. I could never understand why I always got so much pleasure from it. We knew we had problems but always enjoyed looking for solutions.

By the time we returned to Culver City after a night out, we would be at each other's throats. Drunk. Screaming obscenities at each other. Climbing the stairs to our apartments, sometimes on hands and knees, waking up our neighbors in the building. We could not hold our liquor and I finally realized I was allergic to it. Pam grew tired of it as well. Both of us decided that the friendship and our ability to solve problems with the men in our lives was far more important. We waved good-by to our thirties as well.

*   *   *

A year ago

Damn! I wonder whose calling me. I hate this phone sometimes. As soon as I get comfortable and into what I'm doing, the stupid phone rings. I'm not going to answer it. The service can pick it up. It's either someone trying to sell something, or love-sick Eddie. Oh, I'm so tired of him. I wish he would stop calling me. Give a man a night to remember and he expects Carte Blanche. His poor wife died and I swear, he's trying to make me her replacement. Well, Eddie, this kind of pressure is not going to work. You are used to being with someone. I'm not.

After the second ring, the call automatically went to the voice mail center, so I checked it and sure enough, Eddie's voice was there.

'Hi, baby. I wus jus' callin to say Hi an' see how you feelin' this mornin'. You know I really miss shoo. I'll call you lader. Bye.'

Sometimes I feel sorry for Eddie and could probably be a little nicer to him. I was very nice to him two years ago when we first met, but things changed between us. I was happy that he gave me money, money that I needed at the time. He would give me lots of it, and all I had to do was be nice to him. When I realized he was illiterate and could barely write his own name I thought to myself *no problem, I'll read to him.* I encouraged him to enroll in a literacy program at his local public library. My concern for his well-being made him fall head over heels in love with me. He thought I really loved and cared for him and I did, but not in the way he wanted me to. I loved his generosity and desire to please. He gave no indication that he would cause me pain. At the beginning of every month I could expect spending money that he told me might come in handy. But Eddie became too possessive and wanted to run my life. He would call me all day long, and when I didn't answer the phone, he would accuse me of being off somewhere with some other man. This infuriated me because at the time, I was faithful to him. I wish he could have been more grateful, because after all, I chose to be with him, *not* any other man. I don't understand why he can not be more civil and change his cave-man style. I understand the need most men have to be in control all the time. That's a given. I warned him not to push me but he finally did.

Eddie always encouraged me to pamper and take care of myself and would pay for my visits to Glen Ivy Hot Springs Spa. My personal stomping ground. He was always pleased with the results after regular spa visits and tell me that with my soft skin and sexy smile, I would probably find another man and forget all about him. This hurt me because I had a clear conscience about my loyalty to Eddie. And I felt I showed it in numerous ways. But he kept bringing up the *other man* issue. The accusations eventually led to verbal assaults on both of us and it was then that I realized I didn't need the misery and could do much better. I knew I was qualified to be with someone who could at least read a dinner menu. After weeks of pointless arguments about petty things, I decided to get out of the relationship with Eddie because after all, we were not married and had no children together. I no longer drank alcohol and Eddie's occasional liquor breath nauseated me anyway.

    I could not wait to go to the AA meeting Saturday because afterward, there was going to be a dance. Pam was going to meet me there. Belinda and Terri, Pam's neighbors, also sober, were coming with her. The first time me and Pam would party together as sober adults was a joyous occasion. The plan was to get inspiration from the meeting and proceed to make new male friends. I decided to take Eddie's indirect advice and make myself available to someone new, someone whose body was free of liquor. Since it was the weekend and Teddy was with his father, I agreed to spend the night with Eddie, but told him that I would be going to an AA meeting. He told me, 'Baby, you don't drink, so why you need a AA meetin'? You jus' wanna be aroun' a lotta mens so you can flirt!' Lord knows I wanted to say 'You're right', but I stopped myself. I simply ignored him and reminded him once again that we were not married and that he would just have to trust me. I reassured him I would be back at a decent hour to spend the night with him. With anarchy in my mind, I promised him I would be home early. Eddie, unaware his big mouth, was the reason I felt a need to kick up my heels. He wished me a pleasant evening with my friends.

    *   *   *

I enjoyed listening to the inspirational testimonials from strangers at AA meetings.

"When I stopped drinking, I stopped picking up men!" blasted the middle-aged so-so bleached blonde woman at the podium, ecstatic about her sobriety. The image of this woman in a bar, drunk and surrounded by men flashed in my mind and I laughed along with everyone else in the auditorium. I was happy to hear that I was not the only one there whose appetite for men intensified with every sip of alcohol. I listened to and hung on every word uttered by the woman because I had lived it too. Shaquita was in control when I drank. It would have been easier to spot a virgin on the street than to qualify this woman as an alcoholic. She didn't look like one at all. The wire-rimmed glasses that dangled close to the end of her nose gave no indication of her former wild side. I always felt cleansed after an AA meeting. When the meeting was over, I found an empty chair near the door and waited for Pam. When Pam arrived, she made quite an entrance.

She had on black leather pants and leather boots and a purple silk blouse. Belinda and Terri wore notsoexciting dresses, so Pam stood out because she was so classy, and it showed. Every time I see Pam, she has done something different with her hair. Tonight her elegant shiny dooky braids rested comfortably just past her shoulders. As usual, her arrival turned many heads. She was always together.

We made eye contact, hugged, then found a vacant table next to the dance floor.

"Did you have trouble finding this place? I asked, knowing it shouldn't have been a problem. We used to live in Culver City close to where we were.

"No, but the traffic was a *bitch*. I don't know where all those people on the freeway were going. It was really backed up." Pam sighed, as she looked around the room.

"I'm sick of this dead music. I wonder if they have any 2-Pac or Ice Cube. I want to dance," I said. Everybody laughed.

"I know what you mean," Pam turned to Belinda. "Sasha knows how to party." Pam smiled a grin only I understood.

"Who is the D.J.? Anyone *we* know? I looked around the room for the source of the music. I saw the DJ in a corner across the dance floor. I walked over to him and stood there for a moment trying to find tactful words to say to him. Oh, God. This will not be easy. I knew my work was cut out for me. The man looked like he had a real attitude. Must not have gotten laid. I spoke, and he ignored me. I wondered what rock he crawled out from under. He was a poor excuse for a DJ. He had no manners. And he was rude and painful to look at. So I just stood there and kept smiling. Shaquita wanted to scratch his eyes out.

As I put my hand on my hip to say something really nasty, the disc jockey finally spoke. I was relieved to know he had a pulse. I told him what I wanted to hear, the DJ frowned and I went back to the table.

"Some people are so cocky," I said as I sat down.

"What happened?" Pam stared at me.

I explained how dangerously close the D.J. came to an assault from Shaquita and Pam threw her head back in laughter. Belinda and Terri were oblivious to what was going on. After years of friendship there was no need to explain Shaquita to Pam. Pam knew Shaquita quite well.

I was about to tell one more story when I felt a light tap on my shoulder. I looked up to meet the eyes of a beautifully sculpted bronze specimen smiling down at me. He politely asked me for a dance.

"I'd love to."

He reached for my hand and took me to the crowded dance floor. *'We Have Our Own Thing'* by Heavy D was playing at the time which made me even more eager to get on the dance floor. Being over forty energizes me because I don't look my age and never need to lie about it. The rap music beat gets me up and out of a chair. I like the social commentary in rap and occasionally I hear something I can relate to from my childhood in South Central. Rap music keeps my mind young and on common ground with young people.

I danced my own interpretation of the basic two step. Whatever the beat of the music, my body followed in sync.

As I danced up a storm, I noticed my partners' easy moving body, from behind, when he turned as he danced. *Hmm. Tall with the right amount of thickness. Something to hold on to.* It was hard not to eye him in a seductive way. Men are not the only ones who do this. I tried to be subtle with my dark glasses on that night. Halfway through the second dance he asked what my name was.

"Sasha Friend." I had to repeat it because of the blaring music. "What's yours?"

"Rod Sampson." We continued to dance.

I wanted to rest, so I declined a third dance with Rod, and thanked him, for the exercise. Rod laughed as he walked me back to the table. "Are you married?" *Good second question.* I answered quickly, trying not to sound desperate, "No, I'm not."

"May I call you sometime?"

"Sure," I said, smiling up at his imposing body that was only inches from me. Rod vanished as I sat down with the girls and a moment later he returned. Before I could take a sip of my drink, he gave me his phone number and address written on the severed edge of a dance flyer. "Call me," and he gave me the folded piece of paper.

I could feel the blood rushing to my head as I smiled and watched the heavenly creature walk away. My face was flushed and I grabbed Pam by the arm and pulled her to her feet. I told her we had to go to the ladies room. After touching up lipstick in the restroom we sat down near the entrance of the big auditorium, next to an open door. The chilly breeze from outside felt good to me. After all, I needed to cool my body down. I just got me a phone number. Pam lit a cigarette after we sat down and silently watched everyone who passed by.

We looked at all the different men in the lobby, plenty of black men, we were thinking. We couldn't believe it. Some were extremely tall, some unnaturally short, and exceptionally good looking black men with a lot of color, just what *we* liked. We saw brothers that were borderline acceptable because they should have been just a little blacker for our taste. Most were alright but a few were there that should never have come out at all. Just a few, though. We were surprised at the large number of sober men in supply for the evening. Men who could party without booze. Pam took the last drag from her cigarette, dropped it and crushed it under her shoe just as Rod walked toward us. He looked straight at me.

I wanted a new friend and Rod later slipped me his business card. He sure wanted to hear from me. I saw him as salvation from Eddie, but I couldn't let him know what he would be used for; sex only. I got pleasure from thoughts of Rod while sleeping with Eddie that night. I went through the motions of love making and pretended all was well, knowing in my heart I was determined to leave Eddie. Eddie could do nothing to change my mind. I was moving on.

*   *   *

One Year Later

When the phone rang, I decided to be pleasant and answer it. I put the pencil down and lifted the receiver.
"Hello?"
"Hi. Mom, what are you doing?"
"Oh, hi sugar, what's up? I'm sitting here sketching."
"What are you drawing today?"
"Men's shirts and ties."
"Men's shirts, did you finish the red suit?"
"Sure did, why? You want it?"
"I have a concert to go to for my journalism class and it would be nice to get dressed up for a change."
"You can borrow it. What are you going to wear with it?"
"Do you mean, shoes?"
"Yes, well that, among other things..."
I could see my tall striking daughter in the tailored double-breasted suit I made. She was in sheer black stockings and black leather pumps that highlighted the black trim in the suit. Eileen's good looks and beauty continued to

amaze me. I know it's a miracle from above. I didn't look that good.

"Oh yea, Mom" Eileen said. "You want to hear a funny story?"

"Sure."

"Get this. I went to the clinic the other day..."

I interrupted. "For what?"

"To take a pregnancy test."

Oh shit. "What, are you late?" I asked, trying to contain my maternal panic.

"Yes, about two weeks."

I sat straight up in my chair. I didn't know what was coming next. "And?" I finally said.

"Mom, it was so funny. I went into the doctor's office, found an empty seat after signing in and I sat down next to a little girl sitting all by herself. Guess who it was?"

"Who?"

"Tanesha." Her boyfriend Eric's daughter, and someone Eileen likes. "But I didn't see her mama anywhere." The mother had a hatred for Eileen. Eileen calls her the *cow-mother*.

"Eric told me she says she's pregnant again but he denies it all the way. He said she's been screwing some other brother."

"Did *you* see her?"

"No, I just split, but I said hi and bye to Tasesha. The heffa was probably there for prenatal care."

"So why did *you* leave?"

"I didn't want to run in to the hootchie because when I do, it won't be pretty."

"Yeah, well I guess you did the right thing. Did you tell Eric what happened?" He's probably guilty.

"Yes, and he said it's not his baby and she's crazy if she thinks it's his."

"Well, people who have sex ought to learn how to protect themselves. So, when are you going back to the clinic so you can handle your business? Soon, I hope."

"Yes Mom, soon."

"So, if the rabbit dies, are you and Eric ready for that?"

"Eric has *been* ready and my bio-clock is ticking fast!"

"Baby, you're only twenty-one. What's the rush?"

"I don't want to be too old to enjoy my child. I want to be a young mom, like you are."

"I was *too* young, I think." Twenty-one was young for me to begin motherhood but at the time it was the right thing to do. Eileen told me years ago she wanted a long engagement and a well-planned wedding before a baby, so to hear her talk about sacrificing what was always dear to her was disappointing. This x-generation makes shit up as they go along. I am not convinced that young people make sound enough choices for their lives. Eric and Eileen like each other and he is more reliable than her last boyfriend who she wasted so much time with.

Most men don't know how good a thing is when they have it. I tell Eileen to be careful because men are emotionally unstable. Many men never learn the value of a good woman, leaving most of us women in society burned and abused. I didn't want that for my baby. I still have vivid nightmares etched in my memory, and I pray that one day they go away.

*   *   *

December, 1971

Where is he? Why am I even bothering to wait for Sam. He needs a tutor, not me. I was talking to myself.

But since I had a few hours of time to spare, I stood there. I thanked God for the leaves on the tree I was standing under and the shade they provided me. I was glad that it was December. Close to Christmas which I loved to celebrate. Although it was the holiday season in Los Angeles, people still enjoyed some warm sunny days that made it uncomfortable if you wore warm clothing for the season. One was never sure about the weather in California. The fringed tan rawhide jacket I wore felt like ton of bricks. I could feel tiny beads of perspiration forming at my temples and on my forehead.

Shit! I'm taking this damn jacket off. Where is he? I hate fooling around with some black men. They get on my nerves sometimes. Sometimes? All the time. They always make you wait. For them. Always for them. I wish he would come on because now I have to pee. I know I must look like a fool, standing here shifting from one foot to the other. If I leave to go to the restroom in the Student Center he'll come, I just know it. Then I'll really be pissed. Oh, here comes that asshole now. It's about time. This noisy, dusty, ugly Impala's going to stop right in front of me. And look at this fool sitting behind the wheel grinning like he just stole something and got away with it.

I walked around the pile of junk and let myself in because I knew Sam was not a gentleman. I asked myself why people from Watts always had to ride in their cars with the windows down.

"Hi." I said, as I climbed into the wreck and shut the door. "What happened to you?"

"Oh, I had to go to the Financial Aid Office to take care of some business."

And that was it. No apology for making me wait. Nothing. Unappreciative sonofabitch. I knew he didn't care about me standing in the nagging high noon sun about to urinate on myself. Waiting on his ass so I could tutor him and his damn friends.

Sam finally spoke and asked me if I was hungry, "You want a Whopper from Burger King? I'm hungry as hell."

I wanted to tell him he looked like hell, but I didn't. Instead, I said "Yes," because I knew there was a toilet somewhere in the BK building and I would find it.

When we pulled into BK less than a mile from campus, I ran inside to the restroom. I was relieved and ready for a Whopper with cheese. I didn't need a drink. We decided to take the food with us since we were already running late. Little did I know I was being set up.

When I thought about it later, I realized Sam's behavior was different that day, not his usual talkative self. He usually talks about nothing of interest to me. Sam knew I had no romantic interest in him because I made it clear to him that I still loved my husband, Barry, who I was separated from. He had met Eileen before.

Sam was one of those people you could accept as a friend and never imagine having sex with. He hinted at it one day. I ignored him as usual and reminded him that I had a husband and child. I was not interested in having sex with him ever.

J.R., a class member and friend of Sam's was standing on the front porch of his duplex apartment when we arrived. He spoke to us then stepped aside so we could enter the apartment. Two of J.R.'s other friends were waiting inside. I put my books on the coffee table, Sam handed me the cheeseburger I ordered and I ate promptly. Embarrassed about eating so quickly, I wanted to get the study session underway. I was pressed for time and didn't have my car. I was relying on Sam to drive me home afterward.

Sam had no intention of driving me anywhere. When the study session ended, I noticed that J.R. and his friends had disappeared into the bedroom. There was total silence, peculiar for this group of college jocks.

I had volunteered my time for the afternoon and was ready to go home to do some Christmas shopping that evening. I stood up and began pacing in front of the sofa. I heard my name called from the bedroom.

"What?"

"Come here." I recognized J.R's distinct gravely voice.

I hesitated and felt a queasy sickness pass through my body. I knew I was going to be ill. I didn't want to go in the room with all those guys. I didn't trust them that way. Besides, it was unladylike. The scent of pot was coming from the room. "What do you want? Sam, I'm ready to go."

I stepped into the hallway that led to the bedroom and saw J.R. standing in the bedroom doorway holding a large handgun. He continued, "I have something I want you to see." My eyes widened as I felt an ache in my back. I saw a gun and J.R.'s friends taking their clothes off. With the gun, he gestured for me to do the same. "We're going to have a little party." J.R. said.

Numbed by disbelief and the fact that Sam did nothing to stop the assault, I begged him to do something. I pleaded with J.R. to stop the insanity but it did no good. At gun point I was sadomized and forced to have intercourse with everyone there, including Sam. When they finished raping me, I didn't ask Sam for a ride home.

2

Present

Standing before my answering machine I reminded myself that I would not going to live with the shame of my past. The electronic voice on my answering machine reported that I had 'one new message, at 7:05 p.m.' It released the voice of Paulette, my cousin from Oakland. "Sasha, I really gotta talk to you. Buck married that bitch! I'm so hurt I could die. Call me."

What could be the problem now. Paulette must be going through more changes with that old raisin she's been with lately. Twenty years ago she announced that her sexual preference had changed. I was convinced it was a case of monkey see monkey do. At that time, I thought Paulette had socialized with the wrong group of people while on vacation in Chicago. Her two week trip lasted two years and she came back to California a full blown lesbian. But I loved her anyway.

Paulette's a few years younger than me and an only child, too, so we were always very close in our early years. Paulette had more freedom than I did and always had a wild story to tell. We wrote each other all the time and would send pot back and forth neatly wrapped in foil, along with a letter. It's funny how you do crazy shit when you're young. We had big fun and enjoyed our little adventures. Paulette lost her father when she was twelve and after that she always had a boyfriend around. It was during the grieving of her father that she started coming down to L.A. every summer. Paulette loved my dad because he looked so much like her father. Actually, the two men could have been twins, but had just been brothers. Right after she lost her virginity, Paulette taught me how to inhale cigarettes. I was only sixteen at the time. Paulette had already been smoking three years before that. Her mom, my Aunt Grace, would phone my mom long distance crying about finding packs of cigarettes in Paulette's coat pockets back when she was just thirteen. "I don't know what I'm going to do with this girl, she's so wild," Aunt Grace would cry to mama. I would smile knowing that I just got chewed out occasionally for talking back and not for what Paulette was doing.

Paulette's habits were no surprise to me. I remember when she and Aunt Grace lived in Berkeley and Paulette worked in a record shop. Paulette always had the latest top ten 45's. At fourteen, she was sneaking boys in the house at night having parties while Aunt Grace slept soundly in the back bedroom. Paulette came to L.A. the weekend of my debutante ball looking so grown up that I barely recognized her.

"Sup?" I said in my usual way.

"Sash, you gotta come up here. I'm so confused." What's new? I understood her confusion but why she was thinking about death was beyond me.

"Well, what happened?" I used a motherly tone with Paulette when she got upset, especially since her mother's death.

"He said he was going to make her move out so we could be together." crying in the phone she continued, "I'm going to shoot that old motherfucker. He lied to me!"

"Now Paulette, it can't be all that bad."

"But you don't understand. He comes over here all the time, fixes things around here, he buys me clothes, and makes love to me. He promised to be with me! Can you come up here?"

I quickly ran a mental check list. I just had the oil changed in the BMW, It was tuned up last month. My car is in great condition. My Mastercard is not maxed out for once. What the hell. I'm bored and I want to get on the highway.

"I'll be there Friday," I said, reassuringly.

"Really?"

"Yeah, yeah, so try to relax and please don't hurt him, at least not until I get there. You might need a witness."

I wonder who in the hell Paulette allowed herself to get involved with. About six months ago she took up with men again. I was happy because I always thought being a lesbian was a little extreme for swearing off men. But I understand that it's a comfort to some. Different strokes for different folks. Switching back to men should be easy for Paulette. I know she missed the dick, after twenty years. She probably realized she needed male physical strength to get certain things done. He fixed things around her house, did repairs on her car, and she rediscovered penis. And liked it. Like before. She had to learn all over again how to select the *right* one. Not someone else' toy.

I had to decide what to pack for the trip but before doing that I called Eddie, to say good night.

"Hello." Eddie answered on the first ring.
"Hi."
"Oh, hi darlin'. It's so good to hear your voice. Did you watch 48 Hours?"

One thing I liked about Eddie was that he liked to watch intelligent shows.

"No, I missed it. I had the TV on mute. I was on the phone with my cousin Paulette in Oakland. I missed most of it."
"So, how's yo cousin doin'?"
"Not so good. She has a problem with a man right now."
"A man? I thought she likted womens?"
"Well, she switched back and I'm glad. I'm going up there this weekend."
"Oh, you thinkin' 'bout flying?"
"No, I'm driving."
"You want me to come with you, baby, to help you drive? You know I worry 'bout you so much."
"No, that's okay, but thanks."
"What about yo' son, is he goin' wit you?"
"Well, no, and I haven't told him yet either. Eileen will be here. Will you check on him while I'm gone?"

Eddie was good about doing those things. He told me Teddy was old enough to take care of himself, with his sister's supervision. Eddie had done it when he was nine, for longer than a couple of days. 'Jus' make sure he has plenty of food and video games an' he'll be fine.' He eased my mind so well that I knew he was after something, but I also knew he was right about Teddy being responsible. When I talk to friends on the phone I let Teddy hear me brag about his latest achievements, a technique I learned as a teacher. You motivate children to do positive things this way and I know it works. I am very proud of my youngest baby.

"Yeah, baby, you know I'll keep an eye on him. Maybe Saturday I'll come get 'em an' take him to the mall. You sure you're gonna be okay? Did you change yo' oil like you was goin' to? Do you need som' money?"

Of course I need money. "I have money in the bank, a few hundred that should take care of things. And yes, I did have the oil changed. Can I use your Mobil card, though?"

"Sure."

"Thanks, I love you."

Before going to bed I flipped the light switch on in my closet and stepped inside, looking to my left, and then to my right. The clothes that hung on padded hangers on the left side were blouses, lightly starched shirts, and choice intimate apparel, sorted by color and separated by seasons. My clothes were getting crowded because I replaced peach tubular hangers with satin padded ones. They're pretty, but they take up more room. I glanced at the lingerie and thought how lucky I was to have so much. I made all this stuff. Custom made, for me. I remember how I decorated a small bedroom for Eileen, about the same size as my closet. The walk-in closet bulged. All those clothes, business suits, slacks, sweaters, dresses, and a leather collection. The winter coats and jackets screamed for more space in the closet. Everything was organized so grabbing a few things for the weekend would not be a problem.

I reached up to check the heels on a pair of black suede pumps I thought about taking on the trip. Yes. These shoes will look tuff with the black suede strapless and fringed jacket. All suede. My fingers stroked the top of the shoe, just enough of a touch that reminded me I had good taste. I leaned toward the suede jacket so my nose could sniff the sweet smell of leather. The reward of my hard work. After analyzing everything in the closet, I stepped out, turned off the light and closed the door. Then I went to bed.

"Why can't I go?" Teddy face showed signs of abandonment.

"Because this is business, honey, and I'll be real busy. I wouldn't have time to take you anywhere and you would just be bored." I actually hated not having him along because he's great company on the road. But I knew Teddy likes being home alone. He liked to pretend that the condo was his. He liked to hook up his Genesis to the big screen TV in the living room. He enjoyed the bigger than life graphics for his games. My bedroom became his with the king-sized bed and remote control. He fantasized for a few days. With all the things clear he could do by himself in his mind, he did not put up a fight about not going. Teddy knew that our recent day at the Antelope Valley Fair got me off the hook.

"I'll leave your allowance on my night stand, but remember your chores, please."

"How much are you going to leave me?"

"Your usual, plus fifty dollars, if you want to go to the mall." Teddy lit up like a Christmas tree. Good.

"Eddie is going to check with you on Saturday to see if you want to go to the mall, so please be nice to him. Eileen is going to come by, too."

"Okay Mom. When are you leaving?"

"Tomorrow morning, early. I'm packing and shopping for food today. You'd better get out of here so you won't miss the bus."

"Mom, will you take me to school, please?" The pleading look Teddy gave me worked.

"All right, come on." Already dressed, I grabbed the car keys. Teddy loves for me to drive him to school so his friends can see him pull up in front of the school, like an executive, in our 735. The car still looked good for one that was almost ten years old. Aunt Jewel sure had good taste in automobiles, she left it for me in her will. When we got to school Teddy pecked me on the cheek, put on his tough face then jumped out of the car. "See ya later," he waved good by to me.

I was feeling worn out and exhausted when I came from the store, I had towed heavy plastic bags full of groceries. I looked at the kitchen wall clock and saw that it was only mid-morning. I checked the time and realized there was no time for my routine cup of coffee. I had to keep moving. I had a million things to do so I popped a Vivarin in my mouth and chased it with a tall glass of ice water. I walked into the living room, opened the verticals and looked out at the desert.

I loved the room because it was spacious and had a panoramic view. The work area was adjacent to the glass door that led to the patio. It gave me an enjoyable view all hours of the day. Occasionally I would go downstairs to the living room and out to the patio to watch breathtaking sunrises. They reminded me of a *Tequila Sunrise*, making me feel like I was in heaven each time I saw another day begin.

By the time I finished packing it was dinnertime. Teddy and I ordered pepperoni pizza. I was too tired to cook. We had pizza and ice cream and we talked about last minute things. That included setting his alarm clock for school the next morning, what he could *not* have for dinner Friday night and to expect a call from me. Eddie would make sure there were no wild parties. After we finished the pizza, I ran Teddy's shower water, just to be sure he had a recent bath. That would last until next week when I could run it again. You know how boys are.

At 5 a.m. I hummed along the highway, headed north. I reached Bakersfield around 7 a.m., stopped for coffee and a donut at a road side restaurant. I stopped one other time for gas, and arrived in Oakland at 11 a.m.

Her porch was the perfect stage for her luscious plants and flowers. An iron and cedar park bench surrounded by potted vines and small trees was the center of interest on the porch and the plants were well kept. How does she get this shit to grow? Paulette always gave me tips, but nothing worked. The plants that grew inside her house were even prettier.

Paulette answered the door in a silk caftan after two taps on the knocker. With outstretched arms, we hugged a long time.

"I hope you brought your sketches. A friend of mine called this morning and he said..." Her voice was drowned out by the interior beauty of her home. I took another step on the smooth shiny surface of the recently installed tiles in the entry. After waiting nearly nine months she was happy when the imported Italian squares she ordered finally arrived. She said the ship probably got lost at sea. My eyes followed the intricate hand painted pattern of olive trees in the tile until it disappeared beneath the thick textured fibers of the living room carpet. The bright green color of the carpet was a yard for her robust plant and indoor tree collection. The dazzling earthy sight of shiny leaves and graceful branches took you to the tropics. The bamboo mini-blinds carefully filtered the right amount of sunlight in the day, giving way to warm glows of antique tiffany lights in the evening. I admired Paulette's decorating style. She collected Marilyn Monroe and had incredible screens and framed posters of the movie legend throughout the house. Under the oak and glass coffee table was a remarkable assortment of Monroe books and periodicals by every author who ever tried to write about Marilyn. Paulette's adoration for the white woman was not normal. It was testimony to her complex nature.

"What did you say?" I drifted back.

"Chad wants to see your work. He knows someone who might be interested in investing in your business."

"Really? Who?"

"He didn't say who, but it's some guy from the East coast. I've been bragging about your designs."

"Well, it just so happens I have my portfolio with me, and its loaded with sketches." I always took my portfolio whenever I traveled out of town. You never knew who you might run in to. "Come on, you can help me get my stuff."

Paulette and I walked outside past the plants on the porch. It reminded me to comment on how beautiful they were.

"How do you do it? They're always so healthy looking!"

Paulette laughed and said, "I just give them lots of space and lots of food." Space? In this jungle? I loved my two little plants too, but they didn't look like those.

I opened the car trunk to get the luggage and Paulette said, "One of these days, one of these days."

"What?"

"I'm going to buy one of these babies."

"You're not happy with your Volvo?"

Paulette mentioned a timing problem her car was having and that lately she had been wanting something new. Something exciting. Before Paulette could answer I said, "Well, I'll let you borrow mine sometime, so you can save your money."

"Paulette laughed and said, "Right on!"

I took the heavy wardrobe bag and matching beauty case and Paulette carried the third bag and sketch portfolio. We walked back inside the house through the *garden* to the guest room, my spot for the weekend. Left speechless once again by Paulette's decor I decided it had to run in the family. On the queen sized bed in the guest room were fluffy down pillows. Covered with antique white lace trim. The trim was repeated in the outline of the sheer curtains, pulled back by dusty rose satin ribbons. The bedspread was an antique pattern like the cases, had embroidered dusty rose flowers that were the same as the flowers in the wall paper pattern. A crystal vase containing pink silk roses sat beside the bed on a round table draped with an antique lace cover. African violet plants gave life to an otherwise quiet corner of the bedroom, booming with their velvety leaves and white flowers. The plant stand the violets sat on was a baker's rack Paulette found at a second hand store. She did not refinish the rusted edges. No one noticed because of the vibrating plants sitting on it. I was afraid to touch anything for fear of upsetting the pristine order, but Paulette broke the ice when she dropped the suitcase and jumped on the bed.

I said, "Girl, this is so pretty. This room looks like you turned Martha Stewart loose in here. When did you do this?".

"Sasha, I did everything at once. I got a second on this old house because so many things needed to be done. The outside is going to be painted as soon as I decide what color."

Paulette could have been an interior decorator. She had an apartment once that had so little furniture people who came over sat on huge bean bag chairs and slept on army cots. No one complained, because everybody was comfortable. The plants and the way she decorated always made you feel relaxed and well taken care of.

"Sasha, I'm so pissed off," she began her plight. "I called that fuckin' Buck last night and hung up on him."

"Why did you do that?"

"Because I hate him."

"Why? He reintroduced you to intercourse, I know you've missed it for twenty years. You know it's not hate you feel."

"Shut up!" Paulette snapped, "He lied to me!"

"Lied about what?" I cautiously asked.

"He told me he was going to put Peaches out but he turned right around and married her."

"And you believed him when he told you he was going to evict her? Come on, girl, you weren't thinking. I told you not to push that, to just enjoy the goodies and be satisfied. Did you really think he was going to inconvenience *himself* that way?" I knew Paulette did not want to hear this and I crossed my fingers as I said it.

"That's why I'm gay, because men lie so much. This is the same old shit all over again." I didn't realize my cousin was so damn naïve.

Paulette said Buck knew she was in a lesbian relationship when he started coming around. There were some things like plumbing and other small projects he was good at. Her female lover could not do things that required male talent. Duh! She met Buck at a card at game. That night he told her he was good at fixing things if she ever needed help. I concluded that Buck probably fantasized about what lesbians did behind closed doors. Paulette said Buck offered to be of service, sometime. He said he could fix anything. Paulette found him attractive for a little old man. Seventy something and harmless, she said. So she took his business card.

The very next day as luck would have it, Paulette's kitchen sink stopped up. Having no money for a plumber she called Buck. He answered the page right away and began flirting with her over the phone. By the time Buck arrived at her house, she was curious about what the little creature could do. He did not disappoint her.

Buck seduced Paulette. He finished the kitchen sink and started on her. Although somewhat unprepared, Paulette was willing. He shocked her with his other equipment *not* meant for plumbing, and he proceeded to clear her personal channel that afternoon. He laid plenty of pipe inside of her, giving Paulette a new outlook.

I was happy to know Paulette had been laid by a man. I knew she missed that powerful thrust. When she confessed it to me I thought the miracle would bring back her heterosexual behavior. We talked all night on the phone about Buck and his fabulous hardware. Their relationship grew from there and was based solely upon the sex they were having several times a week. Repairs on the house were being done at no cost. Paulette was happy.

From the beginning Paulette knew about Peaches, Buck's live-in girlfriend. Paulette told me Peaches started to visit her at her home, thinking Paulette was her friend. Peaches liked Paulette, but Paulette hated her guts. Peaches used to brag about how she was going to marry Buck and spend all his money. That angered Paulette and made her want Buck more, just to protect him from Peaches. When Paulette visited me in January, I told her not to pressure him, but she didn't listen. I told her that if she really wanted Buck, just use condoms and be patient. Some things are out of one's control. I reminded her there was a man in the triangle If she had been thinking, she would have realized Buc had the best of both worlds: A woman at home and one around the corner. There was always the possibility of a menage a trois. Paulette missed out on valuable lessons about men all those years she was gay.

Paulette planned a small dinner party to introduce me to a few of her friends, Chad was invited. He liked my portfolio and raved about my artistic talent.

"Paulette said you were the best. She wasn't lying."

Gay.

"Thank you," I said as I turned to the next sketch.

"Oooh, is this what Paulette has on?"

"Yes. My daughter wore this outfit in a film. She was an extra."

"Oh, you worked on a movie?"

"Sure did, Wardrobe." The red lycra halter top and biker shorts fit Paulette's body like a glove. At thirty eight she still had upright perky breasts, breasts that turned heads when she was a teen. I knew the outfit would look good on her so I brought it along, knowing it would probably stay in Oakland.

"Have you ever thought about opening a dress shop and sewing for people?" Chad's question was not brilliant to me.

"No, I try to think little bigger than that." I thought he would be more broadminded. My dream is to manufacturer my creations, as in big business and I wished people would see that. I'm not just a seamstress, I'm a designer. After explaining that to Chad, I quietly closed my portfolio and rejoined the party.

I hoped my visit with Paulette helped to ease her mind. Unfortunately, we have to try to fit in the big picture the best way possible. And when you think a situation is going to be resolved right away, sometimes other shit happens.

* * *

December, 1971, continued

When I got dressed, I headed for the door. No one offered me a ride home, not even Sam. He knew how far I had to go to get home. I considered asking for a ride from one of them but instead, I left the duplex screaming, "You'll pay for this!" I was shaking, thinking as I ran away that I couldn't even douche. The lousy bastards. Someone was going to hear about it. I ran to the gate at the sidewalk, flung it open and ran down the street. The few tears on my cheeks became rivers by the time I got to the end of the block. Where in the hell were people in the neighborhood? I didn't see a soul. No one on the street or in their yard, no one to tell my nightmare to. After turning the corner I still didn't see anyone, not even a wino. I had visions of the devastating orgy that gave me little capacity to think. I felt nasty and afraid that when I reported it I would be humiliated even further. I finally spotted a Sheriff's car coming toward me and wandered into the street. I waved my arms at the passing police car. The vehicle slowed and eventually stopped. I kept crossing the street to where the officer had parked.

"I have just been raped!" I frantically screamed. "Those bastards raped me!"

"Okay, Okay, ma'am, calm down. Where did this happen?"

I pointed in the direction I came from, "down there." Someone of authority had come and could do something for me, I thought.

The officer had me take him to the place where the alleged rape occurred. He told me to get in the squad car.

He made a U-turn and called in his location. He then slowly drove back down the long block I had just walked up, and stopped when we reached the duplex.

"There it is, the duplex on the right," I moaned, feeling nauseous.

"All right. You wait here, I'll be right back," the deputy ordered me as he got out of the car. "How many did you say were inside?"

"Five."

The officer walked through the open chain link gate to the front door of the duplex. He knocked several times on the door with his nightstick. Someone answered and I could see the officer talking. I sensed what would happen next, and in less than a minute the deputy stepped back, said thank you in the form of a salute, turned and walked back to the patrol car. From the driver's side of the police car he bent down and looked at me. He asked me to step out of the car and come around to his side. His icy words will forever be etched in the surface of my mind, "There is nothing I can do. They said you were a willing participant." The result of the two minute investigation was the final blow that permanently scarred my soul. I went ballistic.

"They're lying! They raped *and* threatened me with a gun! Do something! Can't you do *anything*?" My plea elevated to an ear piercing level.

"No, I don't have any proof of a crime."

I wanted to show him the sperm trickling down my leg. "Can't you take a report, or something?" I sobbed. I did not believe any of the shit.

"No, ma'am. Now, you need to leave the premises," he said in his acquired tone of authority.

The reality of the horrible action took a toll on me. I didn't feel so smart and strong anymore. It was obvious, I know. I was a victim. Victimized by a group of jocks and the system that should have protected me in my crisis. I wondered who I could tell this to. Who would believe me? The weight of the books I was carrying suddenly became unbearable. I dropped them on the sidewalk. Nervousness, anger, hurt, betrayal and humiliation physically drained me. Emotionally I was a bust.

I couldn't tell my husband Barry about it. I knew he wouldn't understand. He always said nasty things about boyfriends I had before I met him. I knew he was incapable of dealing with a rape, and by some guys I knew? No way. Black men don't like their women to talk about former lovers, so my past private affairs were just that. Private. I kept them to myself. Barry didn't like my attitude and got mad about it. He thought he could physically abuse me. That was his way, but I was not going to be abused, so me and my baby Eileen, left him, even though I still loved him. That's why we were separated.

The police car drove away as I picked up my books from the sidewalk. I started walking down the long lonely block a second time. By the time I got home some thirty minutes later, I knew who I had to call. Dwayne. He would help me settle this. I grew up with Dwayne, who adopted me, and Pam as little sisters. Dwayne would want to know why they chose me to *fuck* with. The rapists made a bad choice. My decision to tell Dwayne about the rape turned out to be a bad choice, too.

He got upset when I called him at work to tell him what happened earlier. He told me to stay put, and when he got off work, he would come get me so I could take him to the slimebags. Since the police took no action, we would settle the score ourselves.

Dwayne and his friend, Bubba arrived just after dark as the sun disappeared into the ocean. I was still visibly shaken even though I had bathed. I washed away the proof of rape when I did that. The call I made to Dwayne disturbed his usually composed nature and the sight of me in my condition added anger and infuriation. I had been violated, by friends. They had to pay.

In a dreamlike state, I climbed into the back seat of the Camaro. In the front seat Dwayne and Bubba checked their guns to make sure they were fully loaded.

"Say man, you need a clip?" Bubba said as he handed Dwayne a long dull metal magazine. He quickly looked at it and slapped it into place.

"Thanks, blood," Dwayne replied, then started the engine. These guys had heart. I felt lucky to have them stand up for me. It bothered me to know that Barry would not have risen to the occasion, like these guys. He would not have understood. The sound of the Camaro engine was the battle cry.

Dwayne didn't talk much on the way, talked just enough to confirm directions. We parked the car across the street from the duplex.

"Which apartment is it?" Dwayne asked, still angry.

"The one on the right," I pointed toward the building. I took a deep breath, gathered as much strength as I could, and said, "Come on, let's go." I leaned forward to get out of the car. I walked through the gate first, with the guys close behind. I asked myself what the *hell* I was doing. What we were about to do took nerve. No satisfaction from the legal system led to the showdown. It was inevitable and necessary.

"You said he had a gun?" Bubba asked.

"Yes, he showed it to me today. He held it on me while they raped me."

"Do you know what kind it was?"

"It looked like a .38, but I don't know, it was big." I stepped on the porch, with Dwayne and Bubba on either side of me. Their guns were concealed under the pea coats they wore. I was wearing the fringed rawhide jacket I had on earlier and jeans hoping the clothes would give me the strength I knew I needed.

It was dark on the porch. "I wonder if this sonofabitch is home," I mumbled as I rang the doorbell. Shortly after pressing the buzzer I could see someone peek from behind a curtain in the window just to the right of the door. The room where the rape occurred. Someone else in the apartment turned the porch light on and the three of us came into view.

We continued to wait under the porch light for an answer to the door buzz. We could hear conversation from the other side of the door but could not make out what was being said. Suddenly the door swung open and J.R. was standing there with the same gun I had seen earlier, at his side.

I opened my mouth to say, "Why did you…" Before I could say "rape me?" he brought the gun up and fired it, right at me, in the abdomen. I could see a woman in the background inside the apartment when I felt my body thrust backward off the porch. All time slowed. A floating sensation envelop my body as I hit the ground. It was then that I realized I had been shot. I tried to get up, but couldn't. "Shoot him!" I faintly screamed as my voice began to trail off. On that order Dwayne and Bubba unloaded several rounds into the small apartment.

"Shit!" Dwayne cried out loud. They scrambled to get me moved to safety. "Are you all right?" I don't think he realized I was shot. It was all too unreal, even for me. We had no business going to someone else's house with loaded weapons. Bubba was speechless, completely shocked. Blood rapidly poured from my stomach covering my jacket with warm dark fluid. The burning I felt turned to nausea and by the time they put me in the car, I was vomiting.

"We gotta get her to a hospital," Dwayne said, numbed by what he saw, looking and trying not to panic.

My first memory after the shooting was hearing someone say, "We've lost her." It was the voice of an emergency room technician.

I woke up the next day in excruciating pain, to find out I had had emergency surgery, necessary to save my life. The mental anguish intensified when I tried to move my legs, and couldn't, because I had shackles on my ankles, attached to the bed in the jail ward at County Hospital. I was under arrest for assault. Dwayne and Bubba were in jail also.

3

Present

I knew I needed change in my life. No matter what I did or how hard I tried, I could not make a relationship work if it was not meant to be. I needed to kick Eddie to the curb. He still did nice things for me but his jealousy was the problem. I had not been intimate with him for months and I wanted an intimate relationship, with someone like Rod. Rod and I were taking it slow, taking time to get to know each other. We decided to date. For the moment, Rod was desirable and made himself available to me.

Although Rod was still legally married, he said that the possibility of a reconciliation with his wife was doubtful. He shared an apartment with a man who, like himself, lost everything to the savage grip of alcohol and drugs. They were recovering addicts. Satisfied with his living arrangement, he enjoyed little things in life like not sharing a bathroom with anyone. Like me, he was organized and had a place for everything.

The long marble top counter in his bathroom was covered with his fragrance collection, some of the best. Egoiste by Chanel, Lagerfeld and Safari sat in front of other colognes bottles. The night I met Rod he was wearing my favorite scent, Eternity for Men. I loved a good smelling man. Certain fragrances just have a hypnotic effect on me, taking me over like a drug. I was helplessly drawn to the scent on Rod's body, and to the joy of my senses. He wore it the first time I went to his apartment.

Rod just returned from an AA meeting when I got to his place. He went to both AA and bible study classes in the same evening. He knew that sobriety was easier if he was spiritually grounded.

He mentioned on the telephone one night that he was having a minor problem with a pinched nerve in his hip. I offered to let him borrow my heating pad to help with the pain, since he didn't have one. He told me he could get some relief with a heating pad. He appreciated my thoughtfulness concerning his annoying problem. He had overworked his body on the basketball court and was suffering for it.

"How often does it bother you?" I asked him, the night before, on the telephone. "Does it interfere with your sexual performance?" I was direct, to the point. Rod was a friend and I was only being friendly.

"Why do you want to know?" Rod asked me.

"I want to know if your condition would prevent us from getting busy sometime, oh, in the future, of course." I wish I could have taken back what I said. He probably thought I was a slut. Then he said,

"No, not at all. No problems in that department." Rod said reassuringly.

"Oh, that's good to know," I released a happy sigh.
"Why, are you interested in finding out?"
"Well, when I'm ready, I'll let you know."
"Well, when you're ready, just bring it on!"

I wondered if I was the only woman who did that kind of shit. Well, I went for it. He didn't seem to mind.

The next day I went to Rod's. I knew the possibility of an intimate encounter was very strong. I wanted to wait and see how things would go first, after all, I was just delivering the heating pad. I wanted to see how he lived, conditions. He thanked me for the heating pad and offered to make me dinner. I declined, made my excuses and said 'good by'. His place passed the inspection. He said he would call me in a day or so to give me a report on the condition of his hip.

I called Rod three days later to see how he was feeling. I didn't wait for him to call me. To my surprise he did not complain about the pinched nerve. In fact, he felt good enough to shoot hoops the day before.

"When are you coming down this way again?" he asked, knowing I had to pass through his neighborhood to get to Los Angeles.

"In a few days. I have a production meeting for a play I'm doing costumes for."

"In L.A.?"

"Yes, the meeting is in L.A. but the play's going to be somewhere else," I explained.

"Why don't you call me when you finish your meeting? Maybe you can stop by on your way back. What day is your meeting?"

"Monday."

"I'll miss my AA meeting if you're coming by."

"Well, okay. It might be late though, around nine, but I can't stay long because it's a school night." I explained that I had to be home at a decent hour.

"Nine is cool. Just come on when you finish with your meeting."

I was thrilled.

The meeting ran smoothly. I accepted the offer for the job and was invited to the audition process the next weekend. I was on a cloud and couldn't believe the sum of money I was offered for doing something that brought me so much joy.

I called Rod from my cell phone to let him know I was on my way. I looked and couldn't find a parking space in front of his building but finally found something around the corner. I thought about how inconvenient the parking was going to be if I decided to make this run often. He is walking me to my car when I leave. I closed the car door, chirped on the car alarm and walked as fast as I could to the entrance of the apartment building. I knocked on the apartment door, and he answered it wearing sweats and no shirt. Oh Damn and Lord have mercy were my thoughts when I focused on his washboard stomach and huge biceps. His relaxed attire exposed a flawless physique, but I knew he had that from the beginning.

"Hi!" I grinned.

"Hi, how'd it go? Did you get the job?" Rod greeted me with a big smile.

"Great. But I knew I had the job before I went. I pretty much knew it last week when I talked to them," I said with confidence.

"So when do you start?" he asked as he closed the door behind me.

"I have auditions next weekend and I guess anytime after that the madness begins."

"Are you hungry? Can I fix you something to eat or get you a soda?" Rod was eager to show his hospitality, again.

"Yes, a soda would be nice." Rod went to the kitchen and fixed a small tray with soda and snacks on it. He escorted me to his room.

The picture of his soon to be x-wife was in full view sitting on his chest of drawers. I tried to ignore it but it was impossible. I sat on a chair next to the bed and tried to blend in. He's got to do something with that picture. I bet that's his wife. I had to overcome the strain of looking at the picture, so I confronted him about it. I kicked off my shoes.

"Is that your wife?"

"Yes"

"What's her name?" I thought I may as well know her name since she's a fixture among his things.

"Gloria."

"Are you still in love with her?"

"No."

"She's very pretty." I lied. Rod said the picture was her high school portrait. I wondered why he had an *old* picture of her. She must look like Shamu now.

"Does the picture bother you?"

"No, but it gives the impression you still have strong feelings for her."

He leaned against the chest of drawers. "She and I have been through a lot together."

"Do you think you will reconcile in the future?"

"I doubt it. She refuses to go to Alanon and doesn't realize we both need a program. She doesn't think she has a problem."

"Oh, that's too bad," I responded sympathetically.

"Yeah, she abused drugs right along with me, but I was the only one who decided to get help."

"Do you have children together?"

"Yes, three daughters," he said with a lot of pride. "She had the oldest when we first met but I raised her."

Gloria needed a joint.

"Oh, well, you must know how to treat women, since you have daughters and all," I said to him.

Rod flashed his sexy smile, then sat down on the bed, close to where I sat. He reached over and rested his hand just above my knee, moved it in the direction of my hip and said, "Now, what were you asking me the other night about my ability to perform?"

"Oh I just wanted to know if it would be a problem when, well, you know." I blushed and tingled inside. I was about to get what I wanted. He leaned over from the bed and kissed me lightly on the side of my mouth. I kissed him back softly on the lips. Mmmm, good was the only thought I had. I wanted more.

"Know what? Do you *want* to find out if my hip's working?"

That's not all I wanted to know about. What about those other parts too? "Yeah, why not?" I decided to live a little and I let Rod undress me. I stood up to help him with the zipper on my slacks. He sat on the bed admiring me for a moment then reached for me, putting both hands on my hips. He pulled me close to him and held me a long time, massaging my back with his big hands and strong fingers. I wondered if foreplay ever got any better than this. Since things were going so well I just relaxed and got into it. Rod stood in front of me, determined and ready to make a real, long lasting impression. He succeeded. I was hooked. We used several black jacks in one hour. I left his apartment walking funny.

On my way home I thought about my new replacement for Eddie. Rod was a very passionate lover and it was a shame I couldn't have stayed longer than I did. There was so *much* of him to enjoy and I savored every moment and every inch.

In my mind I had conjured up thoughts of a friendship/relationship that could lead to marriage. Why is it that when a woman meets a man, she instantly sizes him up for marriage? Especially if she sleeps with him? It's a fact. All women do it. Most women have this need to be married, especially if a woman thinks she will benefit in some way. These same women think marriage will make a man monogamous and commit to a relationship. Period. Marriage works for some, but most of the time men feel trapped and will do anything to avoid emotional issues women struggle with. Why do we fall in love with the man we are having sex with? Even when we don't mean to?

I overlooked the display of Gloria's picture. The explanation Rod gave temporarily satisfied me. After all, we *did* have great sex. He had taken my mind completely off the focus of the picture.

Once in my car I pushed in a cassette tape and listened to Ice Cube describe he stupidity of women. Yes, it's universal. We can't help ourselves.

I called Pam first thing in the morning. It had been a month since we last talked and we needed to get caught up on things. Pookie had been out of the pen a few weeks and I wondered how things were working out, how Pam was holding up.
"Hi, Pam. What have you been up to?"
"Oh, hi Sasha! I haven't been up to very much. Just taking care of Pookie and working my ass off," she sighed. "You know, Sasha, I'm so tired. My back aches. I've been working a split shift at the hospital and it's wearing me out."
"Oh, so that's why I haven't heard from you."
"Yes, and I moved to a bigger place and with the packing and unpacking, its been a nightmare. Pookie's been helpful, though. I don't know what I would have done without him."
You would have done just fine, thank you. "Has he started working yet?"
"He starts next week. His uncle is a landscaper and he needs some help on a project he has to finish."
"That's great! That should be a relief to you."
"Yes, and Pookie's already talking about where he's going to take me out for dinner when he gets his first paycheck. But we have so many bills. Up until now, we've had only one paycheck and the cost of the move set us back, and..."
"Let him," I interrupted. "He wants to romance you and you deserve it! Don't you think he's ready for an intimate

meal, in public? My God, he's been dining with Charlie Manson for eighteen months. I'm sure he would like to gaze across a table at you instead of some sex offender he could never bond with. The bills will take care of themselves. Let him take care of you, for a change."

"You know, you're right, Sasha. He said he was going to take care of things, so I should let him."

"Good girl," I agreed.

"Sasha, he said I'm the only woman he will ever love. He has never loved anyone the way he loves me."

I hope Pookie's not lying to my friend. Pam was putting everything she had in the relationship to make it work. For once maybe one of us can get some results from doing the right thing. From our loyalty.

"I'm so happy for you, but let me tell you what happened to me last night..." I told Pam about the production meeting and my visit to Rod's. We talked about the annoying picture and what little purpose it served.

"Well, Sasha maybe he keeps it there so when his girls come over and see it, they won't think he hates her." I laughed at Pam's evaluation of the situation, even though she might have been right. I realized I would get nowhere on that topic so I quickly changed it.

"I went to Oakland last month."

"You did? Did you have a good time?"

"Sure did. Paulette was upset with her boyfriend and was thinking of doing herself in. So I intervened and saved a life. This man Paulette was fucking had a girlfriend who lived with him and when he suddenly married the girl Paulette was pissed off about it. She was going to kill him so I decided to drive up to calm her down. She was really tripping. You know I had to go see about my cousin, besides, it was nice to get away for a few days. Since she decided to take up with men again, its been a little bumpy for her. She has to learn all over again that men are a luxury, not a necessity. This is the nineties!"

"And that a bird in hand is worth two in the bush," Pam laughed.

"Right on!" We had a good laugh after Pam's remark. Pam and I understood the statement and felt sorry for Paulette who missed out on vital information about men while she was going with women.

"Well, I have to go. I'll talk to you in a few days to see how you and Pookie are doing."

"Okay, I gotta finish getting dressed for work. Talk to you later."

And we hung up.

4

The photograph of Marlene depicted happiness, but I thought about the fight I had with her a few months ago. Instead of getting on each other's nerves, we called a hiatus every now and then. I chose to reflect on the happy times with Marlene and was eager for the period of silence to end. As with Pam, Marlene had unconditional love and loyalty for me. We became friends at one of my lowest points and Marlene welcomed me into her life with open arms. No suspicions. I was recovering from the rape and trying to put my life back together. A late summer barbecue given by a mutual friend, Lou, was where I met Marlene and her husband, Dennis. That day I was despondent, sitting alone in a corner when Marlene came over and said 'Hi' to me.

August, 1972

Marlene introduced herself and asked me what my name was and who I was there with. I told her I had come alone. Lou knew me. He was a good friend. He invited me to the party after he learned about the rape. He wanted to lift my spirits. Dennis and Lou were sports fanatics and attended NFL games together. They were good friends also.

"Do you like football?" Marlene had a disgusted look on her face when she asked me that question.

"It's okay, why?"

"Because my husband and Lou are in the den watching the Dallas/Eagles game and the opening game of the season hasn't even been played yet. I guess I've lost him for the rest of the afternoon.

"You don't like football?"

"Not really. The only time I get interested is when it gets close to the Super Bowl game. It's worth watching then. My husband Dennis, oh, have you met him? He's the one with the big Afro." I had noticed him earlier.

"The one with Lou?"

"Yes, they are sports crazies." She told me how, when the football season was over, Dennis and Lou would dive right into the basketball season. Lou got season tickets for Laker games. That year Dennis took care of the tickets for football games. They went to San Francisco for games to and other places as far away as New Orleans. Marlene gave me detailed descriptions of their betting wins and loses from games. Some wins included nights out on the town, trips to Tahoe, weekend cruises to Mexico, and jewelry, in some cases. Like the three carat diamond ring Marlene was wearing. Her small physique enhanced the beauty of the incredible bauble. It didn't look gaudy. I thought Marlene was so cool, telling me all that personal information. She continued to share stories about her husband's goings on. I knew Lou was a loan shark by profession, so I was interested in hearing about their gambling escapades. Marlene said Dennis and Lou had been friends for years. I had not met Marlene and Dennis because Lou's friendship with me was new.

"What are you drinking? I'm on my way to the bar. Do you want anything?" Marlene reached for my glass.

"Oh, just 7-Up. Thanks." I was already beginning to feel paralyzed by the cognac I had just finished. I liked Marlene. Bonding happened immediately.

Most of the men at the party gathered around the TV in the den to watch the game while the women ate, drank, and talked among ourselves. It turned out to be a great party after all, and Marlene and I exchanged phone numbers so we could talk later.

The next day the phone rang and it was Marlene. "Hello, may I speak to Sasha, please?"

"This is she," I answered in an irritated tone.

"Are you busy? This is Marlene.."

I was relieved to hear a friendly voice. "Oh, hi! No. I'm just sitting here sewing at the moment."

"Oh, do you sew?"

"Yep. It keeps me out of trouble."

"What are you doing later?"

"I don't have any set plans for later."

"Why don't you come over? I want to meet your daughter. I told the twins about you and your baby and they want to see her. Dennis is going to watch Monday Night football with his friends, so come on over."

Marlene gave me her West Los Angeles address and directions to her home.

"Do you like chili?"

"Yes I do." I began to salivate.

"I made a pot this afternoon so you get to sample my cooking." I couldn't believe the generosity of my probable new friend. Two days ago I didn't know Marlene so the surprise invitation to dinner made me begin to feel accepted by her.

Eileen and I arrived at Marlene's house at seven. Marlene lived in upscale Leimert Park, an area in west Los Angeles where the predominate design of homes was Spanish stucco. She cheerfully answered the door after the first push on the buzzer.

"Hi, come on in! Is this Eileen? She's so pretty. How old did you say she is?"

"Eighteen months." I put Eileen down and she began to wander about. "She is trying to talk now. Where are your girls?" I asked as I looked into the tastefully decorated living room.

"In the kitchen having chili. Want some?"

My sense of smell let me know something hearty and tasty was being consumed nearby. Marlene motioned toward sounds of giggling and other gentle noises coming from the kitchen.

"It smells so good in here. Thank you," I said, forgetting she told me she had twins, thinking I was seeing double for a moment when I saw her girls. I picked up Eileen and walked over to her girls sitting at the kitchen table. The uncanny similarities of the girls was dizzying. I had not taken a drink that morning so it had to be real.

"Hi," they giggled in unison.

"Hi," I responded, totally amazed.

"What's your baby's name?" asked one of the twins.

"Eileen, what are your names?"

"Kai," said the other twin.

"And Jasmine," said her twin.

"What beautiful names." They were so cute and so tiny. Marlene could not get a word in the conversation. The twins were handling the formal introductions very well, so she went to the cupboard and got two bowls and a plate.

Marlene was a great cook and hostess, and her hospitality made me feel a little guilty. I wasn't used to being waited on. Eileen and I felt comfortable and right at home. After we ate I insisted Marlene let me fill the dishwasher, at least. She should have been exhausted, but her work was not done yet. She had a set of twins and a husband. She never had a free moment.

Kai and Jasmine took Eileen upstairs to their room where they played with toys. At seven, the twins were years beyond their chronological age.

Marlene invited me into her master bedroom where we continued to talk and visit. I couldn't believe how warm and open Marlene was with me only knowing me for less than 24 hours. I thought about how strange it was for some friendships to be destined. We discovered that we had had similar tastes, were adventurous and loved to travel. We enjoyed camping. I was studying fashion design and Marlene wanted to further her education, possibly earning a degree of some kind. She would go back to school in a heartbeat if she could juggle a part-time job, her family responsibilities, and study time without it disrupting her current routine. Her maid came in two days a week, but even with the help, it would be difficult.

Dennis took good care of his family. He owned a foreign car repair and detail shop he built from the ground up. He did not want Marlene to work at all but to stay home and manage the household and finances of his business. I admired their upwardly mobile lifestyle. I wished my floundering estranged husband Barry would do the same for me and Eileen. We talked about our mothers and compared notes on ways we were victimized with unjust punishment as kids. We shared personal things about each other, including smoking. Marlene said that although she smoked cigarettes, she never tried marijuana. We agreed that smoking cigarettes was a dirty habit.

Marlene understood that after going through what I had been through she could see the reason to drink or abuse drugs, just to get over it. She knew I wanted to forget. "I can't believe the police did nothing," Marlene said in a sympathetic voice. "I would have done the same thing."

It was getting late and I did not want to wear out my welcome. Or get up from the comfortable velvet sofa I had been sitting on in her bedroom. I was completely gratified and hoped Marlene understood why I had to leave. It was past bedtime for all of the girls. Marlene said the next time we came over we could drink some wine and stay in the guest room. It belonged to us whenever we needed to get away.

When I said my prayers that night before going to bed, I thanked God for my new friend. I cried as I fell asleep.

* * *

Present

"Hello," Marlene said.
"Hi, what have you been up to lately?"

"Sasha?"

"Yes, it's me."

"Hi, I was just talking to Jasmine about you. Girl, you're going to live a long time. Superstition."

"I hope you're right. How is Jasmine doing? Did she ever get her fall classes straightened out?"

"Yes, finally. She graduates in December!"

"Whew! I'm so happy. And you said she was taking forever."

"Well, she did take forever. Kai finished college last year."

"What difference did it make? None. Both of your daughters are college graduates now. You should be happy."

"I am, believe me. And I'm broke too."

"Happy and broke. What a combination!" I warmly responded. I knew Marlene was no where close to broke.

Marlene and Dennis had financial problems five years after I met them, but they managed to come out of it and buy a bigger home in Ladera Heights. The mini mansion they lived in had a pool and spa and a custom built green house that sat in a corner of their park like back yard. Marlene grew different varieties of orchids and ferns in her little conservatory. The yard was always perfectly manicured. In the Spring and early Summer the jacaranda tree in the back yard sprinkled beautiful lavender petals over the grass in the yard. Marlene and I enjoyed the dazzling flower shows on Saturday mornings when we sipped lattes on the patio. I was glad Marlene and Dennis got it together and put the twins through college. Last year Dennis bought Marlene a new convertible Jaguar. When her insurance went up she worked extra hours so she could make her insurance payments on time. Her insurance had to wait recently, when fall tuition for Jasmine was due.

Marlene decided to park the Jag and drove one of Dennis' loan cars until she could pay her own insurance. Jasmine's tuition was a priority at the time.

I dreamed of having a perfect marriage like the one I thought Marlene and Dennis had. They made a commitment to stay together, and it meant something. In the midst of astounding divorce rates, their marriage gave me hope. I wanted to be married to a loving husband and have all my children by the same man. But from a very young age, I knew I would face hardship with men.

5

I learned early how easy it was for women to get confused when reacting to advances by men. What you hope for isn't always what you get.

February, 1968

I boarded an airplane bound for college in Baton Rouge, Louisiana, just four days after graduating from high school. While in flight, all I could think about was Larry Mac, the boy who humiliated me all through school. My attraction to Larry Mac began in eighth grade and really swelled by my senior year. He treated me badly most of the time but was civil to me once in a while. I was too young to understand the connection between the beatings I received at home and Larry's occasional piercing comments. I always forgave his obnoxious behavior and continued my quiet devotion to him. I thought he was mean to me because he liked me.

Feeling totally defeated, I took a deep breath and declared that I was sick in the head. I thought I had mental problems. I promised myself I would forget about Larry Mac and find myself a *real* boyfriend. Someone who would be proud to take me out on a date When the plane landed in Louisiana my mind was made up.

My new roommate met me at the airport. Instead of going directly to the college we went to my roommate's parents' house. My roommate Becky, was from Baton Rouge. Her family was home when we arrived at the house so I met everyone. Becky's family was my surrogate family for the time I studied at Southern University. Man, I thought things would be great, especially since Becky had a car. I thought we could leave the campus dorm anytime we wanted to! Unfortunately, it did not work out that way.

Becky's boyfriend, a student at the college also, was lost without her and likewise, she couldn't live without him. He was a football player and traveled with the team throughout the region to play games. Every bit of extra time Becky had after her studies was spent with him. Her absence and my isolation in the dorm from family and friends became unbearable. It forced me to venture out on the campus in search of new friends. Deciding being cooped up for one week was long enough, I wanted to find the Student Union on campus, and possibly make new friends.

I stepped outside of the dorm into cold air as the heavy steel door slammed shut behind me. I tightened my plaid wool scarf around my neck and put on my earmuffs. February was extremely cold in Louisiana, unlike the warm year round weather in California. I was not used to the cooler temperature in that part of the country so I froze.

The green wool overcoat I had on was a Christmas gift from Mama who said 'it might come in handy.' I hated the shade of green of the coat but admitted that it did come in handy, for warmth. I looked down at the pebble and concrete pathway I was following and saw puddles of frozen water the recent rain and freezing temperatures had created. I fumbled when I put my gloves on, dropping one glove that landed on top of the ice. I picked up the glove and tested the ice by pushing my boot onto the icy surface breaking the ice as my shoe traveled to the bottom of the puddle. That caused me to lose my balance. I caught myself before going down. When I looked up I was standing in front of the Student Union.

I learned when one travels alone, anything is possible. Once inside the Student Union, I joined a noisy group of student radicals having a heated discussion about the Black Muslim organization.

"Malcolm X is a racist!" shouted one student. "He preaches nothing but hatred in his autobiography!"

"We've tried to march, and look what happened in Selma. Whitey thinks Martin Luther King is a joke! So far, marching has only gotten people hurt!" screamed another debater. "We need to have our own state, right here in the USA," he continued. He's never been to Watts.

"That is so ridiculous. Where do we get the land from? Do we just take it?" a female student added.

"The Black Muslim movement is gaining momentum all over the place, and we *all* need to get involved," commented the same young man who spoke before. He held his own among his peers. When he caught my eye, I started to focus on him alone. He winked at me and smiled, then continued with the ongoing discussion. Before the debate escalated to badgering, I got up and looked around the room for people that might have been familiar to me. When I did not see anyone I recognized I walked to the door. Just as I reached the door, I felt a tug at my coat sleeve. A voice said, "What's the matter, is the conversation too deep for you?"

I turned my body around to respond and saw it was the handsome green-eyed creature who was so opinionated a few seconds ago. He said, "Are you leaving?"

I thought it was obvious. "Yes, I'm bored."

"So where are you off to? What's your name?"

"Sasha. Back to the dorm. Who are you?"

"Craig Willis. Are you a freshman? I haven't seen you around here."

"That's because I just arrived this semester. Yes, I'm a freshman."

"I'm going that way. I'll walk with you." Craig opened the glass door for me and we walked in the early evening air. It was cooler outside and I immediately buttoned my coat and reached in my pockets for my leather gloves. Craig zipped up his coat and pulled the fur lined hood over his head. He pulled the cord in the hood and tied a knot under his chin. I liked his strong face. No ingrown hairs. I wondered if he shaved. My ears were burning because of the cold, so I put my ear muffs on again. I constantly complained about the icy breezes as we walked toward the dorm.

"Is your roommate home?" Craig asked me.

"No, she's never home. Today she and her boyfriend are having dinner with her parents. They are inseparable."

"So, what do you do in your spare time?"
"Study." That was a lie. I'd been daydreaming lately.
"That's all?"
"Well, I don't have a lot of friends here. They're all in California."
"California. That's where you're from?"
"Yes, Los Angeles. And I miss it."
"Do you have a boyfriend there?"
"Well, no." I thought about Larry Mac and my pain returned momentarily. "There was someone, but you know how it is after graduation. I was leaving and all so we decided to say goodbye." I didn't tell him that Larry Mac treated me like crap and started dating an enemy of mine and took her to the prom. I actually thought that he would ask *me* to the prom and when he didn't I was devastated. Craig didn't need to know that. I could feel his mind working overtime. I saw sparks flying all around him.

"Why don't you come home with me? I live just off campus, down the road a bit. My place is kind of run down but it's warm inside. My rent's cheap so I can keep the heat on."

I thought it was nice of him to invite me over. I knew I did not need permission for the adventure, and I agreed to go home with Craig. We reached the dorm and I deposited my books. I was ready for a journey into the unknown.

Craig and I continued to walk down the pebble path past the dormitory. The sun slowly went down in the distance behind us. The path we followed fed into an old road full of potholes that took us to a railroad crossing. We paused at the tracks to allow a noisy train to go by then crossed to enter a neighborhood that previously held no interest for me.

We approached an old decaying apartment building and I began to wonder about my decision to venture off with the stranger. It was dark and there were no outside lights to illuminate the building we got close to, but Craig led me down a flattened path of overgrown grass that led to his tiny apartment door.

We were anxious to get inside, out of the cold arctic temperature. Once inside the warm apartment, we stopped shaking. It took a few moments for the numbness to wear off.

Craig was right when he told me the apartment was not much to look at. It was a tiny two room hole with old, dilapidated furniture needing refinishing and a prayer. In the bedroom was an old mattress on the floor he slept on. A three drawer chest and lamp sat on a milk crate beside the mattress. Craig had an interesting collection of black lite posters covering one wall. Portraits of Malcolm X, Huey Newton and Martin Luther King were arranged close together on another. He said he spent most of his time in the bedroom where it was the most comfortable place to study. I took off my coat and gave it to Craig. We sat and talked for hours in the privacy of his temporary home. I was happy to have a new friend.

It was getting late and I knew breaking the dorm rules would jeopardize my freedom. We agreed to meet the next day at the Student Union and possibly go to his place again. I liked his little dump. I was safe there. Being with him became my definition of a cheap date.

Our second date was meager, like the first. We ate dinner at the snack bar in the Student Union then walked to his place. Again, we talked for hours, forgetting about our studies for the second night in a row. As we learned more about each other, something happened. The more he got me to open up about my romantic blues, the more relaxed he got. He sensed I had no experience. According to him, I was naïve to think I could keep having intimate evenings with him and not expect to make love at some point. I could not hold an intelligent conversation on the subject of lovemaking with Craig because I had no real experience. I had lost my virginity, but that was it. The act didn't leave me wanting more. Mama always said sex was dirty and never discussed it with me, so when I got my period again after my first time of sex, I never thought about doing it again. That was the extent of my sex education.

Craig reassured me having sex with someone you care about is not a dirty act. He convinced me that making love was something special and I would learn to enjoy it, especially with him. He decided I could use a few lessons.

Craig wrapped his athletic arms around my shoulders and pulled me close to his him on the bed and kissed me for the first time. His gentle touch sent me into complete submission. I couldn't believe what I was willing to let him do to me. Craig unzipped my dress and carefully took it off. My quiet cotton undergarments were exposed, and caused me to blush. I was shy but it began to fade when he caressed and kissed my full still covered breasts. He told me how voluptuous they were, and how much they needed attention. I allowed him to take my bra off. I didn't resist. It was the first time I had been undressed by a man. It was also the first time my anatomy had been referred to in such sweet terms. I began to feel good about the breasts I always hated and thought were vulgar because of their size. Craig covered my dark nipples with his mouth and concentrated on his seduction of me.

His well-trained tongue sent messages downward, where I could see Craig's hand struggling to go behind my white panties. He took the cotton panties off and continued show me things me in his own special way.

"How do you feel right now?" Craig asked as he massaged my vagina.

"What you are doing with your tongue tickles me down there," I moaned.

"When I did this?" and he covered the top of my breast again with his mouth. His tongue did aerobics on my rising nipple and all I could do was close my eyes and smile with pleasure.

"You have beautiful breasts." He kissed me softly all over my bosom. Craig reached for my hand and placed it at his belt buckle. He guided my hand down the front of his pants. I could feel his growing excitement. I wanted him to get undressed so I struggled to undo his belt, and with his help, unzipped his pants. He let them fall to the floor, along with his shorts. I was shocked at what I saw and not sure if I was even ready...He was huge...I wondered what he going to do with that. I was afraid to touch him.

Craig knew I didn't know what the hell I was doing so he took my hand and gently put it on him.

"Go ahead, you can touch me. I like to be stroked." Craig laid down beside me while I stroked him and became familiar with his beautiful body. The heat was brewing inside me as I laid there beside Craig, waiting for the next thrill.

"Please don't hurt me," I whispered.

'I don't want to hurt you. I just want to make love to you. Are you a virgin?"

"No," I said proudly.

"Then it won't hurt, just relax."

He lied about the pain. It hurt at first, but was soon the beautiful act he talked about earlier. I began to see that having sex was not dirty.

I neglected my studies for weeks, letting Craig teach me all he knew about lovemaking. Then it stopped, as abruptly as it began. All of a sudden I couldn't find Craig anywhere. I was in love with sex at that point. He never told me he loved me when we were having sex. *He used me for sex.*

I learned the first lesson of many to follow. Revenge is not always so sweet. Three weeks after we first made love I saw Craig on campus, walking with another female student. I was hurt and embarrassed, and I avoided him, finally figuring out that he had only wanted my body, not my heart. My heart needed a fix. Now he was going after someone else. It brought back memories of Larry Mac. I was trying to forget him. The only difference was that no sex had been involved with Larry who had hurt me deeply. I wanted to get even with Craig. I wanted to make sure Craig heard about me on campus, since he gave me experience in the area of sex and lovemaking.

I was not concerned about my tarnished reputation after my parents saw my mid-term grades. They informed me by letter I would not be returning to Southern in the fall. After hearing the unhappy news from my parents, I didn't care who I slept with, or when or where. My roommate Becky saw I was miserable but couldn't do anything to make me feel better. She arranged for us to attend an Otis Redding concert in New Orleans, to help chase away the blues.

The concert was great fun but it didn't help much. I swore never again to allow myself to be tricked into thinking a man could really truly love me. My higher education was complete for the moment. I learned once again that rejection is inevitable. In May, I returned to California.

6

June, 1968

"What in the devil were you doing down there?" Mama screamed. My secret was no longer a secret and Mama was not happy. I couldn't figure out how my grades arrived on the same day I suddenly became ill and doubled over in pain. Mama rushed me to the family doctor whose diagnoses was an infection, of a sexual origin.

"Who did you have sex with?" Mama demanded to know. In reality, I couldn't remember all the names, so I didn't answer. If she had asked me how many, I probably could have given a ball-park figure. Around twenty? Maybe twenty five? Hell, I didn't know.

I lost count at some point.

"Everybody," I mumbled. Mama hauled off and slapped the crap out of me.

"You whore!"

The verbal abuse and criticism was more than I could bear. I needed love and understanding. I began to cry as

Mama badgered and cussed at me, saying that I would never embarrass her again. I was not allowed to use Mama's bathroom. She ordered me to disinfect my own bathroom after each use. Mama made me feel dirty and nasty. She called me stupid and worthless and told me she would not spend another dime on my college education. In her closing comments as we left the doctor's office, Mama told me I would never amount to anything.

The ride home from the doctor's office was not a happy one for me. I took insults and criticism from Mama. When we got home I went to my bedroom and sat on the edge of the bed. I stared at a seam in the wallpaper that was coming apart. Just like my life. Before I went away to school I was going to repair it and now it looked worse than ever. I wanted to fix the separating wallpaper now that I knew I would be stuck there for a while. Everything around me needed fixing then, since I was such a failure. I didn't need to be constantly reminded of my flaws.

After about two months of criticism and fighting with Mama, I felt I had listened to enough. The situation was taking away what was left of my self image. At the same time, Pam was having problems at home.

Pam's mom decided to run off with a man she was having an affair with. I got a desperate phone call late one night from Pam that made me snap out of my depression. She had taken an overdose of sleeping pills and wanted to end her life. She didn't call for an ambulance, Pam called me. By the time I reached her house, she had passed out and slipped into a mild coma. Pam still had a pulse so I called the paramedics immediately. I was afraid to lose her. I wondered what Pam could have been thinking. The emergency crew rushed Pam to the hospital where technicians pumped her stomach. She slowly regained consciousness. It was a miracle that brought her back. The medics told me later that had I not called when I did, Pam would not have made it. She and I were only eighteen at the time and I could not figure out why we had so many problems. It was only the beginning.

When Pam finally recovered from her attempted suicide we talked about going back to college, locally. We wanted to do something constructive with our lives so we registered for fall classes in Harbor City. Pam volunteered to drive us to class in the 'blue bomb', a convertible Buick her mother gave her when she ran off. She bought herself a brand new Mercedes on her way out the door.

We arranged our classes so we would be out of school by twelve noon every day, no evening classes. The schedule was great for us until we wanted to party at night during the week. Even though Mama had not been so mean to me, she still managed to bring up the pain of my indiscretion in conversations about things unrelated to my current affairs. To drown out the criticism, I began to experiment with drugs. Pam could get red devils and I found a source for pot. After combining our resources many evenings were spent at Pam's house, where we tried to forget our problems. By mid-semester, however, we decided to get full time jobs. School was becoming a burden and we needed a steady cash flow, to buy drugs. We used drugs to try to erase all the bad things we had been experiencing in our lives.

Pam was the first one to get a job and soon after, I was employed. We felt like we had accomplished something for a change and knew there was a God. I got comfortable with my new clerical job with the County, vowing to get my own apartment as soon as I could. I was independent with my own money coming in. Mama criticized my decision to drop out of school and get a job, but I hated asking Mama for money. I wanted to be independent. She couldn't see that.

When Mama insisted I start paying rent, my blood boiled. We argued constantly about how impossible it had become for me to live at home. If you are going to cuss me out everyday, don't expect me to give you anything! One evening after having an ugly scene with Mama, I called Pam and Dewayne for support. They told me not to cry and they were on their way to pick me up. We were going to the motorcycle club to shoot pool and have fun. I took two seconal capsules just before Pam and Dewayne arrived.

By the time we reached the club, I was well on my way to being stoned. Dewayne parked his VW in front of the club, next to a row of customized motorcycles. Pam was tipsy too and we stumbled out of the car onto the sidewalk. It was up to Dewayne to be sure we stayed upright throughout the evening. He was the designated responsible person of the group. Dewayne escorted wobbly Pam and I inside the rundown storefront the bikers called 'home'. We found vacant chairs in a corner near the pool table. Pam and I sat down and did not move.

"You guys want anything?" I heard someone ask the question but the voice was not familiar. I didn't see Dewayne anywhere.

"Yeah, bring me a beer," Pam answered in a slurred voice. Pam didn't even drink beer.

"Would you like something?" the voice repeated.

"No, thank you," I carefully pronounced my jumbled words.

I hoped I would be able to stand up long enough to shoot one game. One game of eight-ball was all I could handle.

Dewayne ran the table. He left me astounded. He teased me constantly, He told me I could not handle getting high. I agreed with him but did not apologize for my condition. I was happy in my condition for the night. I had problems.

The lingering cigarette smoke in the small night club was unbearable. I decided to go outside for some fresh air. I made my way through the crowd and out the front door to the sidewalk. I swayed back and forth several times and saw an old milk crate sitting against the building. I walked over to it and sat down. The fresh air in my face was exhilarating.

"Hi, what's your name?" The voice was familiar to me, like the one that offered me a drink earlier. I looked up and tried to focus on the person standing in front of me. There were so many of him.

"Sasha, what's shore's?"

"Jett. Jett Stream. Who are the people you're with?"

"My girlfriend Pam and our friend Dewayne. Are they still inside?" I focused long enough to take a good look at the strange person. Jett's clean shaven face and bright smile made me pay attention for a moment.

"They are inside shooting pool. Your girlfriend is having a good time."

"I need to go back inside."

"Why? It's nice and cool out here. I'll stay here to keep you company."

"Okay, but in a minute I gotta get up an' walk around some. I'm thirsty. Do they sell sodas inside?"

"I don't know, but there's a liquor store across the street. What do you want?"

"A 7-Up would be nice, thank you." Through blurred vision, I watched Jett J-walk across the street to the store. I liked his medium build and was relieved to see he had a proportioned body to go with his noble face. I looked down at the sidewalk to the dotted pattern of chewing gum deposits made over the years and lazily closed my eyes, wondering why I was sitting on a discarded milk crate, looking at a filthy sidewalk. My depression carried me to the paunches of despair, challenging every principle I had been taught. Sunday School did not prepare me for this.

I looked up to see Jett coming back across the street with a small brown paper bag. He gave it to me. I opened the bag to find a 7-Up, bag of potato chips, Hostess Twinkies and a plastic cup.

"I thought you might have the munchies and I wasn't sure what you'd like."

"Ooh, I love Twinkies, thanks. And thanks for the 7-Up."

"What's a nice girl like you doing in a place like this?" Jett looked puzzled. My conservative look gave me away. I knew it.

"Why, I don't look like I belong?" I moaned.

"I'm afraid not. You look like a nice little college girl who got lost among the hippies."

"Gee, thanks." I opened the soda and poured some in the cup. "Would you like some?"

"No, go ahead. Knock yourself out. Seriously though, what do you do?"

"I was in college but I'm working now. In my spare time I make clothes. What about you? You look out of place too." I worked hard to sit up straight.

Jett was very clean cut. He had on off-white corduroy slacks, a sky-blue sports coat, matching blue alligator loafers and a pin striped shirt worn open at the neck. My focus improved when I realized he appeared decent.

"I know you didn't come here on a bike, dressed like that."

"No, but I do own a Chopper. I'm in my car tonight. I just wanted to get out tonight and get some fresh air."

"Get out? Are you married?"

"No, I'm single and I live alone. It gets lonely sometimes so I come down here to have a beer and hang out with the fellas. Are you married?"

"No, I live with my parents right now. I'm thinking about moving out. Soon.

"Can I call you sometime?"

"Sure." I fumbled around in my purse to get a pen. It didn't take me long to locate one. Jett handed me a business card to write my number on. I turned the card over to read the front.

"Jett Stream, photographer," I said. "You're a photographer?"

"Yes I am. Just write your name on the back. I'll give you another card."

I didn't know any photographers so I was impressed. We continued to chat in front of the club for a while. After a while Dewayne and Pam came outside and found me. They asked if I was ready to go home. I told them I was and Jett said he would call me the next day. I wrote my name and phone number on the back of the business card.

After work on Friday, I went straight home so I could get some much needed rest. The night before was murder on my system and I paid for it that day at work. I wanted to be home if Jett remembered to call. He seemed like a pretty nice guy. I slept soundly that night and Jett called first thing Saturday morning.

After we talked briefly I found out that like myself, Jett was an only child. Unlike me though, Jett was aire to a sizable real estate fortune. He lived in an apartment above a photography studio that was given to him on his twenty fifth birthday. When Jett was twenty, he and his father made a trust agreement that awarded the property to Jett at the time of his fathers' death. His father was losing a battle with cancer and his dying wish was for Jett to finish college. His father's estate included additional apartment buildings and several houses that were being managed by his grandparents and an aunt. There were bank accounts too.

Jett enjoyed boating, horseback riding and cycling. He tried skydiving once, but when his primary chute failed and he barely escaped death, he decided learning to fly would be safer. He took flying lessons and earned licenses to fly twin engine aircraft and helicopters. For a second I thought I was out of my league with Jett, but I had lived a little, too. I had a lot to contribute to the conversation with my own stories of adventure and travel with my family. I relaxed with Jett and felt comfortable enough to accept a dinner invitation that evening. Afterward, he would show me his photography studio and bachelor apartment. I gave Jett my address and he agreed to pick me up at seven.

When I finished talking to Jett I put on a new swimsuit that I had just bought at a late Summer sale. Even though it was early October, it was still warm enough for a swim. I headed for the backyard where the swimming pool was. I studied the still water in the clear pool for a moment then dove in head first. I didn't mention to Jett that I enjoyed water sports also.

He arrived on time in his red MG. Jett had an appetite for seafood and asked me if I knew of a romantic place for us to eat at. I told him I wanted to go to San Pedro and have dinner at the Ports of Call, my favorite place for seafood. I chose that location because as a child I enjoyed watching the cruise ships sail past the dining room window when my family dined there for Sunday brunch. When Pam and I were young kids, we loved to count the passing barges when we ate. After eating we would go outside to the patio of the restaurant and feed the seagulls. We smuggled breadsticks out of the restaurant. It would feel different to be there as a young woman with a man on a date.

I liked being with Jett because he did not criticize me. When I told him about my heartbreak and disappointment in Louisiana, he sympathized and understood my pain and disappointment. It saddened him to hear me talk about the unhealthy relationship with Mama. Before my comments about Mama became downright vicious, we changed the subject. We discovered we both had a fascination for the ocean and other large waterways. Not only was he handsome with a good muscular body, he was charismatic, intelligent and a great conversationalist. We discovered we had lot in common. He had finished college, and thought it was a safe stepping stone for all African Americans.

Jett cheerfully paid the dinner tab and thanked me for the unusual dining experience. He held my hand as we walked to the car. When we reached the MG, he put his arms around my waist and kissed me softly on the lips. It was not a deep kiss, although I would have allowed it. After the kiss, we just stood there and held on to each other.

Jett and I headed north on the Harbor Freeway in the red MG as we began to make our way to West Los Angeles. After exiting the swift moving Santa Monica Freeway Jett made his way north to Venice Boulevard that merged into San Vicente. We drove northwest on the well maintained boulevard until we reached a modern two-story Spanish stucco building flanked on either side by towering medical buildings. Jett parked in the rear of the building next to a freshly painted staircase that led to the second floor.

"I'll show you the studio after I show you the apartment. I like to go in this way at night," he said. He led me up a flight of stairs.

I wanted to see his studio since it meant so much to him. He enjoyed the success and pleasures his work brought him. He photographed Chaka Kahn and Phoebe Snow, and was going to photograph Pam Grier next week. His work with celebrities, mainly singers, was a childhood fantasy he was living.

The apartment was spacious, but cozy. Jett put in a built-in 50 gallon aquarium in the living room that contained a variety of tropical fish. Every room had an aquarium. The oak tables and bookshelves made me feel warm and content. The apartment was well kept, everything was in order.

"Come on Sasha. I'll show you the studio."

He took me by the hand and led me through the kitchen and down a narrow flight of stairs. At the bottom of the stairs Jett stopped to unlock a metal door. He opened the door and flipped on a light switch. We were standing behind a black curtain and could see light from the bottom on the other side. Jett stepped to the other side of the curtain and on to the studio floor. He held his arms out and said, "Welcome to my other world!" I laughed as I followed him in to the studio. "This is where I capture people in print, and make stars, sometimes. My name is getting out there now and I've made some great contacts. I've been asked to do some stills on an upcoming film that's currently in development."

On the walls of the studio were life-sized portraits of famous people, from musicians to actors, carefully preserved for an eternity. 'Jett Stream' was the name people sought after for his exquisite work with the airbrush. He was known for capturing the emotional depths of his clients in print.

"Would you like to photographed sometime? You can wear clothes you've designed, and I'll take some pictures."

After giving me the grand tour of the studio Jett turned the lights off and we went back upstairs to the apartment. I was comfortable and uneasy at the same time. I told Jett I was ready to go home.

The next morning I grabbed the newspaper from the front porch and started looking for an apartment. Pam was not ready to leave home yet so she came over to help me find something reasonably decent for rent in the classifieds. I discovered I needed to have more than the first month's rent to move in anywhere. Security and cleaning fees were required and were equivalent to one month's rent. All ads demanded some deposit be made. Disappointed, I realized I would not be moving as soon as I had hoped. It was going to take some real planning.

The next week I got lucky and found a furnished one bedroom apartment I could afford so I quietly packed my things and moved out when no one was home. I was happy to be going to my own place. No more Hitler-style wake-ups. Jett soon became a fixture in my apartment because he felt I needed the protection. I didn't mind him being over all the time because he always did nice things for me and made me feel special. The first time we made love he called his mother to tell her he found someone special. He had not pressured me to go to bed with him and said he would never make me do anything I did not want to do.

On most days after work I would go directly to the studio where Jett would be finishing his work for the day. I was totally in to his loving side. When his last client would leave, we would romp around the studio, sometimes making love on a prop or in a convenient chair. We did not care who caught us since 'we owned the place,' Jett said. He liked to cook, and would prepare dinner for us at his place before following me home to make sure I was safe. He told me he could never allow me to drive home alone at night. He was conscientious about his male responsibility.

When I got home one night, we discovered the front door was adjar. Someone had burglarized my apartment and got away with my stereo console, a clock-radio and a toaster. Jett wouldn't let me sleep there another night. By the end of the week, I was officially living with Jett.

When Mama learned about my new living arrangement she hit the roof. It was one more reason for Mama to criticize, but I didn't care about what she had to say. I was no longer alone. I had a companion I trusted. Jett promised to take care of me, and he did.

Jett treated me with the love and respect I deserved. On Sundays we went catamaran sailing in San Pedro Harbor. Once, he convinced me to fly with him in a twin engine airplane he borrowed from a friend. I was so scared during the flight that I was speechless through most of it. All I remembered about the frightening experience was the sight of tiny cars and trucks beneath me that looked like Hot Wheels operated by remote control. And the nausea I felt when we landed. I swore I would never fly in anything that compact again, ever. I made the right decision because one week later, Jett died when the Piper Cherokee he was flying fell from the sky, clipped the roof of a house, plowed past two parked cars and crashed into the sound wall beside a south land freeway. It took a long while for me to accept the fact my new love was gone.

7

I had contacted Jett's mother in Dallas the week before and invited her to join us for Christmas. I agonized about the call I now had to make. I knew she would be anticipating good news about our holiday plans. I had words of comfort for Jett's mother and then I informed her of her son's death. She screamed and fell over. She hit her head on the dinner table and started a small fire when she grabbed the tablecloth on her way down to the floor. The heavy sterling silver candelabra barely missed her head when it landed inches from her scalp, sending the flames to the tabletop. She recovered from the shock of the news, then boarded an airplane and flew to Los Angeles.

His mother took care of the funeral arrangements while I tried unsuccessfully to find Pam. Paulette dropped everything and came down from Oakland to be with me. Jett's Mother said it was painful to be in his apartment so Paulette and I did all things humanly possible to make her comfortable. The three of us grieved the surprising loss and managed a decent memorial for Jett. Pam was on vacation and could not be reached.

Within days of the memorial service his mother announced she would be returning to Dallas. She left with a suitcase full of personal items belonging to Jett. I had no idea what she had taken, and I didn't ask. I wished his mother well and promised to keep in touch.

In the week following Thanksgiving I received a certified letter from an attorney in Dallas informing me that I was to vacate the apartment and the premises. Jett's estate was now being handled by his mother, who planned to sell the property. The dirty bitch. Couldn't she have had the decency to discuss this with me when she was here? I then knew what his mother had taken from the apartment. Trust deeds, bank statements and bank passbooks were all missing from Jett's things. Things I had never thought about. I was to be out of the apartment by December 17. Eight days before Christmas.

My sympathy and compassion for this woman quickly turned to rage and hostility. The few days I had spent with her were strained at best and I felt the bombshells of pain would never ease up now that I was being evicted. I was alone again, wondering why this shit had to happen to me.

Paulette stayed with me longer that she had planned just so we could figure out what to do next. We needed housing and my paycheck from work was not enough to get us another apartment. Me and Paulette needed money fast, so we decided to use what we had, and called an escort service. We became hardworking girls after hours, within days. We were no strangers to the bed.

It did not take us long to make enough money to rent a nice apartment in Hollywood. Paulette got a job working as a cashier. We both liked Hollywood and wanted to be where the action was. The 'easy money' we were making came with risks and we wondered how much longer we could pretend to be hookers. Quick money bought a lot of things, like the furniture for the apartment. I maintained my day job and worked the service in the evening. But as expected, guilt began to set in. We were not behaving in the way we were brought up and were exposing ourselves unnecessarily to many dangers.

The guilt resurfaced and got the best of me. I decided to give up the night job and concentrate on my position with my daytime employer. The mental strain of it was making me ill. The burden of maintaining the exclusive apartment was incredible. Paulette wanted a change of pace from all we had done and in January She went to Chicago and I moved back home with my parents. I had no way of knowing the recent events in my life would lead me back to the place I did not want to be.

The criticism began as soon as I went back home and never stopped. Mama told me I had been stupid to move in with Jett and that I was a real loser. The unhealthy remarks were not what I needed to hear. I hated living by myself so for now, living with Mama would have to do.

One year later

My decision to enroll in Fashion Design School came in the months following Jett's death. I was finally getting around to the task of registering for classes to pursue my passion for designing, as Jett would have encouraged me to do. Mama was not happy about my career choice and said I was wasting my time. I couldn't understand why

Mama was being so cruel, knowing that sewing was what made my happy. I was able to get my hours at work changed to an evening shift so I could go to design school full time in the day. The schedule was grueling but worked out perfectly because I was rarely at home. I did not have time to cry about Jett anymore. It was time to get on with my life.

In design school I earned a reputation for being the most skilled sample maker in my class and was soon sought after for correcting the sewing errors of my classmates. The most skilled illustrator in my class was Cindy. We knew right away that each one of us possessed what the other lacked in skill. We easily became friends. If I had a problem with a sketch, Cindy was always able to help me find a way to fix it. Likewise, if Cindy struggled to properly set in a sleeve or zipper, I would make her rip it out and show her an easier way to do it, before the project was graded. We were the infamous couple on campus, because of our opposite skin colors.

Cindy had come to Los Angeles in search of a new life. Her abusive ex-husband had stolen her daughter from her and got full custody. She was out in the cold and with no money to fight with. So when she arrived in Los Angeles she decided to follow her dream to cultivate her talent as a designer. Cindy was a natural artist.

She was sympathetic and cared a lot about my personal bad experiences. She offered me moral support daily. Cindy had problems with her mother, similar to those I had experienced with Mama. Cindy had not spoken to her mother in years. At the age of twenty one we knew what we wanted to do. We wanted to become the most dynamic design duo on the West coast. We would call our label 'Zebra'.

As we advanced in our course of study Cindy and I felt subtle competition from each another that occasionally put a strain on the friendship. We would enter the same sketch contests. If either one of us won first place, which was usually the case, an observer of the friendship would suggest jealousy existed. Cindy and I talked about it and felt it was the others who were envious of our friendship. We rose above the rumors circulated daily. As my sketching improved I became more confident about my ability as a designer.

"Sasha, you did great! First place this time. You're getting better all the time." Cindy was sincere with her words.

"Thanks, Cindy, but I thought yours was much better than mine."

"Well, the judges didn't think so, and I'm happy with my second place," Cindy sighed.

"What are we doing for lunch today? My treat," I said.

"Oh, I can't today. Robert is taking me to lunch."

Robert was Cindy's new boyfriend who was already established in the garment industry as a manufacturer. Robert had a solution for everything. He was fortyish, divorced, and like Jett, wanted to protect his girl. He convinced Cindy that her tiny single apartment was not appropriate for her, even though she enjoyed the ever changing view of McArthur Park in downtown Los Angeles. Robert lived on his yacht at Marina Del Rey and pressured Cindy to move in with him. I admired her predicament. It reminded me of what I had had with Jett. I wanted to meet someone new myself but I had no time for romance, choosing to focus on school instead.

On Sunday I shopped for tomatoes at the neighborhood market and became the object of fascination for a fellow shopper. He was a tall, dark and well dressed. His moves were direct. When he spoke, the baritone sound of his voice commanded my attention. I was his prey.

"Hi, who are you?" he asked.

"My name is Sasha." I didn't bother to say hello.

"Are you married?" His tongue was hanging out. I figured it was the red silk mini-dress that hung on my body like a cheap suit I was wearing that made him react to me that way. I wished he would put his tongue back in his mouth. "No, I'm not." I wanted him to move on because he was standing in my way.

"Will you marry me?"

The look on his face was serious. I thought he was on drugs. "Excuse me, you are in my way," I said to the psychopath.

"Oh, sorry," and he stepped back.

"What is your name?" I asked him, in case I needed to call the police.

"Barry Sutton. You're not married?"

Annoyed, I replied, "I told you I was not married. If I was, I would not be standing here talking to you. I really am in a hurry, so if you'll please excuse me." I continued to make my selections from the fruit and vegetable display and quickly made my way to the checkout stand. I paid for the groceries, picked up my bag and proceeded outside to my car with Barry in hot pursuit. This man must be crazy.

"Can I have your phone number?" he pleaded with me.

"Are you a comedian? What kind of work do you do?" I asked the drooling man.

"I'm a parole officer. I work for the state."

I guessed it was okay to give this fool my number. I wrote it on the brown paper bag he was holding.

"You sure are *fine!*" He stood on the sidewalk smiling as I drove away.

Barry's come on was an original to me. He had the most direct line ever used on me. As weird as it was, I was thrilled that someone told me I was fine before barely asking my name. If he had not been so handsome with a job, I would not have given him a second thought, *or* my phone number.

Before I could return from shopping, Barry had called. Mama reported that some very nice intelligent sounding man had called, "said his name was Barry." He didn't leave a phone number with Mama so I had to wait until he called again. I got busy cutting out a dress I wanted for the weekend. I hadn't quite finished cutting out the garment when the phone rang. I dropped the scissors and rushed to answer the phone.

"Hello," I said.

"Sasha?" Barry's deep voice boomed through the receiver.

"Yes, it's she."

"Are you still wearing that red dress?"

I softly sucked my teeth, exhaled then said, "Yes, I'm wearing it. Why, do you want the dress?" I felt like having a little fun with Barry.

"I want what's inside the dress. Will you be my wife?"

"Will you stop asking me that? You don't even know me."

"But I want to get to know you. Can I come over?"

I remembered the promise I made to myself to go to bed early and I said, "Now?"

"Is now a bad time?" He sounded desperate.

"It's not the best time, but I guess it's alright. But I'm changing the dress." He arrived within minutes.

I was about to change when the doorbell rang. I decided to keep the damn dress on and try to get rid of him as quickly as possible, while teasing him in the process.

The sun was just going down so I turned on the porch light and looked through the peep hole in the door. As expected, it was Barry, looking bewildered. I opened the door to let him in and he grabbed my waist and kissed me passionately. The unexpected move made me mad.

"Take your hands off me!" With a frown I pushed him away. "May I close the door please?"

"It's that dress. It makes you look like dessert," he said with his hungry eyes.

I smiled this time and ushered him into the living room, motioning for him to sit down somewhere, anywhere. Once he regained his composure and began to behave like the civilized person I was hoping for, he suddenly had some appeal to me.

It turned out Barry was knowledgeable about his work and understood what was required of him to get ahead. He was college educated and very proud of his achievements and personal commitment to the community. I was impressed. Barry was a great communicator and storyteller. He would make statements that required me to think intensely before I could respond. I loved his intellectual side and the aggressiveness with which he conducted himself. Barry was a passionate man with all the qualities of a winner.

"How was your weekend?" Cindy asked me as we sat down for our usual Monday morning coffee.

"You'll never believe what happened to me," I said and then proceeded to describe the events of the day before. I liked giving Cindy vivid details of my escapades.

"Wow, how insane, and thrilling! Are you going to see him again?

"Yes, I guess I'll go out with him. He wants to cook for me tonight."

"Tonight? You're going out with him already?"

"Why not? He swears he's a gourmet chef, so I'm going to let him prove it," I said, lifting the coffee cup to my lips.

Barry came through with flying colors. He picked me up from work after my evening shift for a late night dinner. He took me to his third floor apartment of the building he lived in. The elevator was out of order so I was slightly winded when we got to his floor. Barry was used to the climb. Once inside his dwelling I immediately plopped down on the sofa to catch my breath.

Barry put music on the stereo and walked into the small kitchen with the confidence of a master chef. The clanging sound of pots and pans soon gave way to the sizzling sound and smell of T-bone steaks broiling. The rich aromas coming from the kitchen convinced me that he knew what he was doing. So far, Barry qualified himself as a credible candidate for marriage. He could cook.

Following dinner I offered to do the dishes. With Barry's help the task was completed in record time. The seduction began shortly thereafter. Barry poured more wine and put on more music. The combination of the wine, music and his demeanor made me want to know more about the passion I knew existed beneath his confident exterior. It was no surprise to me when he told me very politely how, since he first laid eyes on me, he wanted to make love to me.

There was something special about the way Barry clarified his feelings. There was no beating around the bush. Barry was honest about his physical attraction to me and I respected him for it. I had not made a commitment to celibacy before marriage. I refused to analyze my feelings about premarital sex, in case I did not decide to marry this man. I hadn't known him long enough to say I loved him, nor had he declared his love for me. We were both caught up in the passionate moments that followed several glasses of wine.

I excused myself to the bathroom. When I came out I found Barry pacing back and forth in the living room. As we made eye contact Barry swiftly moved to my side, which kept me from being able to budge an inch. I took steps backward as he continued his Mac truck approach. I knew what he wanted. I was amused by his aggressiveness.

"What are you doing?" I asked playfully.

"I want to make mad passionate love to you," Barry said and he reached to undo the top button on my blouse. He got no resistance from me and he continued to unbutton my cotton blouse. He backed me into the bedroom and stopped his pursuit when we reached the bed. I did not object to anything he did, so far. It was too late to plan an escape, if I had not been so willing. I surrendered completely and enjoyed a very special night of lovemaking. Barry made mad passionate love to me, as he said he wanted to.

"I'm thinking about getting married," I told Cindy the next day.

"How'd your date go?" Cindy asked.

"It was splendid. He's a great lover."

"Boy, you didn't waste any time, did you?" Cindy growled.

"Look who's talking. You and Robert got busy the day you met. At least I waited a day." We both laughed.

For the next two weeks, I spent every night with Barry. In the morning he would take me home early enough to get ready for school. Mama did not like the idea of my staying with Barry all night, so I told her I was thinking about marrying Barry, hoping to appease her. I sensed a sigh of relief from Mama and we began discussing the possibility of a wedding.

"When is he going to give you an engagement ring?" Mama asked.

"I don't know, soon I hope."

"Baby, you know I love you. I truly hope he's good enough for you." The excitement of the possible marriage overshadowed the only moments of open affection I was ever to receive from my mother.

A few days later Barry sent me on a scavenger hunt in his apartment that ended in my finding a beautiful full carat solitaire diamond ring. I was delighted with his exquisite taste and the way he gave me the ring. The carefully crafted bauble was nestled in a cup of crushed ice Barry had asked me to get from the freezer, ending the scavenger hunt.

The following week Barry and I were married in an intimate ceremony at my church. Both sets of parents, Barry's close friend John, the best man, Pam who was the maid of honor, and the minister were there. No one expected the marriage to survive, because Barry and I had only known each other slightly over a month. I told Pam I was in love with Barry. The truth was that in the beginning, I was not in love at all, but one month later when I realized I was pregnant, that changed everything. In the early stages of my pregnancy I began to feel true love for the father of my unborn child.

Our relationship changed after I announced to Barry that we were pregnant. He began to withdraw his affection for me and we started getting phone calls from a person who would hang up whenever I answered the phone. Finally, one day the caller made herself known, asking to speak to Barry. The lady of mystery never identified herself. He took the phone from me and spoke to the person in private, from an extension in the bedroom. Barry became visibly irritated when, after the call, I asked him who the woman was. His irritation turned to rage and he started pushing and shoving me around. Barry turned into a monster leaving me uncertain about my safety. My delicate condition would not permit me to get into physical wrestling matches with Barry. I had taken enough whippings from my father when I was growing up. One day, after all my attempts to communicate with Barry had failed I packed my things and moved out. Barry returned from work that day to an empty house and no dinner waiting for him.

I was hurt and disappointed about my failing relationship, and I felt responsible for all that had gone wrong. Unsure of everything, I was confused, not knowing if somehow the skeletons of my past had paid a visit on Barry's psyche or if he, in fact, had lied to me from the beginning about his own demons. Barry did not show or express any emotion about the problems we were having.

Shortly after I left Barry, his sister told me his ex-girlfriend, who was living in Alaska caring for her ill father, was the mystery caller. They had had a nasty long-distance fight shortly before he met me. Prior to that, they were living together. I was even more confused. I couldn't understand how a husband could ignore his responsibility to his wife. I was his wife and I thought I had rights. I had never witnessed that type of behavior in my parents' relationship. Tradition and my proper upbringing were struggling to find a place in my married life. After all, I was carrying my husband's child. Barry never found it in his heart to apologize for his actions that caused me to leave him, nor did he beg for me to come back. When we eventually talked he only chose to talk about the pain and emptiness he felt when I left. He never acknowled my pain. For months we remained in emotional gridlock, at separate residences.

On the day I went into labor, Barry could not be found. At 1 a.m. my father drove me to the hospital and six hours later, I gave birth to a healthy beautiful baby girl. I named her Eileen.

I chose not to complete the Spring semester at design school so I could take care of Eileen. Barry finally emerged to claim his daughter, only after hearing how beautiful she was. He came around often and bragged about her to anyone who would listen.

We were no closer to a reconciliation when the fall school term began. We made attempts during the Summer months, but no promises were made. I completed fashion design courses at design school and transferred to a community college closer to home. I took general education classes to complete my major. The baby and the new school location placed an unusual strain on my friendship with Cindy. We saw very little of each other and finally lost contact. I missed our friendship tremendously. I'd give a million bucks just to find her.

8

February, 1972

"How do you plead?" The judge sent a piercing stare down at me. My attorney discussed the possibilities of punishment before I went to court. If I had pled guilty to the assault charges, I would have faced three to five years of imprisonment. A not guilty plea would have meant suffering through a lengthy jury or judge trial. I was given the option of a plea bargain that would have reduced the charge against me to disturbing the peace. I accepted it and pled 'no contest'. The punishment for disturbing the peace was probation and/or jail time because weapons were involved. I received both punishments.

I could not believe how the justice system had failed me. The mental scars were still fresh from the rape and the scab from the gunshot wound surgery had barely fallen off. I was immediately taken into custody when the judge concluded his sentence. Actually, I felt like I was about to go on vacation from the tormented life I had been living in Los Angeles.

The three years of probation and sixty days the judge ordered me to spend in jail completely interrupted my life. I wondered why the judge did not consider the fact that I had been raped, raped while attending college, raped after a tutoring session I had just conducted. Or even date raped. I had had to face my attackers every day at school after I was released from the hospital. The judge did not realize that it had been hard to stay in school. His ruling showed little concern for my infant daughter who needed my care. Once again my dignity and self respect had been stripped, leaving me feeling as though I had been gang raped all over again, only this time by the system. I started to cry as I was taken away from the courtroom, embarrassed to watch my father look on with the sadness of a parent losing a child. I was humiliated and consumed by fear, not knowing what my outcome in jail would be. I was scared to death of what awaited me in there. I had never been inside a jail and never knew of anyone who had ever been put there.

I knew I had to be strong and overcome the new battle in my life the same way I had tackled past difficulties. I entered the holding cell, never to forget the experience for as long as I would live.

During my incarceration I reflected on the uncertainty of my life. I was young, almost twenty three but I felt ancient. I wondered how I ended up in jail. I enjoyed a great childhood, full of activity that only privileged kids had. Being in the Girl Scouts for all of my youth did not prepare me for the ordeal. Neither did the piano and ballet lessons. In school I was always the academic achiever, not counting the one semester at Southern. I always had a deep sense of justice, knowing right from wrong. I always believed in doing the right thing, but justice overlooked me for some reason, and I could not understand what it was.

I would not have minded the punishment for assault if the rapists had been punished for their crimes too. The injustice given to me made me more bitter and angry with every day that passed. The bastards were still free to live their lives and do the same thing to someone else.

Barry had nothing to do with me. He refused my collect calls from jail, which made me feel like an outcast. He did not bother to visit me. He was no better than the rapists and just as bad. I wanted to talk to Barry about what had happened even though I knew he would not understand. Mama was too embarrassed to visit me, but my father would come to the jail. I would cry during the painful visits and ask probing questions about my beautiful infant daughter I could not care for at the moment. My father surprised me one day when to my surprise, he brought Eileen along on his visit. There were no tears of sadness that day, only tears of joy.

I hated being locked up with people I didn't know. Near the end of my incarceration I began to sketch costumes and direct my thoughts to being released. Good behavior got me an early release, shaving two weeks from my sentence. Three years of probation was the next hurdle.

After being released, my first concern was to become reacquainted with Eileen. She had grown in the weeks I was away. Mama had taken good care of her and I had to give her credit for that.

I tried to reach Barry by phone, only getting a disconnect message. I called my sister-in-law, Liz, who told me Barry had moved and she gave me his new phone number. Liz also told me Barry's ex-girlfriend was back in the picture now and was probably living with him. I cringed and thought it was fucked up because I didn't want to go back to jail for killing Barry's ex-girlfriend. And if it were true, Barry had a lot of explaining to do. They had been living together just prior to our meeting and she was back from Alaska to reclaim him.

A week after I was released from custody I was able to contact Barry. As suspected, the woman answered the phone, humiliating me further.

"Hello," the woman answered after a second ring.

"Hello, is Barry there?" the sound of my voice was venomous.

"Who is this?"

"This is Sasha, his wife."

The woman dropped the receiver and in the background I could hear her say, "Barry, someone named Sasha wants to speak to you." A few moments Barry came to the phone.

"Hello."

"Barry. What the hell is going on? Why is she answering your phone? We are still married you know."

"Well, things have changed for me."

"I don't care how much they've changed for you, you still have a wife and a baby. You were not around when I was having problems and now you tell me things have changed? It's not right for that bitch to be answering your phone *and* sounding like a wife!..." Barry interrupted me and said, "It's over between us, Sasha. I loved you once, but you left me."

"That was ages ago, and I was not letting you beat up on me. I want to try to save our marriage. Can we talk about it, please? I love you."

"Let me call you back."

I agreed to talk with him later and hung up the phone. Barry did not call back.

Three days later Barry called me from work to tell me he wanted to come by and take Eileen and I to lunch. We could talk then.

During lunch he began explaining to me that the woman who answered the phone was just a friend. Barry didn't know I knew the real truth, so I decided to let him lie like a rug. "She's staying at my place temporarily while she looks for an apartment of her own." Yeah, right.

I wished he would just tell the truth about the woman, but no such luck.

"Well, Eileen and I need a place to live, too. You know I don't get along with Mama very well, and the baby *needs* you," my eyes filled with tears as I begged my husband for mercy, something I thought I would never have to do. There had been no divorce in his family or mine and I felt a responsibility to hold things together, at any cost. I knew I had made an error in judgment when I returned with Dewayne to the scene of the crime only to be shot and nearly killed, but I felt that was no reason to give up on the marriage. If he could get past the rape, we would be okay. I was still very much in love with Barry. "I need to think about it," Barry sighed unconvincingly, then picked up the check, read it, and got up to pay the cashier. I took Eileen out of the high chair. We barely spoke on the way home.

For the next few days all I thought about was the sound of the woman's voice that answered Barry's phone, and his denial of the situation. I was taking too much mental abuse and was not going to sit at home crying my eyes out. I called Pam to see if she wanted to go out.

"The Page Five," I announced with the liveliness of a new birth. "I heard the catch action is great over there. It's a new club."

"Are you still mad at Barry?"

"Yes, but he can go jump in a lake. I'm not waiting around for him. Do you want to party or not?"

"Yeah, yeah, come on and get me. I could use a drink."

When we pulled into the parking lot at the Page Five Nightclub, we saw nothing but expensive and carefully detailed cars. Jaguars, Porsches, Seville's and Coupe de Villes filled the parking lot to its capacity. A paradise for people like myself and Pam, who needed a lift.

The Page Five was L.A.'s latest hangout for aging high rollers who claimed to be the 'cream of the crop'. Everyone who went there was there to be seen. I slowly drove through the parking lot looking for a place to park until I saw the tail lights of a Rolls backing out of its space. We took the parking space, smoothed our midi skirts and pranced up to the entrance. The first person we encountered was an older man who greeted us as we walked in. "Hello, Brown Sugar, who are you?" he asked, wearing a big grin and a gold tooth.

"I'm Sasha, and this is Pam. And who are you?"

"I'm Lou Bates, are you two alone?"

"Very much," I said, smiling. It was great timing.

"Can I buy you two ladies a drink?"
"Thank you, Lou," Pam finally spoke and Lou led us to the bar where two vacant bar stools awaited us. As we got comfortable and pulled out the cigarettes Lou quickly grabbed his lighter to assist us. He was a polite man.

Pam and I ordered Margaritas while Lou drank Black Label on the rocks. I liked Lou because he was an older gentleman who did not mind spending his money. We liked the look of the Page Five. The well-dressed crowd of people in there were having a great time. It looked like everybody was getting drunk.

After our second Margarita, Pam and I wanted to get something to eat. Lou suggested a soul food take out restaurant in the neighborhood and invited us to his home to eat. Since he lived close by, in Baldwin Hills we agreed, and slowly followed Lou's shiny black Seville to the restaurant first and then to his home in the hills.

Lou's home was a comfortable modern two bedroom house that was decorated in very masculine taste. He had a view of L.A. to die for. At forty five, he had been a bachelor all of his life. Originally from Chicago, he served two years in Viet Nam then moved to Los Angeles when he retired from the Army. Lou watched every move I made, eyeing my body constantly then smiling and winking whenever I caught him.

It was late so we made our excuses and thanked Lou for everything. He asked me if I would call him to discuss the possibility of him taking me out on a date. I thought that he might have had other things on his mind, judging from the way he had watched me all night. Earlier in the evening I told him I was separated from my husband and gave no scandalous details. He gave me his number and I put it inside my purse. Lou walked us to the car then kissed me on my forehead through the partially rolled down car window. He made sure we were locked securely in the car. I admired the well-meaning man.

Days after meeting Lou, I decided to give him a call. Through the course of exchanging thoughts and personal philosophies I discovered that Lou was a loan shark by profession. That explained the real nice car, the L-shaped diamond ring he wore on his pinky and the large amount of cash he had that he didn't mind spending. He looked like one of those elegant hustlers from the 'old school'. I liked Lou because he was down to earth, loved women and never bragged about his assets. He had a free spirit and always had a good joke to tell. I enjoyed his company but felt guilty after I allowed myself to be seduced by him on our second date. He was no replacement for Barry. He was a dear male friend I could confide in. That is what the relationship with Lou became. We agreed not to have sex in our relationship but to remain confidants. Lou knew I was still in love with Barry and that I wanted Barry back.

To keep from thinking about Barry so much I thrust myself back into designing and making samples. Barry was taking a long time deciding what he was going to do about the marriage. I called him to find out how we stood as a couple.

"Shall we go for a divorce?" I nearly choked on the words.

"Sasha, I don't want a divorce. I want to try to work it out. When can you come home?"

I sat holding the receiver in disbelief. I pinched myself to make sure I was not dreaming. In our conversation I made no mention of the other woman, assuming she was out of the apartment and out of his life. Barry told me to pack my things so Eileen and I could move back the next day. I was elated to know we had another chance to make our marriage work. But to my surprise it didn't work out that way.

Barry was very distant with me. His passive resistant behavior and heavy drinking did nothing to mend our relationship. There were days when he would come home from work hours after the office was closed. We only lived fifteen minutes away from his job. Other times he would bring a friend home, unannounced, and drink an entire fifth of liquor or more with the friend, past midnight. When Barry and I went to bed he was usually too drunk to perform. I could get no action. There was *no* sex. He curled up on his side of the bed with his back to me. Barry showed no affection toward me and made it difficult for me to respond to him in any way. On one occasion, Barry went to work and did not return for four days. I couldn't sleep while he was gone and later found out that he had gone to Texas. The stench in the car wreaked of low lives who must have traveled with him. I was worried and concerned about Barry and did not know who to call or what to do. I was on the phone constantly with Pam during that time.

Barry concocted some elaborate story about where he had been those four days, but I didn't buy any of it. He had changed. He was a monster. He was not the person I once loved. The abuse continued for more than two months, until the day Barry made the mistake of bringing his ex-girlfriend home.

I had been waiting for Barry to come home from work. I was looking down from the kitchen window, like I always did when I saw a new small car pull up. The car parked right beside our Firebird. I watched him get out of a Vega sedan. A tall, slim, high-yellow red headed woman stepped out from behind the driver's side. I could not believe my eyes. Barry was bringing a strange woman up to the apartment who fit the description of the other woman.

So that's the bitch.

I sized up my competition and had to figure out what to do next. I wondered how many days in jail I would get for kicking her ass.

Barry walked her up the stairs and into the apartment and offered her a seat on the sofa. Without speaking to either of them, I walked past them and down the stairs to the Firebird. I opened the trunk and removed a tire iron. I started striking at the woman's car and continued until there was no glass anywhere on the windows of the car. I totaled it, with its paper license plates and all. It made me feel good. The tramp was next and with tire iron in hand, I went back upstairs to the apartment. I appeared in the doorway only to see the woman holding my baby, Eileen.

"Put her down!" I screamed.

They saw the look of terror on my face and the tire iron in my hand and froze. Barry finally jumped up and wrestled me to the floor. He then pushed and shoved me all over the apartment.

When I recovered from the blows and embarrassment of the moment, I decided that enough was enough. I refused to spend another night with Barry. I begged Barry to take me back to my parents. I could see my dream of a perfect marriage with the animal would never be. Mama was sad about the whole incident. It made her sick.

Mama had not been feeling well but decided to take her monthly trip to Las Vegas anyway. While in Vegas she developed chest pains. She suffered a massive heart attack and died in a hospital in the city she loved more than anyplace else. The funeral was a week after her death, not giving me much time to put things in perspective. It was shortly after these events in my life more than 20 years ago that I met Marlene.

9

Present

"So how was the trip?" How did the graduation go?" I asked Marlene.

"It was great! Jasmine graduated in the upper ten percent of her class. Girl, there were so many people there. We barely got seats."

"Was it outdoors, or in?"

"Both. There was a general gathering in the outside stadium, and the different colleges gave their diplomas out at other locations around the campus. There was so much walking involved I thought I was going to die from heat exhaustion. It was 102 degrees outside. It is so damn hot in Arizona. I don't see how people live there."

"Oh, the weather is no different from the Antelope Valley in the summertime, and you like it out here."

"Yes, but you have air conditioning and besides, you don't make me sit in the blazing hot sun. Hold on a sec."

She clicked her phone over to receive an incoming call. I hate call waiting and had it removed when Eileen moved out. Call waiting was a nuisance.

"Okay, I'm back. Sasha?"

"Yeah, I'm here. Marlene, I think I have a problem."

"What kind of problem? Are you sick?" asked Marlene.

"No, not exactly. A month has gone by and my friend has not shown up."

"What friend? Rod? Eddie?"

"No, silly. You know what I mean. Can I ask you a personal question? Have you gone through the change yet?" I just asked her.

"Girl, yes. Do you remember when I had my hysterectomy five years ago?"

"Yes, I remember."

"Well, they took everything and I haven't had a period since. So I guess you could say I'm going through it now. Why, were you late this month?"

"I can't really tell. I've been so irregular lately that it's hard to say what's going on."

"So what are you going to do about it?" asked Marlene, with a mother's concern.

"Nothing yet. I'm not going to worry about it. Believe me, I don't miss it at all."

"How are things going with the show?"

"Pretty good. Did you start taking hormones or anything after they took everything?"

"My doctor prescribed Premarin and Provera in the beginning because my hormone level dropped. I take it sometimes, less now than five years ago. When they take your ovaries, which they did in my case, you automatically go into menopause."

"Oh. Well, I'll be glad when I get there because it's such an inconvenience."

"Ha, ha, ha! Too bad for you! I can get busy with Dennis anytime I want and I don't have to worry about getting pregnant ever again. At my age it would take a miracle anyway. And if Dennis' sperm was that potent I would have an abortion and not tell him about it." Marlene had abundant energy and did not look like her child bearing years were over. She was the big sister I never had. I can always blurt out any question I have and get an intelligent and compassionate response from Marlene.

"Have you ever had an abortion?" I suddenly realized that after all our years of friendship I never asked Marlene that question. I was getting downright nosy.

"No, just a miscarriage, before I had the twins. What about you?"

"No, and I've only been pregnant twice. I don't know if I would have an abortion. I hope I never have to make that decision."

"Well, Sasha it's unlikely that you will have to decide so don't worry about that. If you accidentally get that way just call me so I can come over and we can stage a slip and fall down your staircase and it will take care of itself!"

"You are sooo crazy." We laughed together a long time.

"But seriously, Sasha, give it a week then take a pregnancy test if you haven't started yet. Hold on." Call waiting interrupted again.

"I'm back, but I gotta go now, it's for Dennis. Call me, luv ya."

"Bye," and I hung up but I wasn't finished yet, so I waited fifteen minutes then called her back.

"Hello," Dennis answered.

"Hi, Dennis, were you on the phone? This is Sasha."

"Hi, no, hold on a minute." Dennis gave the receiver to Marlene.

"Hi, I didn't think you were finished. What's the matter with you, really?" said Marlene. She knew me well.

"Do you have a minute?" I asked.

"Of course I do."

I began by telling Marlene how involved I had become with Rod while trying to break things off with Eddie, and how Eddie was not getting the message. I told her although Eddie was loyal and generous and really cared for me, I found it impossible to return the affection. I didn't share the same passion he had for me and I felt guilty about it sometimes. Sometimes. It was difficult to say nice things to him because he interpreted my gratitude the wrong way. I understood what my relationship with Eddie was about. It had its roots in the life I lived shortly after Jett's death while living in Hollywood. I fulfilled a need Eddie had and he gave me money for paying attention to him. That was it. It would never be anything more. Unlike his wife, I did not run helplessly into his arms for safety with three young children in tow and an abusive husband on my trail. Eddie rescued his wife from physical abuse and poverty and together they carved a life of happiness from her shambles of pain. I had suffered great pain as well but I refused to be saved by a mere mortal who was just like me. I had managed quite well as a single parent for five years and was not eager to change that. I felt a sense of accomplishment and responsibility for once in my life and Eddie fought to take it away from me. He was determined to make me dependent upon him. He believed life would be better for us if we lived together. He said we could save money and have 'more things'. Life *would* be better for him, but it would be a living hell for me, and I knew it.

As usual, Marlene was understanding. She said if Eddie was dumb enough to think I wanted him for life, then I should take him for all he's got. Marlene told me I was too well educated and independent to be tied to someone like Eddie, who lacked the proper communication skills to make it in my world.

"Where can you take him?" Marlene asked. "Be nice to Eddie as long as you care to, but get to know Rod also. He sounds like someone worth getting close to."

"Girlfriend, thanks for listening," and I said goodbye.

I was eager to start my day because I had costume fittings for cast members later on. The auditions went well and I helped the production team decide who would be hired as characters in the play. After the auditions, I spent hours combing through the racks of antique clothing in the theater's wardrobe department, scanning garments dating back as far as the thirties. I had a lot to do. I went through old dusty cardboard boxes and historic trunks full of shoes, hats, lingerie and post WW II accessories. The incredible volume of clothing that I inspected heightened my interest and gave me a clear mental picture of what was available to me. Anything that resembled a clothing item was analyzed and tallied for use. The first order of business was to take measurements of each actor and decide on the costumes that would be appropriate for use in the show.

After measuring each cast member, I appreciated the depth of my commitment to what I do. I enjoy the dominion of deciding the look of a show. While in production, every waking moment was consumed by visions of costumes on occasionally awkward bodies. I chuckled as I remised of past miracles I've had to perform in extreme cases.

The musical 'Grease' brought back memories of an innocent time in American history when there was less crime and violence in society, a time when poodle skirts, pedal pushers and baby doll pajamas were in style. My task now is to recreate that moment in time.

Another week went by and I did not see my period. The demanding work schedule did not give me time to think about it either so I continued to work around the clock on most days. Teddy was understanding about my chaotic schedule, as long as he knew he would be fed a real dinner before 9 p.m.

"Mom, I'm hungry. When are we going to eat?" The look on his face was not a happy one.

"Soon, baby. As soon as I reach a stopping point," I sighed.

"Mom, why don't you stop right where you are? Just put the scissors down and spend some time with me."

I knew the child was right. It was 8 p.m. and Teddy had finished his homework. Earlier he had gone to play with his friends. After that he fixed tuna sandwiches for us. He raided the refrigerator several times and announced that he was eating the last of the banana pudding. After eating all of the junk food in the house, I knew he needed a balanced meal. But where was he going to put it?

"Okay, okay." I stopped cutting out the poodle skirt and laid the scissors down. "I'm not cooking so where do you want to go for dinner?"

"Sizzler. Can we go there?"

"You finished your homework?" I couldn't remember if I had asked him earlier.

"Yes, I told you I did."

"Well, let's go." I was so exhausted I didn't bother to look in the mirror at myself. Thank God for braids. I liked them because they were low maintenance. And I woke up gorgeous every day. I grabbed my purse and car keys and headed toward the door with Teddy close behind.

When we arrived at Sizzler the dinner crowd was thinning out. We didn't have a problem finding a table close to the salad bar. We made the trip to the salad bar twice and could barely get up when we finished eating.

"I feel like a pig," I said as I started the engine of the car.

"Me too," Teddy replied. I silently praised Teddy for concentrating on the leafy salads and seafood choices at the salad bar. Hopefully it would balance out the junk food he had eaten earlier.

I didn't know if I had eaten something at the restaurant that was causing the queasiness in my stomach. The discomfort nearly prevented me from driving home. As soon as I got home I headed straight for the bathroom. Teddy knocked on the bathroom door.

"Mom, are you all right?"

"Yes, darling, you get ready for bed now. I'm okay," I smiled as I greeted my monthly friend. That night I thanked God for one less problem when I said my prayers.

10

Opening night for the play was phenomenal in spite of the pre-production commotion. Last minute cast and crew changes threatened the stability of the show. One of the main characters threatened to make a costume change without my permission during dress rehearsal and became humiliated when the producer demanded that she wear what I recommended. At the last minute she threatened to quit the show, but realized it would have meant unprofessionalism on her part and would make it difficult to get future jobs. Creative differences were always a menace to any successful production, but in this case all discrepancies were ironed out.

The review in the local paper was favorable giving special mention to the beautifully updated 'Pink Lady' jackets worn by the female lead characters. I remember visualizing how the hot pink satin fabric would make the jackets unique. I wanted the royal blue sequined lettering to sparkle brightly under the stage lights, and they did. I was a little disappointed that my name was not mentioned in the article even though credit was given to the costume department.

With free time on my hands once again, I wanted to spend more time with Teddy, and update my résumé. But not necessarily in that order. In the business of show business résumés had to be updated immediately and sent out so the next job awaited when a current job was completed. But that was not always the case, and sometimes designers ended up with more time on their hands than money. When it happened to me I would try to plan activities that included Teddy. I also made the necessary phone calls to follow-up on résumés I had mailed out.

Teddy mentioned wanting to go someplace special after I finished the costumes for 'Grease'. I had one place in mind but wasn't sure if Teddy would be interested. The Danish town of Solvang nestled just inland from Santa Barbara up the coast from Los Angeles was the place I had thought of taking him. There's not much to do there except eat and sight see, but Teddy was excited to know he was going somewhere. I felt he deserved a trip, especially since I had recently gone to Oakland.

"When are we leaving?"

"How about Saturday morning? Do you have a game this weekend?" I asked knowing about his obligation to his team.

"Yes, but I can miss one game. Will you call my coach for me?"

"Why can't you call him? All right, I'll do it. Where's the number?"

I called the number Teddy gave me and talked to Coach Rick. He was very understanding about my wanting to take Teddy on a weekend trip. I explained how Teddy's father had promised to take him to Seaworld last month but his new wife created a financial emergency that took priority over everything else. Seaworld was a second choice for our weekend together, but I decided to let his father take him when he was able to. Teddy and I planned our weekend in Solvang.

I worried about not having a job to go to after a show, and I would pinch pennies and put off taking trips. But now I am grateful to have breaks in between shows and am happy I'm able to get away whenever I need to. I have learned to manage money much better than I used to, when I was married to Teddy's dad. After the divorce, my greatest fear was becoming homeless, but so far that has not happened. Collecting child support had not been a problem although Big Ted's wife tried to make him pay less than he was ordered to pay. He didn't listen to her because he knew he could face financial ruin if the payments changed for any reason.

Early Saturday morning we put our overnight bags in the car and departed on our weekend adventure. We stopped at the bank and got cash from the ATM machine then went to the gas station to fill up. Teddy checked the oil as he always does, then went back to finish pumping the gas. I enjoyed watching Teddy act like a little man. All I had to do was pay the cashier. Teddy decided to buy a few snacks for the road, even though we planned to stop for breakfast later on. We drove the scenic route that took us through remote areas dotted with tiny obscure towns.

Blackstreet was playing on the tape deck when we stopped in Santa Paula for breakfast.

Teddy ordered hotcakes and sausage, his standard breakfast on the road. I ordered a western omelet, coffee and juice. It was pleasant to be able to relax and take time to enjoy the scenery around us.

We replaced *Blackstreet* with *Erikah Badu* in the tape deck as we drove away from the gravel parking lot of the tiny café. We got back on the highway and worked our way north along the picturesque coastline. I was tempted to stop in Santa Barbara but decided to keep driving until we reached our destination. The emerald mountains and hilltops were vivid as we drove the last stretch of highway inland toward Solvang. We knew we had arrived when Teddy spotted the first old-fashioned windmill Solvang is famous for. The windmills dot the countryside of an otherwise tranquil country scene. Numerous businesses located within the environs of the city cater to curious observers and pastry seeking travelers.

We registered at Best Western and quickly made ourselves comfortable. Teddy brought the luggage in from the car and chose the queen-sized bed closest to the window.

"Did you get the scrabble game?" I asked him. I like playing the game with Teddy because it helps with his spelling. For dinner later on we decided that we would order pizza, and play scrabble afterward. I thumbed through a TV guide I found on the desk beside the Gideon Bible just to see what cable had to offer for primetime.

"Yes, I got the game."

HBO was airing "Necessary Roughness" at eight, then "Tales from the Crypt". There was a comedy special after 'Tales', so the entertainment line up looked pretty good. I suddenly felt energetic and wanted to do some exploring, on foot. I put on my leggings and a sweat shirt and dug out my tummy pouch. I stuffed the pouch with my wallet, car keys, the hotel key and an ink pen. I put it around my waist. Teddy was eager to find a McDonald's, but I explained to him the delight of discovering new restaurants while on vacation. He really didn't care where we ate as long as he could have fries.

We ended up compromising when we spotted an Italian restaurant that specialized in lasagna, one of Teddy's favorite dishes. I promised Teddy fries before leaving Solvang. We stopped at every gift shop we passed in search of perfect souvenirs for Eileen, Eddie, Pam and Marlene. Teddy collected Legos and coffee mugs from places he visited, so I suffered while I watched my wallet bleed to death. 'Rick's Shells and Gifts' had beautiful jewelry I liked but I decided not to shop beyond the limit I set for myself for gifts in my budget. Instead, I settled for unusual pastries I could never find at home. After about three hours of shopping and hauling bags that were getting heavier by the minute, we began our hike back to the motor lodge. I was grateful to have worn my Nikes. We stumbled into the room, put the bags down and collapsed on the beds. We rested for about an hour then decided to put on our pajamas and start the Scrabble game. We would order pizza later.

When I prayed that night, once again I thanked God for all the joy in my life. It is times like these that make up for all the former pain. I looked over at Teddy sleeping so soundly and peacefully and thought about the many sleepless nights I spent with Teddy's father whose snoring always kept me awake. Teddy turned out to be the perfect son that any mother would want.

"Mom, this was the best weekend I've ever had. Thanks."
"I loved it too."
The Tudor style architecture began to disappear as we drove away from Solvang toward the highway that would take us back to the Antelope Valley. Teddy snacked on his fries from Micky D's.
There were three messages waiting for me when I got back Sunday evening. A production company was responding to a resume I sent out a week ago. They asked if I'd be interested in doing alterations for a show beginning Monday. Pam called, leaving a stressful sounding message. Eddie also made contact several times during the weekend, sounding bewildered about not knowing where I was. I called him first because I knew he would be the most worried. I dialed his number. Still showing my loyalty.
"Hello."
"Hi, what are you doing?"
"Oh, Hi, darlin'. Where you been all weekend? I been callin' since yesterday mornin'."
"Teddy and I went to Solvang yesterday."
"Solbang, what's that?"
"It's Solvang, Eddie. It's a little town north of Santa Barbara. Do you know where Santa Barbara is?"
"I ain't never been there."
"I didn't ask you if had been there, do you know where it is?" I asked myself why I was getting into this.
"Nah."

"Anyway Eddie, it's a small Danish town where you can but all kinds of Danish pastries." Enough said. "I brought something back for you."

"Oh, baby. You didn't have to do that."

"It's not much, but I thought about you and I felt guilty about not telling you I was going out of town."

"Thanks for thinkin' 'bout me."

"I have to call Pam. She sounded a little strange when I listened to her message."

"You want me to call you back later?"

"No, I'll talk to you tomorrow. I'm going to bed after I call Pam."

"Tell me you love me."

"I love you. Bye." And I hung up.

11

"Pam?"

"Yeah, Hi Sasha." Pam sounded out of it.

"What's wrong? You sounded a little down on the recorder. Is something wrong?"

"I'm pissed off. Do you know what that sonofabitch did?"

"No."

"First of all, Friday morning Pookie told me he needed to use my car to go to the DMV, something about his driver's license. He was gone all day Friday, then last night a eight he called to tell me my car had been hit."

"Hit, how?" I hoped her car was still in one piece.

"I don't know. He told me some crazy story. That motherfucker wrecked my car! And he hasn't been back yet."

"Did you call the police?"

"No, not yet, I'm just waiting."

"Waiting for what? Pam, you need to get your car back and if the police can help, let them."

"I'm calling his parole officer in the morning."

I asked myself why Pam hadn't called the police. "What can his parole officer do about your car? Pam, don't protect him. He disappointed you, again. Was he able to drive your car after he wrecked it?"

"Sasha, I don't know. I just want my car back." Pam was upset and couldn't hold back her tears.

"Pam, I know you're hurting, but please don't get too upset yet. Has he been acting like he would do something like this?"

"You know, he's been talking to a lot of his friends lately, the ones he used to hang out with before he went to jail. They all sling, and as far as I know, he might be smoking that shit. He's been drinking pretty heavily this week, running in and out of the house constantly. He acts like a smoker. And Sasha, he's been trying to boss and control me in my own house. Who does he think he is?"

Shit, I thought. Pookie thinks he's a wise ass who can take advantage of a stupid ass woman. That's *exactly* who he thinks he is. I hated to think it but Pam chose to pay for that. She knew damn well that she couldn't just let a man move in with her. We both learned that lesson a long time ago when another jailbird friend of hers moved in when he got out of jail. When they're locked up they have plenty of time to write those beautiful love letters, promising eternal love and commitment and all that shit when they get out. It always goes well the first week or so but they soon turn on you with fowl language and abusive patterns, like what Pookie was doing. I couldn't believe Pam had done it again, with Pookie this time. I didn't say anything to Pam. I figured she was willing to pay the price, no matter what it cost her. I would have been glad for Pam to stop paying for bullshit lessons, though. I knew it was embarrassing for her to talk about the problem.

"Call me when he comes back." I shook my head when I hung up the phone.

Three years ago when we lived in Culver City, we thought we'd be nice and visit a friend of Pam's who was in County jail. Of course, he had a friend who wanted a visitor also so I was recruited to visit him. I went along with it for a while but realized there was no future in that type of relationship for me. After all, I was a school teacher at the time. I simply knew I could do better and was not that hard up for a man. It was easy for me to walk away, but not for Pam.

She continued to visit her friend in jail. As his release date approached, Pam talked more and more about how much he loved her and how much in love she was. Identical to the same crap she was talking a month ago about Pookie. Girlfriend had a short memory.

When Pam realized that she had made a mistake, we changed the dead bolt locks on our front doors to keep him out. We switched our locks because we had no money to buy new ones. His violent temper prompted us to buy bullets for my rusty .38. I sold the gun right after that. We were then terrified at not having immediate protection, had he decided to retaliate in the night. The obscene phone calls started and continued until Pam got her phone number changed.

I never thought a responsible man should move in with a woman anyway. If a man wants to please a woman and make her his he should be responsible and patient enough to save his own money to get his own place. If he does that he is in a position to call the shots. And in addition, he has shown that he can stand on his own. A man has to do these things by himself if he wants to be treated with respect. I think a lot of men resent the nineties woman with her identity and financial independence. The delayed vocational progress of a previously incarcerated man cripples his ability to provide and compete to some degree. I thought Pam could have been more aware of her choices, after all, she was actually better off living without Pookie, and she didn't even know it.

When Pam called me again she sounded much better than she had the night before. That morning she gathered up all of Pookie's things and paid a neighbor to drive her to his mother's house in Riverside where she dumped everything on her porch. Good move, I thought. When she got back from Riverside she continued to wait for Pookie, who showed up with a friend two hours later. Pookie bullied his way into Pam's apartment and discovered he no longer lived there. He was belligerent and made Pam drive him and his friends to Riverside, in Monday morning traffic. He had been there for the last three days getting high with his friends. Outraged and outnumbered, Pam complied.

Pam was not aware of the additional damage to her car when she got on the freeway. When they were completely off the on ramp that carried them on the freeway Pam heard an unfamiliar noise coming from the engine. She pulled the car to the right shoulder of the road near an emergency call box and stopped the engine. Pookie made no effort to look under the hood for the source of the problem. Pam provoked him by criticizing his non action, and the insults and nasty comments started again. Fed up, Pam got out of the car and walked to the call box. She notified the Highway Patrol of an ongoing kidnapping and car-jacking, gave the location, then walked back to her car. She slid back into the car behind the wheel and lit a cigarette, not saying a word to Pookie. Five minutes later her car was completely surrounded by police cars with officers knelt down behind open car doors armed with shotguns and revolvers aimed at them.

Pookie and his friends were taken into custody but were later released when Pam dropped the charges. All she wanted was her car back, which she got. Pookie would be crazy to bother Pam again, I thought. He got off easy that time.

Our high school class reunion was coming up soon and I needed to decide what to wear. I had no idea who to ask to escort me to the affair. I was thinking of asking Rod and Pam was going to take Pookie, but I seriously doubted it after the incident with her car on the freeway. I was beginning to think we might have more fun if we went without dates.

I had been sketching a black chiffon after five dress and decided to wear it to the reunion. I liked the off the shoulder look with its bouffant skirt stopping several inches above my knees. The dress could show my well maintained upper body as well as my shapely legs. The long rhinestone earrings Mama gave me would be perfect with the dress. Black satin pumps and sheer pantyhose. It was time for me to get my hair rebraided so my hairstyle would be fresh. All set. I called Pam to find out what she was wearing.

"Hello."

"Hi Pam, it's me. Are you feeling better? Still upset?"

"Yes, Sash, I'm doing fine now. A little tired, but I'll be all right."

"I know it's late, so I'll make this brief. Do you still want to go to the reunion?"

"Are you kidding? I wouldn't miss it for the world. We still look good. Are you going to ask Rod?"

"You know, I've been thinking. Why should I ask him? We could have more fun if we go alone."

"Then, that's what we'll do."

"Right on. Talk to you tomorrow."

Pam decided to wear a red strapless halter dress with a matching bolero jacket. She wanted me to help her find the right accessories to go with it. We set a date to have lunch and go shopping since we still had time to prepare for the late October occasion.

I wondered where the time had gone with the summer about to end. Labor Day just one week away. I didn't make plans for the holiday weekend so I could save money. Teddy's father took him shopping for school clothes before we went to Solvang. That was an expense I was relieved of that year. Big Ted surprises me with his generosity when I least expect it.

I added watercolor to the drawing of the dress I planned to wear to the reunion. I was swishing the paintbrush in a cup of water I watched turn gray when the telephone rang. I answered the phone after the first ring.

"Hello." I answered.

"Hi. How are you doing." It was Rod.

"Oh, hi Rod. I'm doing great! What about you? Are you off today?" He rarely called me in the daytime.

"Yeah, doctor's appointment. You are the hardest person to reach."

"Me? You know that's not true." I giggled. "I have been kinda busy lately. I had the play to do but you knew about that."

"I called you last weekend."

"I was out of town."

"How is the play going?"

"I guess it's going okay. I finished that a few weeks ago." All of a sudden I had a flash of the annoying picture of Rod's wife and realized why I hadn't thought about him lately. He hadn't called either.

"What have you been up to lately?" he asked.

"Nothing really, just sketching every day and sending out résumés, you know, the usual." I wondered if he had had sex since being with me. I was ready to go to bed with him again but didn't want to come right out and say it. I was afraid of appearing trashy but I wanted sex right away. "I'm surprised to hear from you so early in the day. What's on your mind?" Sex, I hoped.

"Are you coming down this way anytime soon?"

"As a matter of fact, I'm going to a fabric store on Pico this afternoon. I'm working on a dress and I need to get some fabric. Why?"

"You want to stop by? I'll be back from the doctors' around one this afternoon."

Good, I thought. He asked first.

"Hmm. I might be able to come by."

"What time will I see you?"

"Tell you what. I'll stop by before I go to the fabric store. That way I won't hang you up all day." The truth was I couldn't *wait* all day. I was horney then. It had been over a month and my body craved fulfillment of its sexual need. "I should be there by two o'clock."

I finished touching up the sketch I was working on then cleaned up my work area. All of my thoughts switched immediately to Rod and how he would please me that afternoon.

12

With everything coming together for an erotic afternoon, I thought it was time to start primping, pampering and getting dressed. It was mid-morning already so I had no time to waste. To get in the mood for the seductive rendezvous I decided to listen to the appropriate mood music of Luther. I thought about what I would wear underneath my clothes to make myself sensual for Rod. My bathing ritual was next. A lavishly self-indulgent, peaceful, relaxing bubble bath was a must. I went into the bathroom and lit the scented candles that surrounded the bathtub and added potpourri to a waiting simmering pot.

    Under running water I poured my favorite bath crystals and a package of instant powdered milk. When the tub was full enough I climbed in slowly and inched down until the warm water reached my neck. I soaked and relaxed about twenty minutes then stood up, drained the tub and patted myself dry with a fluffy white towel. I sat at the makeup table with the towel wrapped around me. Rod likes 'Poison' by Dior so I smoothed Poison body cream all over my body, not missing any areas. I sat back down and applied a little mascara and eyeliner to my eyes. I used a tiny bit of blush to accent my cheekbones then applied a radiant red color to my lips.

I attached a black lace garter belt around my hips and carefully pulled on black sheer stockings. The matching black panties and bra were next. I sprayed Poison cologne all over my torso and pulse points. I made sure the scent would not be lost on my way to Los Angeles.

Finally, I pulled a black knit turtleneck dress over my head and on to my body. My five foot eight frame filled the dress to perfection. I slipped my feet into black leather 3 inch pumps. I carefully smoothed my braids and misted them with braid sheen. Putting on the gold hoop earrings was the final step in getting dressed.

I looked in the full length mirror and was assured I had obtained the result I was after. I reminisced about the last time I was with Rod as I wrote a note for Teddy and posted it on the TV. I told Teddy to do his homework, eat some snacks and expect a call from me around six. It was time to go.

Driving into Los Angeles was always a treat for me, no matter what time of the day it happened to be. It was like taking a mini-trip because of the endless vistas I observed on my way while driving through the San Gabriel mountains. I loved to listen to my favorite artist on the tape deck, and was usually in a good mood when I arrived at my destination. My *Luther* tape was blasting on the car stereo when I pulled in front of Rod's building. I sat in my car humming and waiting for the song to end. In the rear view mirror I checked my lipstick which delayed me further. I glanced at my watch as a reminder of how valuable my time was. I grabbed my purse and keys and got out of the car.

Walking up the stairs to Rod's apartment brought back eerie thoughts of the annoying picture of his soon-to-be ex-wife. I refused to think about the impending threat the picture held for me. I wanted to think about how I would please Rod that afternoon.

He answered the door, fully dressed this time. He was smiling, showing his great white teeth. "Hi. You look great. You didn't do all that for me, did you?"

"Hi, thanks. Yes and no." Gliding past him I carefully planted a soft kiss on his full lips.

"Damn, baby. You sure smell good. Is that what I think it is?"

"If you think it's Poison, you might be right. You said you liked it. Have you been here long?"

"I just got here fifteen minutes ago. Can I get you anything?"

Lots of TLC I was thinking, and in a hurry. "If you have soda, I'll take some, thanks."

By the time he poured our drinks I had made myself comfortable in the bedroom. I sat Indian style in the center of his bed, fully clothed without my shoes. I planned to seduce him carefully, with conversation.

Rod gave me a stemmed glass filled with fruit punch and said, "So, what's on your mind?"

Sex. Sex. Sex. "Not much. What's going on with you?"

"Just working hard, going to meetings. My daughters are coming over Friday to spend the weekend with me."

"Oh, that's nice. Any big plans?"

"There's a Labor Day picnic my group is having this weekend so I thought we might go to that. Are you free to go, on Saturday?"

"I'm free but I'm going to stay home this weekend. I'm kind of burned out from travel. But thanks anyway." To be polite, I asked a few questions about the event, then let it go.

"Tell me about your first date," I said. "Where did you go?"

Rod gave me a strange look, then flashed his sexy smile. "You got me. I haven't thought about that in years."

"Do you remember her name?"

"Yes, it was Jeanie." He smiled again and began to describe the events that led up to their going out. He told me that Jeanie was his first piece, too. It was amazing how much conversation I got out of this man by asking him about his childhood. I felt we were on a roll so I asked, "What was your first job?"

Rod talked about being nine years old when he first earned any money and bought sweets with his money for his sisters. He didn't hesitate to talk about his family, but carefully chose his words. Rod revealed a vulnerable side of himself that allowed a warmth and sincerity to come through. I was touched and wanted him to continue talking about his family but he leaned over and planted a sweet deep kiss on my mouth that lasted an eternity. I was getting hot and just wanted to grab Rod and shove him inside of me, but I had to be patient. I hated playing the little mind games with myself. Fully dressed Rod slid his hand between my thighs and raised my dress as far as he could. He carefully pulled the dress over my head, removing it in no time.

"You are so beautiful," Rod's face found its way to my cleavage and he tenderly kissed me there.

I stopped him to say, "You really need to take these off," pointing to the clothes on his body. Watching Rod take off his clothes was torturous for me, I had to wait even longer. I was satisfied with his ability to make me wait for something tantalizing, a wait that was worthwhile. Rod must have been even more eager than I was because he wouldn't turn me loose. We went at it for hours and set a new record for condoms used.

Neither one of us thought about emotional deprivation in the course of our having intercourse. I couldn't bring myself to say the three words that should have been part of the dialogue for a time like that. I couldn't say 'I love you' to Rod because it would have meant committing to something neither of us was ready for, or sure about. He was still married, after all.

While I lay on the rumpled sheets next to Rod I glanced to his bureau and didn't see the annoying picture. He had moved it. I smiled and wrapped my legs around his. To make myself more comfortable I turned my body and scooted backward into his waiting arms and body. As we lay there all wrapped up and content with each other, we heard a pounding at the door. It was not a normal sound. The pounding continued.

"Someone's at your door. Are you expecting anyone else?"

"No, not that I know of." Rod got up, pulled his pants on and went to the door. I could not hear what was being said because he closed the bedroom door on his way out.

I heard commotion in the other room. My sixth sense told me to get up immediately and begin to get dressed as quickly as possible. My intuition was correct because just as I put my undergarments on, the bedroom door flew open and standing there on the other side of it was an enormous woman, in a man's body, screaming loudly at me, Rod, and anyone else who could hear her. This must be Shamu. My God, I thought, please don't let her kill me.

I didn't want someone else's man. I was there for one reason only and it was not to fight a female animal over a man.

Rod was able to hold her back long enough for me to put on my dress and grab my jewelry and purse. With my shoes and stockings in hand, I said my good-byes.

Driving away, I asked myself over and over again why he opened the door. That was not supposed to happen. Rod had told me his marriage was over and the divorce would be final soon. I knew it was his wife because he said her name several times. In the confusion the woman accused him of lying to her, and that it was not over yet. I thought about the size of the gargantuan and what I would have loved to have done to her. I did manage to find some humor in it and started chuckling quietly then laughed out loud. I know the drivers next to me wondered what was so funny when they saw my head bobbing backward, roaring with laughter. I was grateful to get out of there in one piece. Getting laid is not what it used to be.

I gave myself a real treat at the fabric store and soon forgot about the incident. I had no one to blame but myself. The signs were there but I ignored them. The missing annoying picture had been replaced by the real thing.

13

Labor Day weekend was a drag for me and I stayed in bed for most of it. I turned the ringer off on my telephone and checked the messages periodically. There were no important calls made to me that weekend, just Eddie, Rod and Pam. Pam was the only person I really wanted to talk to.

Pam couldn't believe the story about Rod's ex. I told Pam I knew something wasn't right about him. If a relationship is not meant to be, it just won't happen. If former issues of the heart have not been resolved, it is impossible to move on with a new person in your life. The second time I paid an emotional price was just as painful as the first. Rod refused to admit to me that the matter of his ex was uncertain. There was no guarantee that filing for divorce would end a relationship. Rod's ex was living proof.

Before starting on the dress for the reunion I wanted to call Eileen to get caught up on her activities. The last time we talked Eileen had not had her period yet, but was testing negative to pregnancy tests. I dialed her number and the female voice that answered was not Eileen's, "Hello?"

"Hello, may I speak to "E?" I call her that sometimes.

"You want Eileen?"

"Yes." I still didn't catch the voice.

"Just a moment."

"Hello," Eileen finally answered.

"Hi! Who answered the phone? I didn't recognize the voice."

"Oh, that's Valerie. She and I are going to cover the opening of an art exhibit for the school paper. She's in my class.

"Where?"

"At the J. Paul Getty Museum, the new one up on the hill."

"Oh. Do you have a minute?"

"Yeah, but let me go change phones."

Eileen picked up the receiver in another room and started talking, "I've been meaning to call you, because I talked to my father."

"When?"

"Yesterday. Mom, all he talked about was you and how fine you are."

I was amused. "Did he say anything about his wife?"

"No, nothing good. He said she's always sweating him about you. And when she saw a fifty minute call to you on the phone bill, she hit the roof. Daddy told me they fight a lot, mostly about you."

"Well, that's her own fault. I don't want Barry. His wife refused to accept the fact that we were in his life first, and that we aren't going anywhere. She probably thinks I want to sleep with Barry, but I don't fuck around with married men and Barry knows that." Rod was the only exception I knew about. "She's said and done some mean things to you. I don't know what made her think she could interfere with your relationship with your father."

"I know. When I was living with them, there was always friction in the house. Daddy said Betty got jealous, because when daddy hugs me, she thinks he's hugging you."

I laughed because if she knew what he was *really* like, like I do, she might not have married him in the first place.

"He said she resented the fact that you and Daddy were friendly. Mama, you look better than she does even if you are older. I saw her last week and she had died her hair blonde and she's all fat. Now she looks 'county'. Mom, you and I are the same size and Daddy talks about how you get better with age."

I laughed at that comment. He should have been saying this shit twenty-five years ago and I'm not impressed. "Does he say those things in front of her?"

"Oh, no, these are private conversations we have. Mama, Daddy said he would like to tie you up and take you off somewhere and make mad passionate love to you." Again, I laughed.

"Baby, I still love your daddy, after all this time, with all his faults. And as much as I enjoyed having sex with him twenty-five years ago and believe me, he's the best, I would never sleep with him while he is married to and living with his wife. That's just something I don't do. I think he needs to sit Betty down and tell her to stay out of our business. But I don't think he's strong enough to do that. She should have more confidence in herself and some trust in her husband. She will drive him away if she doesn't make some type of adjustment."

"Mom, I gotta go. We're supposed to be at the museum before seven."

"All right, have fun." I never got around to asking about her period.

"Thanks, Mom. I'll call you tomorrow."

I was able to cut out and sew most of the dress by late evening. The telephone did not ring one time Monday and I began to wonder what happened to everyone. Not getting calls back after sending out stacks of resumes was a bummer at times. You know you're good enough, but sometimes without the right connections it seems hopeless. The constant search for work was a bitch.

Lately I had been looking for a small, unknown lingerie company that desired a breath of fresh air in its designs. Several months ago I sent a résumé to a company like that. The name of the company was Pearly's, a very small, low key manufacturing company in Gardena. I did my homework before mailing my résumé out. When I followed up the résumé with a phone call I found out the company was up for sale and that no major hiring was being done at the time. I was told to call back in a few months.

I made a mental note to call Pearly's first thing in the morning. After dialing the number I got two rings, then an answer.

"Pearly's Manufacturing Company."

After identifying myself I was asked to wait. A minute later, a man answered, speaking with what sounded like an Asian accent, "Ahllo?"

"Hello," I said. "My name is Sasha Friend. Are you the new owner?"

"Yes, how can I help you?"

I told him that a few months ago I had mailed a résumé to the company and was told that the company would have new owners soon. I asked him if he happened to see my résumé.

"The former owner took everything. No paperwork here. If you mail me other résumé I look at it, good?" Yoshi Ura asked me what position I had applied for.

"Designer," I said.

"You make patterns, sketching?"

"Yes I do."

"Good. You mail your résumé today? I look at it."

"Thank you, have a nice day," I added before hanging up the phone.

That was the way I wished I could start every morning. Positive phone calls that were hopeful signs for me. I then called a few production companies I had mailed résumés to. One company was putting production off until next spring due to budget problems. The other company I called was crewed up and ready to begin production in a few days. "No openings in the wardrobe department, but check back next week when the designer is here. All résumés are sent over there, we don't keep them in this office.' After hearing the speech four times, I gave up for the day. I opened my desk drawer and removed a résumé to mail to Pearly's. I planned to mail it before noon, or whenever I decided to pull myself together for the day. When I was not working on a production, I tried to get dressed by one in the afternoon, at the very latest. I could always find something constructive to do at home while still in my nightgown. A woman's work is never done.

I got up from my desk and went to the kitchen to make myself a latté before settling down at the sewing machine to finish my dress for the reunion.

By the end of the week I received a call from Mr. Yoshi Ura, who had gotten my résumé the day before.

"Hello," his recognizable voice said, "Ah, Sasha Friend, please."

"This is she. Mr. Ura?"

"Yes it is me. And please, call me Yoshi. Can you come in so we can talk? I got your résumé yesterday and it is veddi strong."

"Yes, thank you. Is Monday good for you?" I said, trying to control my excitement. I agreed to a ten o'clock appointment Monday morning and told him I would see him then and, "and have a great weekend!"

Yoshi's good nature and sincerity was promising. I wondered what he had in mind work wise because he was so vague, but I decided that it did not matter. I reminded myself that I was a designer capable of giving him whatever he wanted, within reason.

"I want you to come down here today," Eddie ordered.

"I can't come today. I have…"

"You jus' don't want to come." Eddie cut me off, "I really need to see you. Whenever you need money I sen' it to you, but you always too busy for me."

"Eddie, I have things here I need to work on. I can't just drop everything right now and come down to Los Angeles." I was tempted to call him the parasite he behaved like sometimes. Things were fine as long as I was there with him. He did not understand that I had a life of my own and I wished *he* would get a life.

"I need you, jus' so you can hold my hand. I'm going through a rough time right now and you don' even care what happens to me."

"Eddie, I do care, but you want to control me all the time and I will not stand for that. You know that," I said with a soft touch.

"I'm not controllin' you. I jus' love you."

I felt sorry for Eddie, because at fifty eight, he acted so naïve. He thought that just because he loved me, I should automatically fall in love with him. Unfortunately for him, it didn't work that way. I was getting nowhere with Eddie. "Look, I have to go now. Can you call me later on tonight?"

"Why can't you talk now?" Eddie almost sounded like a child. "You always too busy to talk to me."

"I'm right in the middle of something." The conversation was emotionally draining for me, so I hung up on him. I refused to listen to his whining and let it screw up my weekend. I turned off the ringer on the phone and tried to forget about Eddie. Just before going to bed I checked the messages to discover Eddie had called five times with each message containing remarks that were critical and hurtful.

Saturday morning I called Marlene to share the prospect of a new, more permanent job. She was happy for me and insisted that I keep her posted. I could sense an eagerness about Marlene that made me think she needed to talk. "What are you doing later today? You feel like driving up here?" I asked.

"You read me like a book sometimes Sasha. I do need to get out of here today. Dennis and I are having some problems."

"Well, come on up. I'll make enchiladas and buy you some Blush Chablis. What time can you get here?"

"Is seven okay?"

"Sure. And you can stay over if you like, but you know that."

Dennis' latest escapade is what Marlene wanted to talk about, "see you later." The nature of the visit was personal so I decided not to invite Pam over. The three of us had not done anything together in over a year and I knew we would all get together during the holidays.

It was rare for me to entertain at home, so I was happy that my very good friend was coming. Teddy got excited when I asked him to run the vacuum for Marlene's visit. She always had something for Teddy when she came over. Marlene referred to him as the son she never had. I did some surface cleaning that didn't require much effort. I knew that I would be needing the energy for later in the day when Marlene arrived.

"Mmm! These enchiladas are good. I like the way you seasoned them."

"Thanks. Let me get you more wine before I sit down," and I reached for her glass. Marlene loved her wine, and I knew that if she was loose enough, she would tell me everything.

Once again, an otherwise solid relationship was threatened by tension. Marlene said Dennis had been running wild with Lou lately. He had been coming home later and later every day, giving some business deal excuse involving Lou. She told me about the phone calls she had been getting lately and how, when she or the twins answer, they get hung up on. This pattern sounded all too familiar to me.

"I think he's having an affair," Marlene said in a repressed tone.

"Oh, you don't know that for sure, but it does sound a bit incriminating though. Are you guys having sex?"

"Yes, that hasn't changed at all. But I see so little of him it seems."

"Does he still surprise you with nice things?"

"Yes, he does."

"Well, what are you griping about? You look good, there's nothing wrong with you. Maybe he's just working on something 'big' with Lou." I know for a fact that Lou can turn a dollar. I also knew the real reason. Marlene is spoiled, by her man. Hell, there's nothing wrong with that.

After talking about things, Marlene concluded that it probably wasn't an affair he was having, but she would have her number changed anyway. If the hang-up calls continued after the number change, she would take further action.

I tried on my finished dress that evening after Marlene went home. I was quite satisfied with how it looked on me.

The interview with Yoshi went well and he hired me as the key designer for his company. The job started right away and by mid-week I was in full employment.

Yoshi purchased the business as an investment and knew nothing about the garment industry. He was in awe of it. Yoshi's uncle was the owner of a textile company in

Hong Kong and promised to export exotic fabrics to him regularly. He gave me the grand tour of the facility and showed me the volumes of fabric on hand. I felt like a kid in a candy store with no supervision. If I needed to hire an assistant, I could do so right away. I could schedule my own hours and if I needed to work late, a Security guard would be provided for my protection. I had a workroom staff of 23 seamstresses, mostly Hispanics, who had been there at least ten years, some longer. It was comforting to know the workers were experienced, and based on the garments I saw, quality workmanship was a priority to them.

I reassured Yoshi that I would teach him all I knew and everything I did not know, we would research together. Yoshi liked my team spirit attitude and expressed a debt to me for being so helpful.

Yoshi came to America from Canton, China two years ago, leaving his wife and children behind until he was able to send for them. Unable to get funding for his business, in the first two years, Yoshi did menial jobs to keep a roof over his head which enabled him to send money home to his family. I admired the little man whose tenacity and great spirit clearly made him a big success. I hoped to enjoy the same success one day.

A week before the reunion, Pam and I shopped and had lunch. I took her to an earring shop in Santa Clarita where she was thrilled at the variety of choices available to her. She couldn't decide on one pair, so she bought three. I was able to find shoes the same afternoon, and had them dyed to match my dress.

On the night of the reunion we met at my dad's house to get ready. The affair was held at a hotel near the LAX airport. "Ooo, you gals look hot!" my father said, beaming with pride. Yes, we looked sensational and we knew it.

"Thank you, daddy," we said, together.

"Where are you off to?" he asked.

"The reunion. Can you believe it's been thirty-five years?," I added.

"Has it been that long? he said looking sad, "I wish your mother could see you now."

"I'm sure she's watching, daddy," I said with a smile.

Eileen and Teddy took lots of snapshots. Daddy posed for some pictures with us while Teddy snapped the shots and then handed me the camera. "Mom, don't get lost in the hotel and don't pick up any strangers."

We walked into a room full of laughter and screams coming from long lost friends, enemies and retired teachers. Although the ballroom at the Marriott was beautifully decorated, the scene took on a carnival atmosphere. People who were merely skin and bone all through school were now bulging and pot-bellied. Those who had full heads of hair lost it either to balding or graying. Most wore name tags because without them, there was no real proof of what their identity used to be. Pam and I stood out, because we had managed to retain our looks, and really, did not feel as if we belonged there. We were suddenly reminded of why we were so glad to graduate from high school. There was no one there either one of us liked, except Paul Britt, my first piece, but after talking with him for a short time, he became dull. Just like all of the others there, he had put on weight and had a phony story to tell.

We wandered about the room looking for familiar faces but found none. Couples who managed to stay together over the years had begun to look alike. Is this what years and years of marriage would have done to us?, I asked myself. Pam and I looked at each other, glad to be single. "Let's blow this joint," I finally suggested.

On the way home we stopped at Denny's to get a bite to eat. We agreed the reunion should have been put off another week so that it could have fallen on Halloween. That way there would have been an excuse for the way those people looked at the reunion.

14

Immediately following Halloween, I started baking pumpkin bread. The tradition began ten years ago when I decided to make use of the jack o lanterns I had always discarded. It seemed like a disgrace to throw away good squash. I stumbled upon a recipe for the bread and have been a loyal baker of the delicacy ever since. I bake tons of it so I can share it with my friends. I have enough to freeze for the upcoming holidays.

Teddy picked a gigantic pumpkin this year for the jack-o-lantern and I managed to make twelve loaves from it. Popping the last two loaves onto cooling racks, ended my annual ritual. I stood in front of the bread struggling not to cut into it, finally unable to deny my senses I gave in to an extra thick slice. As I opened my mouth to have a bite the telephone rang. "Hello."

"Sasha, Marlene. You will never guess what happened today," an excited Marlene couldn't wait to fill me in, "I went to the bank this morning to make a withdrawal from our business account and I asked to see the balance after the transaction. Sasha, Dennis deposited twenty thousand dollars in the account, yesterday!"

"What? Is that unusual for Dennis?"

"Cash deposits that size usually are. Sasha, I could have withdrawn every cent if I wanted to. Normally, when he makes deposits on Monday it takes three days for the larger checks to clear. Any unforeseen emergencies would have to wait until Wednesday or Thursday. Not that I have an emergency. But I wonder where it came from," Marlene said with concern.

"Did you ask him about it?"

"I haven't had a chance to. And I don't think I'm going to."

Friday evening Marlene and I were changing airplanes in Houston en route to Seven Mile Beach in the Cayman Islands. Marlene was treating herself and a friend, me, to a weekend in the Caribbean, on Dennis. Communication between Marlene and Dennis had not improved so she took action. Dennis would pay attention to her after her latest move. Marlene was sure.

The same day Marlene had made the discovery at the bank she withdrew five thousand. She called me back that night to ask if I would be able to leave work early on Friday. Jasmine and Kai were happy to have Teddy stay with them at their house for the weekend. We would be back late Sunday night. I could not refuse the offer. Leaving work early on Friday was routine for me anyway, so there were no visible barriers to a great weekend.

Once we boarded Cayman airway in Houston Marlene and I settled back and toasted with the free flowing Mai

Tai's and sodas. The flight attendants did not allow any cups on the plane to get empty. By the end of the one hour flight from Houston, Marlene was tipsy and eager to get off the plane. The sun was setting when we arrived. I enjoyed what remained of the day as we waited impatiently to get through customs. The ever frustrating inconvenience was always associated with traveling outside U.S. borders. We were finally cleared after an hour and were allowed to take our luggage.

Finally, Marlene and I were standing in front of the airport, negotiating a ride to our hotel. I felt a painful slap on my chest when out of nowhere an island woman appeared right in front of me. "The mosquito was going to eat you. We have big mosquitoes here," was her remark. I wondered if I was supposed to thank her. I just smiled instead and went back to helping Marlene decide which cabbie to hire.

We finally picked one and followed him to an old beat-up station wagon he called a cab. He loaded our belongings in the back of the car. In a thick British accent the cab driver spoke to Marlene, "How long will you be with us?"

"Just for the weekend," Marlene slurred. The effect from the flight was quite evident. "Where's the party?" she said.

"Do you like to party?" the cab driver asked.

"Sometimes," I answered, wanting in on their conversation.

"Tomorrow I get off early and I can show you where to party."

Things began to look good for the weekend. Marlene asked him for his number in case we decided to go out Saturday night. The cab driver pulled up in front of the hotel that sat at the end of a long gravel driveway. We could hear the fizzing sound of water pounding on the beach as we checked in.

Marlene and I were shown to our room. The beautiful suite had two full-sized four poster beds in it, a desk and a large window that faced the ocean, as did all of the other rooms in the hotel. The hotel was not fancy but was quaint and had a character all it's own. The single-story structure did not try to compete with the other big hotels in the area.

I got up early the next morning and put on summer clothes I was wearing just a few months ago at home. I stepped outside the room onto powdery white sand that led to the water that lapped at the sand about one hundred feet away. The sight of the clear aqua ocean prompted me to remove my thongs and put my feet in the warm water.

It was the perfect time of year to be in the Caribbean. Summer vacationers had long since departed, leaving the virgin sands to me, Marlene and a few mosquitoes. Marlene soon joined me near the water's edge, to tell me that continental breakfast would be served to us just a few feet from where we stood. A few moments later two very tall, ebony native waiters approached us carrying a large silver platter and a blanket they carefully spread out on the sand. The waiter set the tray down on the blanket and asked if we desired anything else. Marlene told him "no", thanked him and tipped them well. We sat on the beach and talked a long time about men and anything else we could think of.

Marlene confessed that Dennis knew nothing about her weekend trip. She wanted him to worry about her. Dennis knew we were together, but the twins were sworn to secrecy about our location.

We took naps after lunch to rest up for an evening of dining and dancing with the locals. Marlene made contact with the cab driver who said he would pick us up at eight.

I climbed into the back seat of the cab drivers' shiny green jeep," What's your name?," I asked. Marlene sat in front.
"Wilbert Long. Have you tried our turtle soup yet?"
"No, but we're going to the Turtle Farm in the morning," Marlene said.
"Well, you can't eat turtle soup there so I will take you to a café that makes the best on the island!" His upbeat attitude was contagious.
We were warmly greeted at the café and treated like royalty. After dinner their 'driver' took us to a popular disco of the locals. An old renovated barn was the place to listen to R&B cuts by American artists. As we danced to the late night hours, the DJ blended slow R&B with true island reggae, eventually playing nothing but reggae until the night ended.
Marlene rarely sat out a dance and partied like there was no tomorrow. Every time she finished a dance, a new dance partner would appear. Exhaustion overtook us around three in the morning and we called it a night.
Marlene and I overslept Sunday morning and had to rush to meet the tour bus that took us to the Turtle Farm. We each bought souvenirs for family and realized our weekend was quickly coming to an end.
When our bags were packed we took last minute snapshots of the room that we spent the last few days in. We arrived back in Los Angeles at nine o'clock Sunday night. Marlene was completely satisfied. So was I.

I spent the night at Marlene's and drove to work Monday morning from there. Marlene brought Teddy to the job just before I got off work, making it easier for us to drive directly home to the Antelope Valley from Los Angeles.

Teddy explained how much he enjoyed a day off from school. He had a lot of questions about the Caymans. We talked non stop all the way back to the Antelope Valley.

I was strangely revitalized after my weekend adventure. The work week breezed by with me having energy left over at the end of the week, so Teddy and I packed a lunch on Saturday and went hiking at Vasquez Rocks. A recycler newspaper was all I could find to read in my car, so I began to thumb through it while we were having lunch. I was interested in finding a good deal on fishing tackle when I stumbled upon the Computer Dating section. I wondered what kind of people would be hard up enough to go through a dating service to get a date.

I scanned the columns to see what qualifications were in demand and analyzed the types of men who were looking for dates. One particular request perked my imagination. 'Seeks intellectual type female, 35+, smoking and drinking OK, open minded for 42 yr. Old black male, has own business, likes to cook', was how it read. The ad gave his phone number and permission to call after 7 p.m. I realized later that I should have had my head examined for calling that number.

I waited a few days before I called. I had to get up enough nerve to be willing to accept the outcome, whatever it was. I talked to Marlene about it first, and with her encouragement, decided that I had nothing to lose. I dialed the number. A very deep, mellow sounding voice answered. The intrigue continued as he said, "Hello?"

"Hi, my name is Sasha Friend, is the person who placed the ad for a date there?"
"I'm Zeeke Small, I placed the ad."
"Do you have a few minutes to spare right now?"
"That depends upon what I'm sparing it for."
"Me."
"Well, in that case, yes I do."

Initially, I was satisfied with the conversation I was having with Zeeke. We talked a short time, less than ten minutes, just long enough to introduce ourselves. The recent disaster in my love life was enough, I thought, to give him my phone number. I thought maybe, just maybe, he could turn out to be that person I'd been waiting for. He sounded romantic on the phone and based on the description he gave of himself in the paper, he could be someone I might have enjoyed being with. To top it off Zeeke worked in show business, as a street musician, and was hoping for a big break. My mistake was that I felt sorry for him to begin with, but I wanted someone to kill some time with. Most of his days were spent on the boardwalk at Venice Beach.

After talking on the phone for several weeks, we decided it was time to meet in person. Zeeke suggested we have dinner at a favorite Italian restaurant of his, located near his home in Hollywood. He told me I could easily spot him by the large hat he would be wearing.

I had no problem recognizing Zeeke when I walked into the restaurant. I was to meet him in the bar of the restaurant, where I found him wearing an oversized top hat that looked like the Empire State Building. My initial reaction was amusement, then embarrassment. I couldn't believe I had agreed to meet with the clown, but then

I understood why he found it necessary to solicit companionship in the newspaper.

Zeeke was gregarious and totaling entertaining but I sensed a dark macabre side of him I could not figure out, until I saw where he lived. He wanted to show me his place that was a few blocks from where we dined. It was an old recording studio that had been abandoned for years. He convinced the owner not to demolish the building and allow him to lease the basement area for living in. That way he was able to live in Hollywood, not far from the activities on Hollywood Boulevard, for dirt cheap. His environment was in sharp contrast to mine.

We went to the apartment and as we descended into the basement of the building I was reminded of scenes of torture and Satanism I had seen in movies. I didn't know how in the hell I had let him talk me into going down there.

There were no windows, which further added to the mystery of the man. I started to shiver in the dark and cold interior. The squalid odor made me sneeze constantly as he gave me a tour of the dungeon he called home. Dimly lit rooms and passageways made me fearful so I held onto Zeeke's arm, never allowing him to stray too far ahead of me. "It's like living in hell," I finally said, "aren't you ever afraid?"

"My grandmother used to say 'if you weren't so bad, you wouldn't be scared'," he laughed but I found no humor in the comment. Zeeke could sense that the creepy concrete walls and exposed plumbing pipes were overwhelming me so he led us back to the entrance, up the stairs and out of there. It was too deep for me. I thanked Zeeke for dinner and the tour of his tomb and said goodnight.

I realized as I drove back to the Antelope Valley just how truly blessed I was. I asked myself how anyone could live where there was no natural sunlight. Zeeke told me that living in basements was common back East and that I had overreacted. You damn right, I thought. I was still convinced that he was hiding something perverse, possibly from his childhood. I wanted to get to the bottom of his desperation without insulting him. I allowed my curiosity to get the best of me, wanting to know more about this man if we were going to be friends.

In our conversations that followed Zeeke revealed a strong dislike he had for his step-father. He and his two younger sisters were regularly abused by the man his mother married. Their terror continued until they became grown and moved out. I had the feeling he wanted to talk about his pain from that but he withheld it because he probably was not sure how I would react . We were cautiously exploring a friendship, and I knew that what Zeeke needed more than anything was a friend, not sex.

Zeeke kept in touch with me in the weeks following. Our frequent conversations touched upon his past relationships and disappointment he felt when they ended. He had never been married but came close to it once. With no explanation his fiancé called it off, never saying why. When he tried to call her by phone, she had refused to talk to him. Overwhelmed with doubt about his devotion and commitment, Zeeke could not ignore the terrifying echoes of rejection. And like me, he became cautious about involvement's of the heart.

My favorite time of the year, the holiday season was upon me before I realized it. I celebrated Thanksgiving at home with the children. I cooked enough for an army. Eileen invited Eric to dinner and they drove up from L.A. the evening before so she could help me cook. Eric registered at a nearby hotel where he and Teddy spent most of the evening playing video games. It worked out well because Teddy was temporarily out of the way. I enjoyed any time alone with Eileen since I didn't see her as often as I would have liked. When we finished preparing the food I drove Eileen back to the hotel and brought Teddy home.

At the last minute Marlene, Dennis and the twins accepted my invitation to dinner. Pam, Lou and Zeeke were surprises as well. I was delighted that everyone was able to come, as I had hoped. Zeeke put on a magic show after dinner, which was a total surprise for everyone, revealing yet another side of himself that I did not know about.

An earthquake tremor woke me up early the morning after Thanksgiving. I opened my eyes to see the bedside lamps on my night stands shaking, accompanied by the sound of rattling perfume bottles on my vanity. The wake-up call, although surprising was welcomed. I forgot to set the alarm the night before and needed an early rise for the day ahead.

It was early, and I had just fixed myself a latté when I heard a knock at the door. I opened the door to find Pam standing there, wearing a warm-up suit and a big smile. "Good morning!", she said.

"Well, hello!" and I stepped back so Pam could come inside, "where are you off to this morning?"

"I'm on my way to see Pookie. Sasha I couldn't take it any longer."

"He knows you're coming? When did you talk to him?"

"A few days ago."

"And you didn't mention it to me last night," I said, almost scolding her.

"No, because I wasn't sure what I was feeling. But I realize even though he hurt me, he still satisfies me in bed," Pam said, as she plopped down on the sofa. I knew what it was leading to but I did not say a thing.

"Well, go for it! Want a latté?"

"No, I had two cups of coffee before I left home."

"Did you feel the earthquake?" I asked as I got my latté from the kitchen counter.

"No, when was it?"

"About thirty minutes ago. It woke me up," I joined Pam on the couch.

"Maybe that's what I felt when I was on the freeway. I thought I was having a blowout, but I just bought a new set of tires. And I was listening to a tape in the car, so I didn't hear about it on the radio."

"So, what's the plan for you and Pookie today?"

"There is no plan, but I'm staying over tonight."

"Would you like some pumpkin bread?" I asked as Pam got up. I walked over to the kitchen counter to slice some for myself.

"No, thanks, and I'd better be going. I just stopped by to surprise you."

"Well, you did. Have fun. I have to go to work myself."

I got dressed for work and said good bye to Teddy, but before I could walk out the door, the telephone rang. It was Eddie.

15

"Eddie, I really can't talk right now. I'm walking out the door."

"This will jus' take a minute," Eddie persisted.

I wondered why I answered the phone. "What is it?" I demanded.

"You know, you sure can be nasty when you want to."

"Is that what you called me to say? This damn early in the morning?"

"No, but can't you be sweet to me?"

"Eddie, I'm trying to be civil with you, but I'm also trying to walk out the door. *I* have a job to go to."

"You and that damn job! I don't know why it's so important. You..."

"Eddie, I don't know why you are calling me anyway, after the nasty messages you have been leaving on my service lately. Haven't you noticed that I have *not* been returning your calls?"

"Baby, you know I love you, please don't be mad at me."

"Good bye, Eddie, I've got to go," I said just before hanging up on him.

On my drive to work, I thought about the many times I had hung up on Eddie, times like that morning. I hated doing it, but when he cuts me off in the middle of a sentence I get frustrated. I hadn't taken any money from him in a while, knowing I wanted to end the relationship. It was too stressful to engage in conversation with him. I always found myself arguing and disagreeing with him, and defending myself, constantly. The aggravation was too great and my pulse would rise with every conversation I had with him. I decided that the relationship was not worth the money.

Many times I wanted to end the relationship with a letter, but realized he couldn't read it. Verbally dismissing him would be best. When that didn't work, I refused to take any more of his calls. Teddy started complaining about Eddie's calls, noticing how upset I would be after talking to Eddie on the phone. 'Why don't you quit him?' Teddy would ask me after one of the calls, and 'I don't like him anyway,' he would say. I demanded that Eddie stop calling, but he continued. I was an obsession to the man and it frightened me.

The last time I was at Eddie's place I saw his phone bill, that was laying out in the open on his dining room table. One page of the bill had nothing but my phone number on it. The entire sheet was a continuous print out of my number that he had dialed daily, up to ten times in one day. It was scary for me to see that. Something told me to take the page, which I did, so if necessary it would serve as proof of his instability and obsession. My number was printed fifty times on the bill with the time, date and charges for every call he made. When I looked at it later I was convinced this was a sick man.

I had heard enough about domestic violence to know what the signs were that led to its eruption. I had recently read about a man who lost his job of twenty years. The man, who was in his fifties, became distraught over being laid off from the aerospace job he loved. His frustration over the loss of income led to the killing of his wife, daughter and son-in-law. Without turning the gun on himself he shot and killed his entire family. By comparison, I knew the case was a bit extreme, but one never knows how a controlling and overbearing person will react in an emotional situation. Eddie frightened me, because he had nothing to lose.

When I got home from work, I learned that Eddie had called and left several messages on the service. Teddy answered the first call then turned the ringer off so the calls would not disturb him. I felt it was time to take action in the form of a letter. I didn't care if he couldn't read it. I needed to write down on paper what he refused to listen to on the telephone. I wanted the relationship to end, once and for all.

I mailed the Dear John letter to Eddie immediately with the knowledge that he probably would not read it. That meant the person who would read the letter to him would know about Eddie's personal drama, and he would probably be humiliated and outraged since he could not suffer in private. I hated the thought, but there was no other way.

When Eddie received the letter, he called me. "Why did you wrote me dis' letter?," he asked me.

"It's over, Eddie."

"You know I din't ment whut I say'd to you," there was sadness in every word he spoke.

I tried to explain once again, "You have no respect for me, Eddie and I am tired of you bullying me all the time. So please stop calling me."

We began to argue. In the letter I told Eddie it was time for him to move on with his life and that I was doing the same, there was no hope for us ever, and that I would never agree to marriage under any circumstances with him, or anyone else. "Eddie, I loved you once, but I don't like you very much right now. Please get some help because you have a hard time dealing with reality," and I wished him well.

Apparently, Eddie did not understand the contents of the letter. He said he ripped the letter up and that it did not mean a thing to him. "You know I love you, Sasha. Why do you wan' to hurt me like dis'?" Eddie wined and pleaded.

"Eddie, if you don't stop calling me, I'm going to do something you might not like."

"What?" he said.

"I will call the Sheriff and tell them you are harassing me."

"You mutha fuckin' bitch!" He hung up the phone after that. For now, at least, I got him off my back.

There had been only one other time in my life when leaving someone was difficult. The first time I left Barry years ago, I needed help to do it. I knew of no one who was available or willing to do what was necessary for me. What I wanted was someone, preferably a strong man, to help me take all of my clothes and personal belongings out of the third story apartment Barry and I shared, down three flights of stairs, in less than two hours, without Barry's knowledge. On Saturday mornings twice a month, Barry worked overtime, usually until noon.

A few days before I left Barry, we had had another ugly fight. I ran out of the apartment, down the stairs and onto the street in tears. I didn't know where to go. All I knew was that I had to get away, so I continued, walking down the dimly lit street, in the direction of my mothers' house. In my pathway not far from the apartment building Barry and I lived in was a small strip shopping center with a pool hall that had an entrance allowing people to go in and out from the sidewalk. A man standing in the doorway watched me rush by. "Where's the fire?" he asked, following me with his eyes.

I kept walking but looked back over my shoulder and saw a very well-built man holding a pool cue. "Wait a minute, where are you going?" he demanded.

I picked up my pace but he caught up with me before I knew it.

Al became my one man moving team and a temporary companion. On the Saturday following our meeting Al and I moved all of my things out of the apartment in record time while Barry was at work. I rented a motel room where I stored my things. Al was unattached at the time so I let him stay there with me. I was acting out of impulse, not knowing what else to do. Even though I was afraid, I knew I could stay there indefinitely with Al, but Al had different ideas.

By the time I was ready to make my next move and possibly reconcile with Barry, Al was in love with me. I didn't realize how deeply committed he had become until I announced that it was over. Al held a hunting knife to his chest and said he would kill himself if I was going to leave him. I just looked at him and wondered how I had managed to get myself in *that* situation.

I was not going to fall for that trick though. He was not going to force me to stay with him. If he wanted to die because of me, I refused to take responsibility. I had enough problems. I asked Al to please step away from my clothes hanging in the closet so he would not bleed all over them. After the incident, he realized that I was wiped out emotionally and just wanted to be left alone. Al departed, never to be hear from again.

I wondered why Eddie couldn't do the same thing as Al and just go away. That was why I was convinced that Eddie had a mental problem. It was not normal for anyone to take the sort of abuse we generated toward each other. It just did not feel right. Verbal abuse was never right. Eddie did not handle rejection very well, but that was not my problem.

I had not heard from Eddie in about a week and I finally began to relax. I started making plans for Christmas and thought about inviting Paulette down for a few days. The last time we talked she was equally torn between men and women as sexual partners.

Yoshi decided to close the company Christmas eve and not reopen until four days later. That gave me plenty of time to plan an interesting Christmas weekend.

I wanted to have a brunch on Christmas morning for my close friends. That way we could all be together before the end of the year. We could loosen up with enough champagne and sparkling cider to analyze the major events and accomplishments of the year. I wanted to spend the special holiday with the ones who had always been there for me, no matter what.

Paulette was not sure if she could get a flight out of Oakland Christmas Eve, but assured me that if it was necessary she would drive down. Pam said she would probably spend the night Christmas Eve and Marlene would drive up Christmas morning. When I told Eileen about the gathering and that everyone would be there she offered to come up the night before and help me get things ready. I had finished my shopping early in the month so I would not be faced with last minute chaos. I waited a week before Christmas to buy a tree so tree dryness would not be a problem. Teddy insisted we have it flocked and trimmed with blue ornaments.

"Who sent the roses?"
"What roses?" I walked in the front door from work and saw a bouquet of two dozen long stemmed yellow roses just delivered. "My, God, they are so beautiful!" I said, surprised.
"Yeah, but who are they from?" Teddy questioned me again.
"How should I know? Who brought them here?"
"A man from a flower shop delivered them," he reported.
"Is there a card?" I walked closer to the flower arrangement that sat on the dining room table searching for a card. I could not find one. With my nose almost touching the yellow petals, I inhaled the fragrance of one rose. "I'll bet that damn Eddie sent these."
I had to admit the flowers were gorgeous and because of their beauty I could not throw them out.
"Are you ready to go find a tree?" asked my excited son.

"Sure, let's go." I loved the excitement the holidays always brought joy to the faces of my children.

Teddy and I ordered Dominos deep dish pizza and decorated the tree that evening. We were delighted with how incredibly awesome the tree looked with the snow-like flocking and its tiny flickering lights accented by the brilliant blue ornaments. We put a pine wreath on the front door that concluded our annual hanging of the green. Completely exhausted and full of pizza, Teddy and I returned empty boxes to the garage as well as ornaments, some broken, we decided not to use. Just prior to retiring for the night, Paulette called to say she would be arriving late Christmas Eve. She decided to drive.

The brunch I served on Christmas morning was fit enough for royalty. We enjoyed honey baked ham, eggs Benedict, fruit salad, cranberry babas, orange eggnog and butter croissants. At the end of the feast everyone was so stuffed we could barely move. We cleared the dining room table while everyone else wobbled into the living room to have coffee and to open gifts.

I was creative in selecting gifts for my friends. Marlene was the first to unwrap her gift and screamed as she held up the crotchless panties I had so carefully wrapped. Pam and Paulette were equally amused when they discovered they were going to be new wearers of thong panties. We had a good laugh together and shared stories with each other. In the middle of the fun, the doorbell rang.

Eileen answered the door and brought a brown padded envelope to me, just delivered by a messenger. There was no return address on the envelope, only my name. I didn't recognize the handwriting.

"I wonder what this is." The intrigue and excitement made me struggle to open the flap. When I finally got it open I reached inside and pulled out red tissue paper that was wrapped around what felt like a small box. I soon realized that it was no ordinary small box. It was a ring box. I opened it to find a diamond ring inside. Eileen picked up the envelope and a tiny card fell out of it. It was signed by Eddie.

"I don't believe this! That man is insane." I said.

"I thought you guys were finished." Paulette commented.

"We are. He's just plain crazy and this proves it. How dare he intrude upon my holiday?" I was truly inflamed.

"Let me see that. So, what are you going to do with it?" Marlene asked, after carefully analyzing the precious stone in its setting.

"She ought to take it to a pawn shop. That's a pretty big stone," added Pam.

"Don't tempt me." My mind began to race. "No, I'm just going to send it right back with a big sheet of paper with the word 'no' written on it in big letters. He should understand that!" I slammed the box closed and tossed it under the tree disgusted.

Eddie still managed to bother me on my family affair even though I had not spoken to him in weeks. I refused to let it spoil my day. If he had been the man of my dreams it would have been terribly romantic.

"Sasha, what did you do to that old rascal? What's your secret, girl?" Marlene joked and we laughed it off.

"I don't know. Maybe it was the thong panties." Laughter filled the house.

Eileen took Teddy with her to L.A. to deliver gifts and visit friends. Marlene and Pam left shortly thereafter, leaving Paulette and I to finish the job of cleaning up and putting away the holiday china.

For the remainder of the afternoon we relaxed and enjoyed each others' company. At sundown we went back into the living room, turned on the tree lights and just sat there quietly, staring at the tree, enjoying the final hours of a very beautiful day. We were blessed and we knew it.

16

Paulette and I got up early the morning after Christmas and planned our day over lattés. Eileen called to say she and Teddy had plans for the day and would probably not come back until the end of the weekend. That was fine with me because we wanted to shop anyway and take advantage of after Christmas sales. I rewrapped the ring Eddie sent and made the Post Office my first stop.

"Are you sure you want to do this? I wish someone would surprise me that way," Paulette sighed as we walked into the Post Office.

"Then *you* marry him, shall I give him your phone number?" I snapped.

"Sasha, you didn't even call him to say you got it."

"And I don't plan to. Paulette, I've tried to quit him all year long but he won't go away. I'm tired. If I call him I would be going against everything I believe in. It's better this way." I handed the package to the postal clerk and paid the amount due. "Do you have any plans for New Years?" I asked Paulette as we got into the car.

"Buck, with his two-timing ass wants me to meet him in Tahoe."

"Well, are you going?"

"I really don't know. I met this chick and she's having a few friends over for New Year's Eve. She invited me just before I came down here. I've been thinking about her all weekend. I wanted to call her but, you know, I didn't want to appear overanxious. You know what I mean?"

"Yep. So what are you going to do?"

Paulette shrugged her shoulders with a confused look on her face that I knew very well. "I don't know," she said. "I'll think about it when I drive back tomorrow. What about you?"

"You know I don't go out New Year's Eve. I prefer the sanctity of being at home."

We found great bargains at the mall, but spent very little money. I bought a few things for Teddy. Paulette bought a sweater for my dad. We had a late lunch then headed home so Paulette could get ready for her trip back to Oakland. She left early the next morning and promised to call when she got home.

Sometimes I think about how my involvement with Eddie began. It started one day when Marlene and I were on our way to a wedding. We had stopped at a neighborhood store in South Central to purchase film for her camera. Marlene waited in the car while I ran inside to make the quick purchase. As I approached the check-out line I noticed an extremely tall, very dark handsomely aging gentleman waiting in line. It was rare to see a man that tall without a petite woman on his side.

I watched him for a moment to be sure he was alone. When I saw there was no one was attached to him, I walked to the end of the line, and stood right behind him. He didn't notice me at first, but as he approached the checker, he turned and glanced at me from the corner of his eye.

"Hi!" I looked at him with my dangerously flirtatious smile. He bashfully smiled down and said, "Hi. How ya' doin'?" That was all he said. The silence continued for a few moments and I wondered if I had offended him. I was determined to know more about him so I pursued. I wanted to know if he was single, but after I got his name. "What's your name?" I asked.

"Eddie." There was more silence, so I proceeded. "My name is Sasha. Are you married?" Bold, huh?

"No. I'm not married. Is you married?"

I recognized his poor grammar right away and answered, "No, I'm divorced." The grammar should have been a clue, but Eddie's gentle way obscured the obvious.

"Do you live 'round here?" he asked, smiling now.

"No, not anymore. I'm on my way to a wedding with a girlfriend."

"Where is he?" his eyes looked around as if in search of someone.

"It's not a he. *She* is waiting outside in her car."

"When's the wedding over?" Eddie paid for his merchandise.

"I'm not sure. There's a reception afterward."

"Can you call me tonight, if I gih you my numba?" He reached into his pocket for a pen and wrote his number on his receipt. The checker repeated my total a second time and I apologized for not hearing her the first time. I told Eddie if he did not hear from me later I would call him within a few days. I took my change and merchandise and said goodbye to him.

    I got into the car with Marlene and told her what had just happened. I looked at the name and phone number he wrote and thought about the difficulty he had when writing. His irregular handwriting resembled that of a youngster learning the fundamentals of the skill. I decided he was probably a stroke patient, and made nothing of it. Marlene and I went to the wedding and reception as planned, but got back too late for me to call Eddie.

    When I called Eddie in a couple of days he was happy to hear from me. He asked me out right away and I accepted with no reservation Eddie asked me to make a special trip to L.A. for dinner and he would make it worth my while. I was surprised to learn he lived only blocks from my dad. I could visit Eddie and my dad on the same trip into Los Angeles.

    My heart went out to Eddie when he told me about the deep sorrow and loss he felt when his wife died. He lovingly nurtured and cared for her during a long illness before her death. The painful time came when all nine children were emancipated and the two were looking forward to their golden years together. He murmured sorrowful tones when he spoke of his wife and his love for her. The sadness in his voice made me cry, as he exposed a hurt and vulnerable man. I thought his humility earned him a front row seat in heaven for the devotion he showed his wife. I could see that Eddie needed someone who was able to give him love he deserved.

I was happy to return to work after Christmas. I had been in the middle of a new collection before the holidays and felt pressure to get it completed. Yoshi liked my idea of showcasing our latest designs in the upcoming Trade Show in New York , just weeks away. I convinced him to use the opportunity to introduce the line and interest future buyers. Our latest fabrics that came in from Hong Kong were exquisite and it was hard not to visualize our finished garments in competition with some of the best designers in the world. Yoshi was willing to invest in my ideas which made me more dedicated to the idea. Pearly's had been a supplier to a discount chain, but with the higher quality fabrics we were getting, it was necessary to upgrade our outlet.

I found myself putting in extra hours at Pearly's simply for the sheer joy of the work involved. I took work home and would labor well into the night. It was difficult to leave an unfinished idea at the workplace. Designers were required to approve all patterns before they reached the cutters and had to meet crucial deadlines imposed by the company. I taught Yoshi techniques involved in cutting layers of fabric.

He showed his gratitude by giving me a holiday bonus. Since he was passing out money, I suggested he fatten the paychecks of the workers as well, and he agreed. I felt they deserved it because we could count on quality craftsmanship with each creation.

Things were going well and we completed the collection samples by the end of January. With my help Yoshi could make arrangements to go to the Trade Show in New York. He needed a Sales Rep for Pearly's who knew the line and could travel with Yoshi and the collection to the show. I opted not to go due to self imposed deadlines and the work load at Pearly's. Yoshi would have preferred my presence there, but I told him to save his money on a ticket for me. "You know the line, Yoshi. I have friends in New York who will show you the ropes and take care of you."

Pearly's continued to supply the demands of the discount chain but the old styles seemed dowdy compared to our new collections. Yoshi wanted to reserve the finer imported fabrics for our latest venture, and knew the customers of the discount chain could not appreciate it's value, or afford to pay for it.

I managed to get Yoshi's approval to use a printed polyester that resembled silk to make peignoir sets with coordinating panties, camisoles, tap pants and thong panties. The items sold quickly and the store wanted more, but unfortunately we were not able to duplicate the pieces because the fabric was discontinued. I found the situation quite amusing because the shoppers, not the store, were smart enough to buy the items at the time they did at bargain prices. It was almost like tossing a bone to a doggie.

I contacted one of my business associate in New York City and she was happy to oblige my request to assist Yoshi while he was in town. She put me in touch with a Sales Rep who was a close friend of hers. Space was still available on the trade room floor. When Yoshi made the hotel reservation I could see him getting all pumped up. He walked around on a cloud the entire week before leaving for New York.

17

"Mom."

"Oh, hi baby. What's going on?" I walked in the door from work when the phone rang. The sound of Eileen's sweet voice was refreshing to hear after my long day at work.

"Guess who I talked to."

"Who?"

"My father."

"Oh, so what's his story?"

"He moved out."

"You're joking, right?"

"No, he really left Betty. He called me from Tucson."

"Tucson?"

"Yeah. And he's staying with Aunt Liz for now." Liz, Barry's sister, and I became good friends during and after my marriage to Barry. We had always remained cordial, still making contact occasionally to talk about happier times.

"Is he planning to stay in Arizona?"

"That's what it sounds like. He has a job already. He asked me for your number."

"You must have told him you got engaged. Did you?"

"Yes, and he got upset." I could hear disappointment in Eileen's voice.

"Why did he get upset?"

"He said that Eric must be a bum because he didn't ask *him* for my hand in marriage."

"Oh, so now he's the concerned parent." He should have been there all those years.

"He is not giving me away at my wedding. Grandfather is. I really don't want him there."

"Well, baby, do you think humiliation would do him any good? Don't worry about it right now. Have you set a date yet?"

"Not yet, but we want to do it in the fall so we can have a candlelight wedding."

"Ooo. That sounds so romantic."

Immediately after talking to Eileen, Marlene called with a bit of scalding information for me. On the weekend we spent in the Caymans, Marlene met a Jamaican businessman from Los Angeles who was there to close a business deal. At some point that weekend they became intimate. Since then, they had been meeting secretly at the Snotty Fox Motel on Western in Los Angeles. He was married too, which freed Marlene of the guilt associated in those matters. She decided to have an affair because Dennis was increasingly preoccupied and spending less time with her. Marlene told me her new lover was talented in bed and that she walked funny for days after being with him.

When they were leaving the motel one afternoon, she saw a friend of Dennis' driving his Rolls. He pulled up right beside them when they stopped at a traffic light. The heavy tint on the windows of the car she was riding in saved her that time. It prevented him from seeing her.

"Sasha, I was scared shitless!"

"Girl, you are brave. You know Dennis is crazy."

"Dennis would kill me if he knew what I was doing."

"Well then, you had better be careful. Are you using protection?"

"Yes, I am. He told me he's not having sex with his wife though."

"Don't believe it. If he lives with her, he's having sex with her."

I was slightly depressed after talking to Marlene, who I thought had it all. She had two lovely daughters, a husband who provided a beautiful home and an unlimited cash flow. Why would she risk all that for some Jamaican? I could not figure it out.

"Who sent these roses?" I began to wonder after receiving them from the delivery man. He gave me no details, only that they were from a 'secret admirer'. The bouquet was identical to the one I received mysteriously six months ago. Yellow roses with baby's breath throughout. How did the sender know it was my birthday?

After a long period of non-communication, Zeeke called me. His career was finally taking off. His magic act caught the eye of some important people in a major studio in Hollywood. Since I had last spoken to him he had traveled to New York to participate in a regional talent search sponsored by the studio. He placed first in the competition and received a cash prize. He also traveled to San Francisco and Las Vegas to perform his act and was well received in both places. We were talking about our professional gains when the conversation got personal.

"Have you had time to go out lately?" Zeeke slipped in.

"Well, yes and no. When time permits, I usually save my energy, and lately I haven't had much, energy, that is. I work so much, I rarely think about going out."

"Yeah, I know. It's a grind. I'm taking a week off, beginning now. I'd like to see you. Can we get together?"

I thought about his offer and how stimulating parts of our conversation had been. "Yes, I would like that," I said.

"Oh, you would? You mean you would make time for a small fry like me?"

"You are in no way a 'small fry', Zeeke." I thought about his big, thick physique and giggled.

"I love your laugh. It's kind of sexy."

Thoughts of dungeon whoopie flashed in my mind as I suggested a day that would be good for me. What the hell, I thought, it might prove to be productive. It had been what felt like years since I had a memorable sexual experience or even entertained the possibility of being happy with someone. At that very moment, I could have thrown caution to the wind and kept an open mind.

We decided to order pizza from Zeeke's place instead of going out. When I arrived, Zeeke was standing outside the entrance of his building, waiting to escort me down the stairs to the basement. This time I took a tiny flashlight so I could have a better look at the floor I was walking on. I knew it was insulting but I needed to feel safe and see where I was going.

Like before, the cellar was dimly lit. We made our way to the big room he called the den and something clicked in my mind. There was no way I would become intimate with Zeeke under any circumstances. We would eat pizza, watch a movie, and talk. That was all.

Zeeke was a nice man but had a troubled family. Recently his nephew was arrested for raping a close family friend and was now in a correctional institution back East. His younger sister could no longer hide her crack habit, and after numerous attempts to help her, his mother made arrangements to have her kidnapped and committed to a recovery facility. The information was too much for me to bear. I began to think about Eddie and how much better he now seemed compared to that. None of Eddie's family members were dysfunctional. I felt nothing but sorrow for Zeeke and knew it impossible to conceive of a long term relationship with him. When I left him that night I told him I would talk to him later, and thanked him again for the lovely pizza. But I knew in my heart I would probably never see him again.

"I would like to speak to Miss Sasha Friend, please." announced Barry.
"Oh, hi Barry."
"What's this I hear about Eileen getting married?"
"I'm fine, thank you. What about you?" I asked.
"I'm okay."
"I'm surprised it took you so long for you to call me and bitch."

"Well, you know, I've made a change and with the move and all."

"Are you happy now?"

"Yeah, I couldn't take it there anymore. I just went off."

I though to myself how lucky Betty actually was. When Barry 'goes off', you don't want to be around. "You guys didn't fight in front of your son, did you?"

Barry gave me ugly details of his confrontation with Betty. I was blessed it was no longer me and thankful the burden was no longer mine.

"I packed my bag and hit the road to Tucson."

"Tucson? So, you have a place there now?"

"I'm at Liz's right now. I just got a job here and things are working out for me. I sure would like to play with your 'cookies' right about now."

"Barry, I'm sorry things didn't work out for you and Betty. Why don't you write to me so we can talk about it? Maybe I can help. You know, after all we've been through, I still love you."

"I love you too."

The love I referred to was the love a mother has for the father of her child. I hoped he understood my genuine concern for him and not interpret my words as something lusty. As usual though, he took it the wrong way.

The first letter I got from Barry talked about his admiration for my accomplishments. He wondered how I could still find some worth in him after all the pain he caused me years ago. He finally acknowledged his lack of responsibility during my rape crisis of some twenty two years ago. He had many regrets about the disappointment he brought to me by the truckload and how he has cried since then over mistakes in his life. I was pleased to learn after all this time he realized he had defects. I managed to survive it all, however, and decided not to gloat over his confession. If Barry chose never to write me another letter in his life, I would have been satisfied. But he continued to write. Barry's second letter read:

Dear Sasha,

I need to be close to you for several reasons which I'll discuss in future letters. But, if you like you can paint your own picture. My mind switches so rapidly now that it's almost like operating an adding machine. I'm truly amazed that now that the fog in head and heart has lifted, I have always known that I would take this road. But yesterday I didn't know it would be today that I'm having one of most joyous times of my life, if I never pass this way again. Perhaps all of my trials and tribulation was for or not for naught, I pray that whatever ties that bind us would only grow stronger and not weaker, that truth should prevail in all matters, and that doubt not find a way to pull down, and that trust become so prevalent that previous history becomes mute. Today as I pray, each prayer is for happiness and the desire to right. It's so consuming within me that I cry when I think back.

I often wish I could put down on paper or receive credit for tunes like 'Your Precious Love', especially that part that says 'your precious love means more to me than any love could ever before when I wanted you I was so blue that no other love could ever do." Just think about what the word 'do' means and once you've read the definition apply it (do) to us.

Perhaps in a month or so I'll have the means to have you here for a weekender. In the meantime, keep fresh batteries in your hand warm.

Barry

The letters that continued to come were more God-driven than before as he spoke of his new stronger belief in the divine. He was optimistic about his current set of circumstances and how they could aptly shape his future. All of this coming from a fifty year old man who chose to desert his adolescent son and second marriage, so he could go find himself. I found it hard to believe. His new found belief should have taken his ass back to Los Angeles to make an attempt to work things out with his wife, for the benefit of their child. It sounded very much like the situation Barry left *me* in. It became increasingly difficult for me to feel compassion for Barry as his letters became more graphic about his sexual fantasies with me. I felt insulted by his assumption that I would be stupid enough to want to pick up where we left off years ago as though I had no life of my own now. Barry thought because I was single he could easily talk his way back into my bed. I played along with his game by answering his provocative letters, but I refused to surrender completely.

After receiving the sixth lusty letter from Barry, I decided it was time to end the charade. I knew it was a complete waste of my time. He was getting total ego gratification from it, so I considered allowing him to drown on his own, and he did.

Barry called me on Tuesday evening and said he would be in town. Saturday. I thought it would be a great idea for us to have dinner and talk about Eileen's wedding. He had other things on his mind and made no secret of it.

When I did not respond like he expected, Barry tried to dismiss his thoughts and said he looked forward to seeing me on the weekend. When he did not call or show up when he said he would, my suspicions were validated. He had not changed his disrespectful ways, and I was off the hook without needing to reveal Shquita. I *did* take the time to write Barry a note stating that he had abusive patterns he needed to break and that some professional help might get him on the right path. His letters and phone calls ended abruptly.

Barry and I never discussed Eileen's wedding. He never offered any positive feedback about Eric either, so we decided to invite him, not involve him.

Eileen and Eric chose a September date for their wedding. With the date set, final decisions about the design of the gown had to be made. Since Eileen and I designed it together, she was recruited to help sew on pearls by hand. I knew once that tedious task of detail was complete, all else was easy.

The first week in July was the date to sew on pearls with us stopping only to eat bar-b-que on the fourth. Paulette came down toward the end of the week to offer suggestions for a unique veil. She once worked at a bridal shop and knew what worked. Marlene and Pam wanted to help out too, so by Saturday night we had a party going on.

"This is so pretty," Pam said as Eileen modeled the nearly finished gown. I needed to check the hem length one more time and note adjustments in other places.

"Thanks, Pam. That was a lot of work. I've had no love life for months."

"Oh? Who's really in the picture now? I can't keep up," Paulette said.

"Then don't try to," I snapped. "It's been difficult keeping track of myself. I have a hard enough time keeping track of myself and making sure I don't miss important meetings I schedule at work."

"Have you talked to Eddie?" Marlene sounded concerned.

"He still calls, saying he loves me. I don't know what to do about him."

"Mom, just talk to him," Eileen added as she turned and pranced out of the room.

"If he would just shut up once in a while and let me finish a sentence without interrupting, we could get somewhere. It's frustrating because he is the only man I've ever dealt with who has taken my rejection and continued to love and care for me the way he does. Do you know he sent me cash in the mail last week, even after I hung up on him?"

"Sasha, what kind of lover is he?" asked Marlene.

"Oh, there's no problem in that department at all. In fact, his back ailment disappears while he's in action, he says."

Marlene suddenly burst into laughter, but not at what Sasha just said.

"I had to go to the emergency room Sunday evening," Marlene laughed.

"Why?" I looked at Marlene.

"My friend got a little carried away. He got a little greedy." Marlene laughed again.

"Please spare me the details," I smiled back at Marlene. She was thinking about keeping her Jamaican lover around for a while, and had privately told me dumping him would require a considerable amount of discipline, which she lacked at the moment. He had completely disarmed Marlene with his insatiable appetite for her.

Eileen returned with the gown and gave it to me to put on a hanger.

"Mom, when would be a good time to measure for the bride's maids dresses?"

"As soon as they can get here."

Eileen decided to have only two bridesmaids and no maid of honor. She chose her two closest friends.

"Coquise and Dana will be in town next weekend. Is that okay?"

"Sure. Have you spoken to your scandalous father?"

"No. I'm not talking to him right now. Oh, Eddie just called while I was on the phone. He wants you to call him back."

"Eddie?"

"Yeah, oh hi baby. It's good to hear from you," Eddie said, cheerfully.

"Eileen said you called."

"I heard you had company. I tol' her I'd call you later."

"That's why I'm calling you back. How have you been?" I thought about the first time Eddie and I kissed.

"Oh, I been okay, I guess. 'Cept I have a hard time gettin' ta sleep lately, I jus' can't sleep at night."

"Why not?"

"Cause you not here. These people 'round here ain't 'bout nothin' an' I ain't had no pussy since you was here. You jus' don't know how you hurted me, Sasha. I ain't never loved nobody like the way I love you girl. People 'round here think I'm crazy I know, but I ain't met nobody like you and I don't want nobody else. I love you, Sasha." Well, buddy, they aren't the only ones who think you're out of your mind.

"Eddie, slow down, darling. I don't understand why you still have these feelings for me after I treated you like shit. I have been thinking about things."

"What things? You been thinkin' 'bout me?"

"Of course." I though about how good it felt to be in Eddie's protective arms sometimes and how nurturing and caring he was capable of being. I felt an urge to be with Eddie.

"Why don't you come over here tonight? I'll give you a massage an' cook for you."

"Eddie, I have a house full of company."

"When are they goin' home? They not goin' to be there all night, please please come over. I need you so bad."

"Eddie, I gotta go. Can I call you back later?"

"Of course you can."

Going to Eddie's would have been a nice departure for me, had I not been so tired. When I called him back later that night, he became very upset that I decided not to get away. I promised Eddie I would get a good night's rest and call him in the morning.

Pam called me late that night when she got home. She had been quiet at my house earlier and I sensed something was troubling her. I was right. Pam announced she was eight weeks pregnant with Pookie's baby and didn't know what to do.

"Does Pookie know?"

"No."

"When do you plan to tell him?"

"Do I have to?"

"Pam, this is no joke."

"I know, I know. Sasha, you know what my health history is." I knew all about it. Pam had never had children due to unusual complications during her pregnancies. A botched abortion performed years ago caused her to hemorrhage badly and she had miscarried three times since. During her last pregnancy five years ago, Pam got as far as her eighth month and began having labor pains. By the time she reached the hospital emergency room the baby had suffocated and was stillborn. It was a girl and Pam vowed never to suffer through anything of its kind again. "I really don't want to have an abortion either."

I felt bad for Pam and once again, could sense her fear. I searched for something comforting to say. "So, when would it be due?"

"Late February my doctor said."

"Well, that gives you plenty of time to take real good care of yourself. And since you don't know what to do, maybe you shouldn't do anything." Before saying goodnight to Pam, I convinced her not to worry, just be still.

After our conversation, Pam hung up the phone and sat Indian style on the edge of her bed. She stared straight ahead of her at the blank powder blue wall and did not move her eyes from it. Her body jerked when the air conditioner came on automatically. Her eyes glanced in the direction of Pookie's picture sitting on a table beside her bed. She removed her petite body from the side of her king-sized bed and walked to her dressing table and sat down on an upholstered bench she recently purchased for herself. Another picture of Pookie on the mirror in front of her was a reminder she was not alone. She would not have to make any decision by herself. She decided to tell Pookie.

18

The wedding date approached with me having headaches. Growing demands at work compounded by last minute wedding details rendered me energy deficient by the end of every day. I had nagging headaches. Yoshi gave me permission to hire an assistant designer to help out during peak times in the season. Adding interviewing to an already hectic schedule, I thought the headaches were caused by the parade of inexperienced design school graduates seeking fame. But the headaches continued well after I hired Troy Bates.

Troy was confident and well trained but he lacked experience. I admired his portfolio and outgoing personality which helped in my decision to hire him without references. I wanted to give him the opportunity denied to me so many times.

Troy blended well with the team at Pearly's, making friends easily. His good looks could have gotten him in any door. He was tall, extremely thin but not emaciated, and wore his bald head like a trophy. The diamond earring in his earlobe sparkled in unison with his perfect white teeth every time he smiled. He was unaffected by distracting flirtatious gestures of women in the shop and his work took priority over everything else. Young, witty and talented best described Troy.

Able to expand very basic ideas I had little time for Troy exploded with creativity. He was as amazed as I at the lavish supply of quality fabrics coming from Hong Kong and we shared many professional similarities. We were able to enrich collections that otherwise had little promise.

I received a call from Eileen two weeks before the day of her wedding. Totally frustrated, she announced that there would be no wedding.

"What happened?"

"Eric has been in his own world lately. Whenever I mention the wedding, he shuts down on me. Today I found out why. That cow had the baby."

"She did? What did she have?"

"A boy."

"How did you find out?"

"I heard through the grapevine she went into labor and went to the hospital. I didn't know which hospital, so I called around until I found the one she was admitted to. I got up early this morning and went over there to see for myself. Mom, the baby looks just like Eric and she gave it Eric's name. First and last names." Eileen began to cry and couldn't talk any more.

"You don't want to marry him now?" I asked. I was so happy.

"I do, but there's always going to be problems with that bitch and those kids. I decided that I don't want to deal with it at all."

Cheerfully, I began making the appropriate cancellation calls. Quietly thanking God for yet another blessing.

"Sasha, you are such a snob!" blasted Pam. She meant pompous bitch.

"Well, you know how I felt about that relationship. Eileen can do better. She didn't have to start out with a ready made family. And the baby's mama. It was to much."

"Did you see someone about your headaches?"

"Yes I did. And I'm taking medication but it hasn't worked. I'm calling my doctor as soon as we hang up. My head is killing me right now. I just want it to stop."

When we finished talking, I carefully placed the receiver in its cradle. Any slight movement tightened the gripping pain. I slumped backward on my bed and grabbed my head with both hands. The agonizing pain paralyzed me. I prayed that my head would not explode. Tiny beads of perspiration had formed on my face when I heard Teddy's voice.

"Mom! Are you okay?" Teddy stood over me looking down into my watery eyes. "Mom, you don't look so good."

"It's this stupid headache that won't go away. I'll be all right." I continued to lay there then asked Teddy to bring my medicine. I took enough medication for a blissful night of uninterrupted sleep denied to me in weeks. I decided to call my doctor in the morning. Teddy covered me with a blanket and turned the lights out in the room.

I awoke the next morning to hammering on the side of my skull. The annoying headache had returned. I tried to get up to go to the bathroom but was knocked back on the bed by a stabbing pain just below her left breast. Labored breathing caused me to perspire. I was barely able to call Teddy in my weakened state so he insisted we call 911 first, then my doctor. My breathing was stifled when I arrived at the hospital which generated grave concern.

"You have a mild case of pneumonia. We looked at your x-rays and we saw a dark area on your left lung. That's why you had the sudden attack of pain," the teen-aged looking doctor announced.

"And the headaches?" I asked.

"The headaches should go away. I am going to start you on Gentamicin and see how you respond. If you are feeling better in a few days, we'll let you go home. But you must rest. No work for two weeks."

Spending a few days in the hospital sabotaged a heavy work schedule. I had been burning candles at both ends, driven entirely by my work. The stress from preparing for a wedding that would not take place and the strenuous work load at Pearly's did me in, I was sure. Poor eating habits might have contributed to my diagnosed ailment and I thought maybe, just maybe, I may have bitten off more than I could chew. Eileen cared for Teddy at my house while I was in the hospital. She did not want me to worry about her brother and she still felt guilty about the canceled wedding.

"It's my fault you're in here, you know," Eileen spoke softly, her sad eyes burdened with tears that quickly ran down her cheeks when she blinked.

"Don't you dare say that! I was a little exhausted from work and not eating properly. As a result of that, I developed pneumonia. You had nothing to do with my being run down. I would do it again." I knew the IV was upsetting for the children to look at, so I insisted they not worry about me.

"Why don't you and Teddy go get a pizza and bring me some? I could use some real food." I gave Eileen money and they both kissed me on the cheek.

I was released from the hospital three days later when the headaches subsided. My weak body began to fight the pneumonic infection. I thought I only needed a few more days of rest and I'd be as good as new. The doctor recommended I take longer to recuperate if at all possible. But something was telling me I needed to get back to Pearly's.

Eddie responded quickly when he heard of my being admitted to the hospital. One afternoon when I was comfortably resting I was awakened by a ring on the doorbell. Not expecting anyone I was surprised to find a delivery man at the door holding an arrangement of wild flowers. That attached note read 'hope you feel better, love Eddie'. I thought it was a sweet gesture no one else thought of. Yoshi had sent a get well card but no flowers. I called Eddie right away to thank him for his thoughtfulness.

"Eddie, the flowers are so lovely. Thank you so much."

"Well, I though you could use some cheerin' up. You is workin' too much. You need to stop workin' an' let me take care of you."

"Eddie, we've talked about this so many times. You know how I feel about that."

"You din' have sense enuf' to take car o' yoself. Dat's how you ended up in the hospital an' who took care o' yo son while you was in there?"

"Eddie, I'm going to hang up now. I just called to thank you for the flowers."

"You need to buy you some Sleepytime tea so you can res' yo nerves. What food did you eat today? It was probably junk 'cause I know dats all you like."

Damn. I didn't need that shit. "Thanks, Eddie for the flowers," I said, then hung up the phone.

The phone rang immediately after I hung it up. Thinking it was Eddie again, I yelled into the receiver.

"What is it?"

"Sasha, this is Marlene. How are you feeling?"

"Oh, I'm sorry. I thought you were Eddie calling me back with his recipe for a happy life. I had to hang up on him again. How are you doing?"

"I'm fine. But I'm not the one who's sick right now. Eileen called and told me what happened."

"Yeah. It was pneumonia they said."

"How long will you be off work?"

"Just a few days. I'm going back next week. I can't take this confinement much longer. When I call Pearly's I'm not getting straight answers to the questions I'm asking. My new designer acted kinda cocky the last time I called. I don't know what he's up to."

After three weeks of bed rest and a proper diet I felt strong enough to go back to work. Yoshi greeted me at the door and rambled on about how smoothly things had run in my absence. According to Yoshi, 'God' was Troy's new name. He bragged about how Troy completed a collection I started and that he was in the middle of something new and exciting for the holidays. I threw myself into the work at hand and tried not to notice how the warm climate at Pearly's had cooled.

Yoshi's family had arrived from China while I was out sick. Getting his family settled kept him away from the shop for extended periods of time leaving Troy in charge.

The unusually warm October weather was leaving me limp from exhaustion after long work days at Pearly's. I ignored the discomfort of the first migraine headache I had after returning to work, deciding it was the unusual humidity everyone was experiencing. Yoshi refused to lower the thermostat in the workroom and by the end of the first week back I was having shortness of breath and full blown headaches again.

Friday came with my leaving work early and driving myself to the closest hospital emergency room. I collapsed just outside the entrance. I awoke several hours later in the company of a medical team.

"Hi. My name is Dr. Einstein, and this is Dr. Harlen. Do you know where you are?"

I began to focus and could see people dressed in white standing around me. Some were moving about in the space I occupied. My breathing was still labored as I gasped for enough air to answer.

"Where am I?"

"You are in ICU. When you were brought into the emergency room we didn't know what was wrong with you. Lucky you were here when you passed out." Dr. Einstein smiled down at me with concern.

"Doctor, what's wrong with me?"

"We are going to run some tests on you that will include work ups for tuberculosis, pneumonia and meningitis. Tell me about your headaches."

"How did you know about my headaches?"

"I spoke to your daughter. We found her name in your wallet as the person to contact in case of emergency. A lovely young woman, too. She's been here for hours and is worried about you."

I explained the patterns associated with the chronic headaches to Dr. Einstein. I told him about the shortness of breath and other complications I had undergone since the beginning of my illness. I told him about my recent hospitalization for pneumonia and that after several weeks of recuperating at home, I had returned to work. Just a week ago.

The doctor was not convinced it was pneumonia I was suffering from. He ordered a diagnostic spinal tap and other tests that would eventually determine what the problem was. I looked away from the doctor and began to scan the glass-walled cubicle I was in. Digital displays on the machines I was attached to emphasized the seriousness of my condition.

I wondered if my body could stand another trauma and if this setback would affect me the same way being raped and shot had affected me more than twenty years ago.

I didn't know if I would be fortunate enough to survive the ordeal. I imagined months of confinement as a guinea pig for research of unexplained diseases. Doctors had failed to make me well so far. I no longer viewed medical professionals as omnipotent. Endless questioning and unusual requests by technicians made me feel alien to my own body.

A closed window framed a gloomy overcast sky on the outside. I held the weather responsible for my relapse. It was the humidity in the atmosphere that was keeping me ill. Yes that was it.

Eileen contacted everyone I cared about from the hospital. When she was finally allowed to see me, she managed a smile, in spite of the worried look on her face. I smiled back at Eileen and raised my arms for a hug accidentally jerking the life sustaining IV line that was attached to my hand.

"Shit! This hurts." I held Eileen a long time before I looked down at my hand. Just beneath the tape that held the IV needle in place I could feel throbbing and stinging brought on by escaping fluid. I had unknowingly pulled the needle out of my vein creating a rapidly rising lump under the tape. My discomfort was metaphoric of what would be routine while I was in the hospital.

I pleaded with the nurse to alleviate my pain. Eileen was asked to leave momentarily so the nurse could reestablish the flow of medicine. It was agonizing for me to endure the attempts made to restart the IV because I had no visible veins, anywhere. Due to the swelling in my hand it was rendered useless a second time for an IV.

The nurse poked and prodded in my opposite hand until a reliable vein was found. I was in tears when Eileen was allowed back in.

"I don't know if I can go through this." I reached for a tissue with my free, swollen hand this time. "I don't know what to do about Teddy, my job, anything."

"Mom, I've already talked to Grandfather and he said he would stay at your house to take care of Teddy, so you don't have to worry about him right now. And when I leave here today, I'm going straight to your house."

"Have you talked to Teddy?"

"Yes, I told him what happened and he wants me to come and get him. He had just come home from school when I called. I told him I would be there later."

"I know he's worried about me."

I was awakened by a nurse early the next morning who was there to take my blood pressure. A Sunrise a lab tech came requesting more blood for testing at the same time. At the early hour I wanted to eat, but was refused any solid food because I was being fed intravenously. I was informed that next I would be going to the x-ray lab so additional pictures of my chest could be taken. After the x-rays, I would then be transported by ambulance to another facility with more advanced equipment, that would aid in the determination of my medical problem. The Tylenol they gave me for the headaches was not working and I continued to suffer. I needed Morphine and knew there had to be a stash somewhere in the hospital.

When I returned from the ambulance ride to the laboratory I demanded to be fed and sedated, but was told that my doctor wanted me to remain on the liquid diet until the test results were analyzed. They offered me more Tylenol.

Around dinnertime Dr. Einstein came to see me. He approached my bedside wearing the white coat and a smile. He reached for my hand.
"Hi, sweetie. How are you feeling?"
"Exhausted and hungry. And my head still hurts. Otherwise I feel fine."
"It's good that you still have you sense of humor. I have some news for you. First of all, it was not pneumonia or TB that made you ill. That's the good news. What you have is rare, though. You live in a geographical area that has a high concentration of fungal spores that become uprooted from the soil and dispersed in the air. Anyone can breathe it into their system and people are more at risk to exposure when they are outside on a windy day. The potentially deadly fungus settles in the lungs and will usually disappear after normal bed rest. This is usually the case for most people. But in your case the fungus has disseminated throughout your body and into your central nervous system, causing the chronic headaches you have been having. Have you ever heard of Valley Fever?"
"No, I haven't."
"The clinical name for this condition is disseminated coccidioidomycosis meningitis, or 'cocci'."
"Cocci. I think I've heard of that. Can't people die from it?" I remembered reading an article about the disease a

few years ago. How it was more toxic in people of color and how a black man died from the rare form of meningitis.

"There is treatment for this and eventually you can recover."

"Eventually? How long will it take?"

"You must understand that some people have lost their battle with this disease because they did not follow through with the treatment. It is not very comfortable."

"What does it involve?"

"Right now we are treating know cases with a drug called Amphotericin B which is given intravenously. The only way to reach the infection in the central nervous system is by injecting it directly into the spine."

I cringed as I listened in silence to Dr. Einstein's horrible description of the procedure I needed to undergo to save my life. At that moment, I was unsure of my ability to overcome the painful process of recovery. Dr. Einstein made it clear that I would have to fight to get back to normal. It could be done. I told him I needed time alone to contemplate.

It did not take long to decide to go through the treatment series. The near death experience gave a renewed sense of my mortality. I had come close to a complete physical breakdown. Being told that a mending required additional agony dissolved any thoughts of arrogance I may have had. I also knew any thoughts of self pity could prevent my restoration. My children needed me and that was reason enough to undergo over seventy spinal taps in the projected period of six months. I would be allowed to go home after three months. understanding that I would return twice a week to continue the treatment. Dr. Einstein had to be convinced that I had overcome the most difficult period of my recovery. I was advised not to return to work for at least six months. Everything I chose to do had to be done in moderation.

My prognosis for work was grim. But the thought of being able to stay home for a while was comforting, too. Dr. Einstein assured me that proper steps would be taken to guarantee my long term disability. Being under financial stress alone could cause me to relapse.

Thought's of Pearly's hounded me constantly causing emotional stress. I talked to Yoshi often when I was in the hospital. He told me not to worry about anything. Just get better. But I wondered about Troy and what he was doing behind my back, with my work. Yoshi said that everything would work out fine.

Eddie visited regularly when I was in the hospital. He brought me flowers and doughnuts. His sweetness caused me to imagine being married to him. Due to the delicate procedures that required total isolation Dr. Einstein requested a private room for me.

Eddie was allowed to stay past visiting hours because the nurses liked him. The nurses would tell me how loyal he was for being there and that he really loved me. If they only knew the real Eddie, the other side of him. Although my recovery was slow I began to look better. My familiar salacious appetite returned. Eddie just happened to be visiting me at the time.

He sat in a chair next to the hospital bed I laid in. He massaged my feet and legs using a technique he knew got to me every time. I started to shift my body in an attempt to suppress the growing exhilaration inside of me, but to no avail. I looked at Eddie's face and saw that lusty expression I had come to know, accompanied by a growing bulge in his lap. It was now or never, I thought, and lacking further thought I climbed out of bed and onto his lap.

"Baby, you know you cain't be doin' dis in here."

"Eddie, I'm not concerned about hospital rules right now." I unzipped his pants. Luckily, no one came in.

"I can't believe you've taken up with Eddie again." squealed Pam.

"Oh, shut up, Pam. You act just like you've never been horny. What is your problem?"

"Yeah, you're right. I know what it's like," she laughed. "You guys screwed in the hospital?"

"You bet. And he brought me flowers every week. It was great!"

"Sasha, you're asking for it again, you know."

"Asking for what?"

"More pain, more, agony, more of his bullshit criticism."

"I haven't heard much of that lately. He's just real protective."

"Sasha, think about this shit you're telling me and call me tomorrow.

I wondered why Pam didn't just tell me to go soak my head. Which was exactly what I did. I got out of bed, grabbed a towel from the bathroom then went down the stairs to Teddy's bathroom. I occasionally took long steamy showers in his bathroom.

I removed the terry bathrobe then stared in the bathroom mirror at my nude body for a long time. I saw a vulnerable, frightened and emotionally mixed up human being who desperately needed answers. Eddie had remained loyal during my confinement.

I found a bottle of shampoo among Teddy's toiletries and turned on the water in the shower. I wanted to wash away all the pain and guilt that was consuming me which probably contributed to my poor health. Dodging Eddie had become a game to me. I had taken advantage of his elder age and pathetic demeanor. I thought of the times I had nothing but contempt for Eddie and wished him dead. Then he would do something nice. Like give me money. And I would forget about how mean and unfair he had been to me. I had always felt Eddie had no right to criticize me. But he felt since he had lived longer he knew best.

I allowed the warm water to soak the top of my head and run down my lean body, drenching away the sorrow and death of another relationship. I poured aloe shampoo on my crown and massaged my scalp. I prayed I would be able to sever the bond I had had with Eddie for years. I turned my back to the jutting stream of warm water and tilted my head back, indulging myself in the cleansing ceremony. Seeking the peace in my life I desperately needed.

When I rinsed the shampoo out of my braided hair I turned back around to indulge my face. I grabbed the shampoo bottle and squeezed more soap in my palm, continuing to wash away the false perception of Eddie as someone else. Pam forced me to examine myself and realize how confused I had been about Eddie.

My baptism complete, I turned the water off and stepped out of the shower. I grabbed my towel and blotted my wet hair and skin dry. I put the robe on my freshly bathed body and went back upstairs to my bedroom to spend the remainder of the evening pampering my needy body and spirit.

I continued to be amazed at how easy it was to be deceived by the signs of an unhealthy relationship. Pam and I had discussed the issues for years. Not to mention the lesions of talk shows we watched that offered insight. We knew women were capable of leaving bad relationships when they were equipped to do so.

I knew in my heart in the very early stages with Eddie that it would not last. Just knew it. Yet I allowed myself to be drawn into his life because I liked the attention from him, and it did not matter if it was negative at times. I felt I could deal with his possessiveness constructively. And teach him a few things, like accepting me the way I was. After all, I wasn't a bad person. I never killed anybody.

At one time I even had visions of him reading me the newspaper in our old age. The only picture Eddie had had was of *me* in bed waiting for him. His creepy borderline abusive behavior became crystal clear to me. A stinging slap he once called 'playful' left a bruise the size of Texas on my thigh. The two times he forced himself on me after I said 'no' to sex were no fun. After it happened, he told me a woman liked for a man to be aggressive. He felt and showed no remorse for the slap he had given to me. His cave-man style sent chills down my spine.

He told me one night he would kill me if I ever tried to leave him. I believed him. I refused to imagine my children hearing about how I died at the hands of a jealous, uneducated fool from Oklahoma on the eleven o'clock news. I pictured the headline announcing 'A crime of passion, desperate man loved woman to death'. Oh, hell no. Not me. That fucker better stay away.

I watched the news before going to sleep flipping past the channels using the remote. I stopped when I recognized a familiar face. It was Zeeke, rapping in a commercial to convince people to buy a popular product. I was elated to see him working and making money.

19

I checked my messages as soon as I walked in the door from Los Angeles. Marlene was on the verge of leaving Dennis. She called me from a hotel in Westwood and left a number where she could be reached.

"Girlfriend, what is going on?" I called Marlene immediately. This could not wait.
"I'm leaving Dennis."
"Shit. What happened?"
"Do you remember when Dennis' friend saw me leaving the 'Snooty' with Gil?"
"Yes, I remember."
"Well, the sonofabitch was at the motel and he saw us coming out of the room. About a month ago."
"Oh."
"Dennis has known for weeks and didn't say anything."
"Marlene, what did you expect him to say?"

"I don't know. Something. Anything! All I wanted for him to do was just talk to me. He refused. Sasha, it's been pretty bad this last year. Dennis just takes off and goes. Sometimes he's gone overnight."

"I'm sorry, I didn't know that. Is he out with Lou when he's out?"

"He says he is. But you know how Lou covers for him. You know what I did?"

"No, what?"

"I'm a blond now. I dyed my hair."

"No kidding." Marlene did things in grand style so I was not surprised to hear that.

"I called my lawyer today and told him I was leaving Dennis."

"Did he give you any advice?"

"I can't get into it right now. Are you going to be home tomorrow morning? I'm driving over to Vegas and I want to stop by your house on my way."

"Sure. Come on."

Marlene arrived early the next morning. I thought she actually looked kind of cute with blond hair even though I'm not crazy about it on black people. Marlene's fair complexion made it easy to digest. The dark glasses made her look splendid.

"Hey, you look great! You want a latté?"

"Yes, thanks. I couldn't talk last night because Gil was there."

"The Jamaican?" I set the coffee on the table in front of Marlene.

"Yes. I kept him out pretty late last night. He wanted to spend the night, but..."

"His wife couldn't wait, right?" I finished the sentence for her. "How long are you going to be in Vegas?"

"That depends upon how much money I spend. I have a thousand on me and the American Express."

"I wish I could go with you, but I'm under doctor's orders to rest, and I have Teddy."

"I know you'll be glad when you can take off when you want, like when Teddy goes to college."

"Marlene, I have the toughest decision to make." I gave a deep sigh.

"What?"

"I don't want to stop working at Pearly's but I'm in no condition to return to work yet. My doctor told me that if I want to live, my treatments have to continue for a while longer. He said that I should focus on myself and my family."

"He's right, you know."

"I know he's right, but I hate to let Yoshi down. I told him I would give him an answer this week about work. The last time I talked to him he was thinking of hiring someone to fill in form me while I was on sick leave. Troy's been complaining about the work load. But I know that slick bastard is up to something. I just know it."

"So, what are you going to do?"

"I don't know."

We decided that my health was more important than any job. Since I had the resources, I decided to stay off work for a while and concentrate on getting better. Marlene's problems seemed more complicated however, because I knew Marlene was still in love with Dennis. She felt humiliated and hurt when Dennis had casually revealed her secret a few days ago.

Marlene was speechless as he described the make and model of Gil's car. And the name of the condoms she'd been using all year. She couldn't bring herself to dispute any of the charges because in her mind she wanted him to find out. Marlene's brooding over Dennis' loss of affection caused her to make mistakes in her actions and to be unsure of her devotion to him.

Her attorney advised her to file a legal separation for now to give her time to think about what was at stake. A divorce at this time could be very ugly. Marlene needed time to think and she would do it in the next few days in Vegas.

Soon after Marlene left, the phone rang. It was Eddie. I froze when I heard his voice on the machine. I got up immediately and unplugged the telephone. I was determined not to allow Eddie to talk his way back into my life. The last time we talked it was ugly. His last words to me were 'you're not the only fish in the sea' to which I replied 'well, go fishin!' And after discussing the matter with Pam, I finally felt I had the strength to keep my word.

It was not difficult for me to adjust to a new role. Being at home everyday had it's advantages, so I would make the most of it. Instead of allowing myself to become bored I decided to take out a sketch pad and take a stroll down memory lane.

I had added features to the face of a sketch I had just drawn when I saw Cindy's face again. The face looked great on the gown I had drawn.

The next day I awoke rejuvenated and eager to start working on my new ideas. I concerned myself less with Pearly's and more with myself and the direction I wanted to take. Designing high fashion gowns became the objective. I stopped working long enough to fix myself another mug of latté when the telephone rang.

"Hello."

"Sasha, please."

I recognized Yoshi's voice immediately. "This is Sasha. Yoshi?"

"Yes, yes, it is me."

"How are you doing?" I though he was calling to find out what my decision was. I was not prepared to give him an answer yet.

"Not so good. Everything is gone."

"What are you talking about, Yoshi?"

"My company burned down. There is nothing. Nothing but ashes now. Nothing."

"Burned down. My God. Yoshi, you had insurance, right?"

"Yes, but all my inventory is destroyed. Everything!" He sounded like his life was over.

In a strange way I was relieved. Two problems had been solved with one action. Troy was now out of work also.

I gave Yoshi my condolences and told him I would pray for his financial recovery. After talking to him I felt I was on the right track, so I worked all day long. I stopped long enough to cook for Teddy then went right back to sketching. I had received no telephone calls from Eddie all day which surprised me. He usually called and harassed me throughout the day if he knew I was there. He would get drunk after I would hang up on him, then he would take his pain and rejection out on me all day long. But he didn't bother me at all.

Marlene called me from Vegas to let me know she was all right. I was instructed to call Jasmine and Kai to let them know where their mother was and that she would call them in a couple of days. Marlene wasn't sure where she was going to live when she got back. She and Dennis owned rental property in South Central and were currently having problems with one of their tenants, who they were in the process of evicting for not paying rent. That was a possibility for temporary housing, Marlene thought, even if it was on the wrong side of town. I could not believe Marlene was willing to move from Ladera Heights to South Central, where she and Dennis originally came from. They had had accomplished so much together. On the phone, I begged Marlene to go for family counseling when she got back because I felt a huge mistake was being made. I believed if they talked to someone, it may have been pointed out to Dennis that emotional neglect was abuse just as damaging in any relationship. His behavior had led to her infidelity and with therapy, they may have been able to save their marriage. Lord knows they could have afforded a therapist. So far, Marlene had gone through two fifths of Remy Martin and smoked all the Indo she took from Dennis' stash. Yes, therapy would do them some good.

I digested all the incredible events and revelations of my long day then knelt down to thank God for my life and my own set of circumstances that seemed easier to cope with than Marlene's. Even though I was not physically fit enough to run a marathon, there was so much I could still do for myself. I was not faced with having to make decisions that could change my life so dramatically.

I lay in my bed watching the late news when it was reported that a horrible accident involving a car and a train had just occurred. The driver of the car was unaware of the approaching train because the flashing lights at the crossing were not working. The car was dragged nearly three hundred feet before the fast moving train stopped. The driver was killed upon immediate impact.

The next morning when I read the paper I was horrified when I discovered the person who died in the accident the night before was Eddie. Traces of alcohol were found in what remained of him. There were absolutely no words to describe what I felt at that moment.

20

Good news came in the announcement of Eileen's new boyfriend, J.T. I was elated. They began dating shortly after Eileen started working at the television station. She had given herself time to get over her failed engagement and was ready to move on. He was immediately attracted to her fresh and intelligent approach to news writing and her great sense of humor. She admired similar qualities in him and was thrilled to have someone who shared the same interests. J.T., in his last year of film school had hoped to see his first work in production next year. Unlike other boyfriends of Eileen's, J.T. had no children of his own, did not want any until he was married. His parents were still happily married after twenty five years. Hearing Eileen talk about these people brought tears to my eyes. It made me believe there was still hope.

When he returned from a promotional tour with a production company, Zeeke called me. It was nice to hear that all was good for him. He talked about the places he'd gone and the work he had done. He saw his mother who was delighted about his surprise visit. I told Zeeke about the horrible accident that took my dear friend, without mentioning a name. Zeeke could sense talking about it was upsetting, so he offered a prayer and hoped it would cleanse me of guilt feelings regarding my friend. Even after death, Eddie continued to cling.

I needed a lot more than a prayer, though. I hoped Zeeke understood what I needed but I knew he didn't. He was a nice guy and I hated to just tell him I was horny and wanted to fuck. Zeeke had never come on to me in such a direct way.

A woman has to walk a fine line when she wants sex with a man she's not married to. In order to get the respect she wants, she has to pretend to be timid and shy. But being diffident and coy takes time and I felt because of my age, I had to get things moving. I felt most men wanted sex only anyway. So, why waste time? I had grown tired of playing games with men just so I wouldn't get hurt. I wanted someone in my life who loved me as much as I loved my work. Someone who respected me because it was the right thing to do. I wanted a man who was not afraid to say 'I love you' and really mean it, a man who did not want to buy my love then expect complete control over me in return.

The main reason Paulette gave up on men had to do with those feelings. In a recent letter she talked about her difficult return to the straight life. I always felt the sexual preference of my cousin was based on how she viewed men, not genetics. I also thought she could be wrong in her thinking. In the letter, Paulette said men always made her feel invisible and she never felt loved. Buck was not capable of giving her enough affection and kept saying he would leave Peaches. She was fed up with his attempts to control all her thoughts, so she decided to end it with him and remain in the gay community. Her unhappy life as a straight woman in the nineties was not what she expected. It was full of new versions of old pain. The 'real thing' wasn't as good as the 'same thing', as she put it. The letter sounded like an apology, but there was no need to be sorry because, I understood.

Zeeke must have someone I don't know about. How can a man so highly visible not have a woman? He's out and about all the time, constantly traveling the country, meeting all kinds of people. Maybe the real question was why would he be interested in me? I'm was just an ordinary person who believed in love. My suspicions continued to grow concerning Zeeke. Many Hollywood types live their fantasies totally unaware of a spiritual connection associated with love. Love is the most powerful force in the universe yet people seek success without its blessing. Well, no more games for now. I'll just buy myself a vibrator.

Pam finally got over her latest trauma. Even though she chose not to end the pregnancy, she struggled with her decision not tell Pookie. Pam continued loving Pookie, even though he violated his parole and was sent back to jail. She didn't know if telling him about the pregnancy would have led to a different outcome. She was angry with herself for allowing the set of circumstances to invade her life. Like me, she often had to settle for leftovers in men, but would still risk bringing a child into this world if it had a father that was hardworking, loving, and faithful. But not this time. She miscarried in her third month while Pookie was in jail. She didn't have to tell him about the abortion she had scheduled.

When Pam felt better, she went to New Orleans for a long weekend of food, jazz, and rest. It was then that she decided to cool it with Pookie, for a while, at least. She was tired of accepting collect calls from prison and receiving pleading love letters he mailed to her almost daily. Pam told her postman not to deliver any more letters that were addressed in pencil. I laughed when she told me that because Pam knew damn well she still loved Pookie. And nothing's wrong with that.

Eileen and J.T. became an item. He told her he never met anyone as attractive and intelligent as her. He sent beautiful flower arrangements to her at the station and at home. Once, after a silly misunderstanding, he sent a group of his friends to deliver a singing telegram to Eileen. After singing a course of 'I'm Sorry', they presented her with a bouquet of colorful mylar balloons with a note attached asking her forgiveness. Eileen conveniently forgot what the disagreement was about. When he called her at work after the delivery was made, he told her he really loved her. After hearing this, I thought maybe the sound of wedding bells was not far off and there would be an occasion for the wedding gown after all. Eileen told me about her date the day before with J.T.

"Mom, you'll never guess what we did."

"You're right." I held my breath.

"We went to his parent's house. J.T. wanted me to meet his mom and dad."

"So what happened?" I pressed for information.

"You would like his mom. She's a snob, just like us." Eileen burst into laughter.

Marlene looked like a Zombie, frail and trembling like a leaf when I walked in. The nurse that escorted me to Marlene's room warned me she might not respond to my being there. The meager chamber Marlene occupied was in sharp contrast to the extravagant surroundings she was accustomed to. Marlene's daze was uninterrupted as I sat next to her on the bed and placed a hand on her vibrating arm. I said nothing. I was overwhelmed by Marlene's obvious anxiety and I couldn't speak. I glanced at the nurse and assured her by nodding that we would be alright. The nurse nodded back and walked out the door closing it behind her. Before I could think of comforting words, Marlene looked at me.

"Sasha, I want to die."

"No, no, not yet. We have some things to do first."

"I'm loosing my mind Sasha, and Dennis thinks I'm crazy."

"Marlene, Dennis doesn't think you're crazy. He just wants you to get better. That's why you're here. Besides, for a while, you get to do absolutely nothing."

"They put me in a straight jacket."

"Goodlord, Marlene! Last night you shot up someone's house then tried to stop an airplane that was taking off to Hawaii. Marlene, they still don't know how you managed to cross the runway without being killed."

"I was wearing black." Marlene slurred. "It must have been the hair. I should have curled it first." Marlene smiled.

"This shit is not funny, Marlene."

Marlene's head looked like the burning bush in 'The Ten Commandments', Don King style. She was not the same girlfriend who stopped by my place on her way to Vegas. Marlene threw her head back, shook it, and tried to run her fingers through her hair jerking her head further back instead.

"Ouch!" Marlene moaned.

Marlene was a mess. And I felt responsible for her condition. When I told Marlene what I knew about Dennis' activities, I was only trying to help her overcome the guilt about her affair with Gil. She had been torturing herself and excusing Dennis in the deterioration of their affairs. Dennis' friend, Lou, got drunk one night and called me to give details of his latest adventure with Dennis. Lou should not drink because he forgets what he says and who he says it to. He never omitted details or descriptions, or people involved in his audacious ventures.

I realized the abundance of misdoing by Dennis and Lou and I was blown away. I couldn't tell Marlene what I heard from Lou because it was too disgusting to repeat. So, I found someone else to do it for me.

My detective work yielded a description and street address of a known participant in the scandal. I passed that information to Marlene several days after her return from Vegas and she didn't take it very well. Marlene tried to call Dennis before she came back from Vegas to discuss her future and their labored marriage, but he was no where to be found. The twins didn't have a clue about where he was. They were simply told by their father not to worry, and were given cash for any unforeseen emergency in his absence. Jasmine and Kai knew nothing but wished their parents would behave like responsible adults, and not like them.

The harbinger made it possible for me to remain uninvolved, but as everything unfolded before my eyes, I found myself right in the middle feeling just as lousy as Marlene.

The nurses entered the room with medication for Marlene, so I decided to end my visit. I told Marlene I would see her tomorrow. She just looked at me.

I visited Marlene at Norwalk Hospital daily for the first week of her hospitalization. Dennis committed her and she refused all his visits. In her neurotic state, she imagined he would do her great harm. He brought her personal items from the house so she could feel more 'at home'. She took all the items from Dennis, but refused conversation with him. Marlene knew she would have to convince a panel of doctors that she was sane enough to be released from the hospital, so she opted to save her energy for the more important task.

Thorazine three times a day made it easier for Marlene to cope with confinement. She said being in a mental hospital was like being in jail, the only difference had to be the non-combative state everyone was in due to the drugs they were on. The staff made sure the patients were heavily medicated which, of course, made their jobs easier.

Rumors spread rapidly about a man who was brought in wearing nothing but a g-string. He said clothes made him itch. The man was transported to Norwalk wrapped in a sheet and refused to put anything on his body.

Marlene's recovery demanded my full attention. I had to help get her out of that place. After two weeks of watching her struggle to gain control over her actions, I decided it was time for me to become serious about getting her out of there. First things first. Marlene needed to look sane.

I went shopping for Marlene. Marlene had a Master Card with her when she was apprehended. I used it and began shopping at I. Magnin on Wilshire and worked my way up to Marlene's favorite lingerie store in Hollywood. I carefully selected each item mindful of how she would be perceived by the staff of professionals who determined her sanity, or insanity. I bought three jumpsuits, each one impeccably designed reflecting strong sanity and style. Robins-May had a shoe sale so I grabbed several pairs of sandals I thought went well with the new outfits.

Marlene was surprised that I guessed her shoe size, a 5 1/2 narrow, half my shoe size. As Marlene emptied the shopping bags, I began to notice signs of recovery. The light at the end of the tunnel was not an oncoming train after all.

Marlene was pleased with every item, and began to try them on immediately. Nothing excited Marlene more than shoes. She once purchased fifteen pairs on a shopping spree because she was convinced there would never be another sale of its kind.

Along with the new purchased things, I gave her a long silk ecru night gown that I had designed for her birthday, with matching feather boa satin slippers. Lounging around the asylum would have new meaning for Marlene.

I contacted my beautician friend Thomas, and for a price, he consented to visit Marlene after working his hours to fix her hair. A reluctant manicurist went with him on the visit.

I was pleased with the results of the makeover. On my next visit following the beauty change, I took my camera. I snapped pictures of Marlene in her room lounging about, and then made her change into the red jumpsuit she liked so well to take pictures outside. When I think about it now, I am reminded of how together Marlene was when I first met her, and how sick she had become, overnight.

Marlene convinced a panel of psychiatrists that she was healthy enough to go home. I was happy because one month of Marlene being in that institution was all I could handle.

I wanted to get away after all I had gone through with Marlene, but before any excursion, I had to get caught up on my responsibilities at home. I was not able to respond to inquiries relating to my availability to work. Marlene had been more important. Teddy was helpful about keeping track of important personal calls made to me in the evenings. Zeeke made several calls to me, as well as Liz, Paulette, and Pam.

"Hi, Sasha, how have you been?" When Liz answered the phone she sounded out of breath.

"I've been okay. I apologize for not getting back to you sooner, but I've had a crisis going on here."

"Are the kids alright?"

"Oh, yes they're fine. My crisis had nothing to do with the children." I didn't want to discuss Marlene's affliction. "Where is Barry?"

Liz giggled before she spoke. "I've been trying to get in touch with you."

"Why are you out of breath?" I asked.

"Oh, girl, I was in the backyard doing jumping jacks. I was trying to burn off my lunch." She took a very deep breath. "Have you seen or talked to Barry?"

"No. You don't know where he is?" I asked.

"Yes, I know now. Betty called me last week."

Liz filled me in on Barry's latest. After hearing what she said, I concluded that my rejection of Barry, combined with Betty's realization of Barry's long list of character flaws, made her take a new lover. It was probably what pushed him over the edge. He went back to see Betty while in a drug induced rampage, and went off on her in his crazy manner, and got himself arrested. After hearing the details of his capture and confinement to a mental hospital, I realized that the man wrapped in the sheet who was brought to Norwalk during Marlene's convalescence there was Barry. I didn't mention that to Eileen. She would have been hurt.

One month later.

More than frustrated with recent events, I knew that taking a leisurely drive through scenic Leona Valley would do me good. The green rolling hills and low lying pastures of the valley reminded me of a more peaceful time, a time that was not rushed, a time probably in my former life. The area of Leona Valley where I took my drive had not been exploited yet by money hungry developers who often rushed to destroy the quiet essence of small communities like those. I drove my car on the narrow two-lane road past a car pulling a horse trailer. I accelerated my speed to maintain my position in the lane I was driving in.

Known for its annual cherry picking season, visitors flocked to the cherry orchards that dotted the landscape of an otherwise sleepy town.

At the very edge of Leona Valley was Elizabeth Lake, my favorite place to be when I needed to think.

I hadn't determined what captivated and charged me emotionally each time I drive through the Leona Valley. I just felt connected some way. It was hard to explain. The beautiful vistas always summoned me to explore and I never resisted an opportunity. I would conjure up crazy thoughts of what life would be like with my very own Prince in that valley, but knowing myself like I did, I doubted I would meet him there, but if someone happened along who was humorous, witty, had a neat appearance, was hard working, loved his work and career, loved to laugh, was handsome, sexy, a great communicator, had great teeth, was tall (at least 6' 2"), had some money or land or both, smelled good all the time, was healthy, generous with his time and money, was great in bed, had a car, a hobby, and did not restrict himself to any particular ethnic group, I would probably consider him.

The simplicity of the small valley held a spiritual value for me no one understood. Sparsely scattered homes and ranches along the main road always competed for the attention of passers-by. One ranch, in particular, always caught my eye every time I drove past it.

Intense curiosity pertaining to this particular parcel of land almost caused me to have a collision when I barely missed a curve in the road. I was looking at its Spanish stucco horse stables. The stables were in alignment with nature, surrounded by practice arenas and pastures. Horses ran freely racing each other and occasionally I would see horses being led by workers back to the barn. I had seen horses on a carousel, having the time of their lives. I wanted to know more about the place holding my attention so strongly. Every time I drove past the stables, the seduction would persist.

One day I made the made the connection. As a youngster, I enjoyed visiting my grandfather's farm in Lodi, where he would let me ride on the tractor with him while he worked in the field. Grandpa Lake taught me how to ride horses and I could never get enough of it. I liked the way I felt when I sat on top of a horse. It made me feel big and important. I would ask my dad take me to the stables in Paramount or Griffith Park every other Saturday, just to ride a horse. One Summer when we were teens, Pam went on vacation with us to Yosemite, where horseback riding was part of our daily fun. The most exciting event on that vacation occurred when, for some unknown reason, my horse spooked, reared, then ran off of the trail into a thick forest. The horse wove between trees and past startled picnickers with me hanging on for dear life. I still remember the rush I got from the thrilling ride. By the time the tour guide caught up to us, we had slowed to a walk. He explained to me that the horse had a desire to lead that day and he was only going to the head of the line. I related.

I gave in to my curiosity. On my way back from Elizabeth Lake I slowed my car as I approached the ranch with the Spanish stucco stables. I asked myself what I was doing.

'Arabian in America' is what the sign read at the gate. I turned my car into the driveway and followed the long narrow road onto the property. There were no 'no trespassing' signs posted so I enjoyed the adventure of not having permission to snoop. I wanted to know more so I kept driving toward a structure that looked like a small office building. I stopped the car and could see someone moving inside the office through a window.

21

Guy Royce, better known as 'G.R.' at the ranch, worked tirelessly on the display shelf making sure it was properly adjusted so it could be mounted in its designated spot. He looked at the wall and back at the shelf on the floor beside him. G.R. decided this time it would fit, so he quickly grabbed the shelf and attached it to the wall. He stood in the middle of the room examining every detail of the work he had just completed. Did I forget anything? he asked himself.

G.R. struggled with the thought of being by himself. The idea of being without a wife did not set well with him and he recalled a conversation he had had earlier with his long time friend and attorney, Deon.

"I'm not getting any return. I give her everything and she's never here," G.R. had pouted in a manly way.

"Well, man, you knew it was going to cost you," replied Deon.

"Something tells me to let her go, but that's too easy," G.R. smiled.

The conversation with Deon took him nowhere, because G.R. knew what he had to do. He had to continue working to pay his bills. That's all he knew. If Dora wanted a new ranch mink to go with her growing collection of furs, it was no problem. For a moment, he thought he might miss making monthly cash deposits into her personal luxury account. It had become a habit of his to completely satisfy, and have no excuses for another failed relationship. Money was not a problem. G.R. told himself that money could never buy true happiness. He vowed to continue giving of himself hoping someday he would be happy.

The ranch was his baby and Dora knew it. Her taste was different, though. She preferred the bright lights of Atlantic City and Miami where she spent most of her time shopping and visiting friends. The sudden knock on the door startled G.R. The door slowly opened.

"Hi, is anyone here?" I asked, as I opened the door and stepped inside.

G.R. was bending over to gather the tools he had worked with. He quickly turned his head toward the door to see me standing there.

"Hello, I was just finishing up here. Can I help you?"

My, my, my. This white man's kinda cute. And he's got a body, too. "My name is Sasha and I drive past here all the time. Do you actually breed Arabians here?"

"Yes, but we do other things too. Do you own horses?"

"No, but I love to ride. Well, I confess its been about ten years since I last rode, but I love horses. Is the owner here?"

"I am the owner, Guy Royce." He extended his hand to shake mine.

I should be so lucky. Well, here goes. "I am interested in grooming and training horses. Do you have an apprentice ship opportunity here for that kind of work?"

G.R. eyed me up and down first then gave me a general overview of the activities and programs he offered at the facility. He told me as soon as he made a few staff changes, an apprentice ship might be possible. He had never done this sort of thing but was interested in trying something new and different. G.R.'s warmth and friendly nature made me feel better about my stupid idea of thinking I could learn to train a horse. His physical build was average and he was tall with a big chest and evenly tanned complexion. His face lit up when he talked, showing a set of perfect white teeth. The wide set deep chestnut eyes and dimples added to the overall handsome appearance of G.R. He kept me interested with the discussion of his horses and childhood experiences growing up in Cleveland. He told about his racially mixed neighborhood and his black friends who defended him against the neighborhood thugs. Each time he smiled, I melted a little bit more. He said he gained a lot from growing up with the adversities he faced as a child. Being the only white kid in an all black neighborhood was not easy.

I looked around the room at countless colorful ribbons won by his wonderful Arabian horses. Plaques and trophies were displayed as well making me think this man must really be a 'winner'. And what made me think he would be interested in teaching me about horses? I prayed he would give me the opportunity to expand as a person, and pursue another interest I had postponed for years. I thought caring for horses in my spare time would possibly give me the lift needed.

G.R. had no pending business so he gave me a tour of the ranch. The imposing stucco stables were home for his prize winning Arabians. Five years ago when he purchased his first Arabian, he had no idea how fulfilling his hobby would become. Walking through the main barn with G.R. was like reliving the memory of a former life. I felt like I had finally returned to the life I was destined to be a part of.

"Where have you been? I've been trying to call you for days," Pam tried not to sound solicitous.

"Hi, I was just about to call you. It's really been crazy lately." I wanted to tell Pam about G.R. and the ranch but Pam started her story first.

"Do you remember that rich black lady I told you about that comes to the hospital from time to time?"

"The one with the heart condition?"

"Yeah, that's the one. Well, she came back to the hospital three weeks ago. She had a series of strokes and collapsed at home. Her maid found her laying in the bed with her eyes open, staring up at the ceiling." Pam told me she couldn't speak for several days while she was in I.C.U. During that time, Pam observed she had no family members other than the maid who stayed with her during the slow recovery. When Pam was assigned to her care for the difficult patient she began to understand why the rich lady behaved the way she did.

Needa couldn't believe it had come to that. She knew it was pretty serious though, because she was in I.C.U. She was thinking that the last episode could be her very last. She had begun to realize how close to the end she was, and what would happen to all her money if she did die. Needa had no living heirs, and every time she thought about the tragic loss of her son twenty years ago, she would cry. No one understood her pain, she thought. Whenever one of the nurses asked Needa about the pictures she always brought with her to the hospital, she barely responded. Once, when in an awful mood, she reached to the small table and turned all of the pictures face down. On that particular day, Needa was deep in thought about an individual whose picture had not been displayed like the others. "None of your business!" Needa was extremely rude and abrupt that day. She was an expert at hiding things. The real truth about how she became wealthy would not be told yet. She wanted to let people continue to think that it was all amassed through her hard work.

Needa wished for a daughter now who could receive the dark secret that had been quietly gnawing away at her for years. Pam was the only nurse Needa found suitable enough to confide in.

Pam released the blood pressure cuff and removed it. "The new medication must be working because your blood pressure is down quite a bit," Pam said. "How are the dizzy spells?"

"I haven't had one yet today," said Needa.

"That's good. You look a lot better today, too!" replied Pam.

"Oh, thank you," Needa managed a smile for Pam, at the same time looking at her small collection of pictures that sat nearby on their special table.

It was only recently that Pam became curious about the collection of small portraits on Needa's linen covered table. Since Needa had softened, Pam felt it was safe to take a closer look at the pictures. She leaned over to look when Needa spoke, "Is it alright for me to call you by your first name?"

"Of course it is. Pamela is my name." Pam was shocked by the sudden interest in her name. She hoped Needa was feeling better because she cared for her. Six months ago she would not have cared if she lived or died, now they were bonding. What could be next, Pam wondered.

"Have you ever been in love?" Needa wore a very serious look on her face when she spoke. Pam was caught completely off guard. An image of Pookie flashed before her, she was slow to answer.

"Well, if I say yes and give you the details, you may think I'm crazy."

"You let me be the judge of that. Love is a funny thing, Pamela."

"I know."

"And its painful too, especially when you are unable to shout it to the world."

Pam understood what she was saying because there was no comfort in knowing what her co-workers might say about her involvement with Pookie, with his unstable past and present. Pam wondered why Needa chose the topic of conversation.

"What about you? I know you were in love with your husband. Based on what I've seen, he must have loved you a whole lot."

"Yes, he did," said Needa, but the face Needa saw in her mind was not that of her deceased husband. The face she was seeing was the face of someone else's husband. Pam was astonished and couldn't believe what Needa was about to confide in her.

Years and years ago in a small Texas town where Needa grew up, she answered an ad in a newspaper for a girl Friday type position. The gentleman looking for help was a wealthy, married, well-known city official. When Needa applied he was taken by both her beauty and youth, hiring her on the spot. Needa was so grateful to have the job working in the mansion of the rich white man she offered to work weekends, if he needed her. And, of course, he did. Needa admitted how naive she was, although she enjoyed the opportunity to make money and possibly move away from her alcoholic father's home. Needa realized that working beyond the call of duty made her dreams materialize much faster. Her blue-eyed middle-aged pudgy employer fancied her presence and made every effort to make her feel at home. As time marched on, he began to give her gifts in addition to her paycheck, that was always slightly inflated. Needa told Pam how she began to fall for this man who was so good to her, unlike her father. Much effort was put forth to ignore the feelings she had for this married man but to no avail. She finally gave in and allowed him to take care of her outright. He purchased a small cottage for Needa to live in not far from his sprawling estate and they became lovers. She soon had bank accounts and was able to establish herself in the community.

Before long people began to question Needa's swift rise in social status and suspected her high-profile employer had a lot to do with it. As his concubine, she was told not to listen to the gossip because people could not prove what they could not see. When pressures became too great, Needa wanted to get out of the one-horse town she was living in. She knew her lover would never leave his wife, but he promised her love and support for as long as she wanted it.

Needa moved to Dallas to start a new life, away from the talk of scandal in her home town. Shortly after arriving in Dallas she met her soon to be husband and one month later they were married. She became the victim of verbal abuse by her new husband which soon escalated into physical abuse. This drove Needa to call and seek the comfort of her former boss. He did not find out about the marriage until he arrived in Dallas. He insisted she move right away into a house he had owned for years in a suburb of Dallas, Oak Cliff. This would give him an excuse to drive to Dallas twice a month. Needa had her prompt marriage annulled and remained a very well-kept woman.

Needa's problems began in Dallas when she found out she was pregnant. She wasn't sure who the father was, but decided to have the baby anyway. Nine months later, Needa delivered a handsome seven pound brown baby boy who looked exactly like his father, old blue eyes. The birth of the child made him love Needa even more and to show her how much, he deposited one million dollars in her bank account. Needa and her lover agreed to keep the secret and he promised to support the child as long as she did not put his name on the birth certificate. In the early years, the child was told his father died before his birth, and that the white man who came around occasionally was an investment counselor. Needa eventually married again, this time to a well-known attorney. Her second husband adopted the boy and raised him as his own. Needa began to cry as she concluded her sad story.

"I loved that old white man and he loved me, but we could never be together. He took care of me even though I had remarried. I invested every penny he gave me, and my husband never knew how much we were really worth. When my husband became ill with cancer and had to stop working, our standard of living never changed, it got better. When my husband died, old blue eyes was right there, on his Lark, at the funeral. A year later I lost him too. Five years later I lost my only child in an airplane crash."

Pam reached for the tissue box sitting on the table with the pictures. She looked closely at the pictures and could not believe who she saw. A picture of Jett, sitting right in view all the time and she never noticed it.

By now, Pam was upset, but she gave grieving Needa several tissues to wipe away her tears anyway. "This was the witch who evicted Sasha over twenty years ago when her boyfriend Jett died!" Pam was very angry with herself for not putting two and two together.

"Pam, please don't get upset. It's not worth it," I told her. "That was a long time ago."

"Sasha, you always said she wasn't right. You knew what you were talking about," Pam said.

"Did you tell her who you were?"

"No, I didn't. I wanted to talk to you first."

"Well, thank you. So, what are you going to say to her?" I asked.

"That depends. I wonder if she has a will."

"You nut!"

Pam called me the next day from work to tell me Needa's long battle was over. She passed away during the night when her heart failed while she slept. Any business Needa had planned to take care of in Los Angeles would now have to take care of itself. God bless her.

"Hello."

"Hello, is Sasha Friend there?"

"Yes, this is she speaking."

"Hi, my name is Jennifer Lawson of Arabians in America. Mr. Royce asked me to call you to see if you would be available to begin your apprenticeship next week."

I was in shock close to three days. I envisioned myself on top the fabulous animals that were so well taken care of at G.R.'s ranch. I met with Jennifer the next day. The initial meeting went well. I was relieved to see that Jennifer was much younger than I was, about Eileen's age, making the situation comfortable for me. After all, we could learn from each other. I was eager to show her my willingness to learn from a younger mentor. My training began right away.

Jennifer told me before I was allowed to ride I had to learn the proper way to prepare a horse for its rider. Jennifer would also teach me how to groom.

I was amazed when I watched Jennifer handle the horses. Years of experience with horses gave her the expertise to teach others what she knew. Her slim frame could have easily been crushed by any horse, yet she maneuvered them with such grace. She complained about her waist-length chestnut hair being a problem when she forgot to put it up. Once in a while, a horse would try to bite at her locks which caused her to take disciplinary action.

Her Jewish features defied the genetic code for her race. She had unusually dark skin, slanted almond shaped brown eyes, and the look of a descendant of an American Indian tribe. The shade of red lipstick she wore bled slightly around her mouth adding fullness and some character to the pretty smile she had. She was a beautiful young woman.

On our first day of working together, Jennifer led the horse she used for demonstration out of its stall and into a breezeway in the barn. She then placed it in crossties . Jennifer explained to me that crossties were used as a stabilizer for the horse, but were not needed if a horse was well mannered and not a discipline problem for its owner or trainer. Occasionally a sound or object would cause a horse to spook then rear without warning which could cause serious injury to its caretaker. I paid close attention to what she was saying.

My thoughts were on memories of my designer friend, Cindy. We once thought the name 'Zebra' would be an appropriate name for our label if we ever decided to start a business together. I imagined irregular black and white stripes on the grey Arabian mare we were brushing. Where in the hell was Cindy anyway and what was she doing now all these years later? I wondered if she was designing like she said she would or had a critical journey through life like me. The most fiendish plot would involve a cheerful reunion with my old buddy.

"Ouch!" I felt a pinch on my elbow. I stepped aside as Jennifer smacked the horse we were grooming. No more thoughts about Cindy today.
"Knock it off!" ordered Jennifer. She scolded the horse for nibbling at my sleeve. "You got to be real careful with this one. The Duchess loves to play," said Jennifer.
"I see."
"Next we need to apply fly spray." Jennifer sprayed the insect repellent on one side of the mare beginning at the long curved neck. She sprayed until the entire side was slightly damp. Then she directed me to use a softer brush to evenly distribute the solution into the coat. Jennifer then sprayed the other side of the horse the same way. We finished brushing the enormous body and legs of the animal and Jennifer showed me how to brush and comb its long wavy mane and tail. It was a great to be a horse and receive so much attention.
The feet and hoofs were all that remained. Jennifer ran her hand down the back of a hind leg and the Duchess lifted her hoof. With a firm grip and a small tool in her hand, Jennifer scraped and removed debris from each horseshoe. The thoroughly pampered creature was ready for a saddle.
Jennifer selected a durable western saddle and a thickly woven pad from the storage in the tack room. The well seasoned saddle she carried equaled her weight but she carried it as though it was light as a feather. First she tossed the up the pad then slung the saddle into place on

top the Duchess. After securing the saddle on the horse, she asked me if I was ready for my first riding lesson.

I noticed improvements on my body after several weeks of riding. I no longer needed to use the Thigh-Master. I found that wrapping my legs around the torso of the horse and applying varying amounts of pressure required strict discipline of my leg muscles. Without acute reflexes, one ended up on the ground. I learned that proper positioning of the legs is what kept you on a horse.

I stood in front of the mirror, nude, trying to decide what I was going to put on. The white silk robe I just finished making was a bit much for lounging around in, so I grabbed an oversized T-shirt from my closet and pulled it on over my head. I forgot the panties.

Teddy was spending the night with a friend, so my Friday night was my very own. I went downstairs to the dining room to work on a sketch I had started several days ago. As I settled into the chair and reached for a pencil, the telephone rang. It was Pam.

"Hi, how are you doing?" I was happy to hear from Pam.

"Hi Sasha. I don't know for sure. I guess I'm okay," Pam said.

I recognized a familiar tone of uncertainty in Pam's voice, "Uh-oh. What's going on?"

"It's Pookie. He's getting out next month and I'm nervous."

"What are you nervous about?"

"I don't know, I guess I'm not sure about how to act."

"What do you mean?" I got a little irritated with the notion because Pam's behavior had always been socially acceptable. I could tell Pam was confused so I said, "You are not the person with the social problem."

"I know, and Pookie says in his letters he still loves me."

"That may be true, but when will he show you he loves you and stop going to jail?"

Pam was quiet for a moment.

"Pam, nothing has changed. What do you want from him? I know you've said the sex is great, but that's not all there is to a relationship."

"Is there something wrong with me?"

"No, Pam, there's nothing wrong with you. I just think you are hoping for a miracle that will change him. I understand what love is. I know all too well."

By the end of our talk, Pam felt better and was able to relax about her situation. But I knew the advice I tried to give would go in one ear and out the other. As soon as I hung up the phone, it rang right away. Pam must have forgotten to mention something I thought, as I picked up the receiver.

"What did you forget?"

"Hi, beautiful." It was not Pam.

"Who is this? I asked.

"You don't know who this is?"

I didn't want to insult the caller and was in no mood for playing games. I put the art pencil down on the table.

"What are you doing?" he pursued.

"Playing with myself." After the comment, I realized who it was. It was Zeeke.

"Can I come over and play with you. I promise I'll do all the work."

"Zeeke?" My fingers were crossed.

"Yeah. I'm around the corner from you, at the 7-eleven." I could hear the traffic in the background.

"Zeeke, it's so late, it's after midnight," but I thought about my temporary freedom and the lascivious images I was having said, "Well, come on."

I answered the door five minutes later dressed in the oversized tee. Zeeke lunged at me, and backed me into the entrance of the living room.

"Hello, Zeeke, may I close the door, please?" I figured he had probably smoked something before he arrived because he had quite an appetite. After closing and locking the front door, he came after me again. This was great but I had never kissed him. Instead, I allowed him to hug and hold me, and I successfully ignored a passion I felt inside. I finally gave in to a deep affectionate kiss I enjoyed until I pictured G.R. I pushed Zeeke away. I was momentarily satisfied and wanted to get back to my work. That was not going to be a booty call. Besides, I wanted to keep the safe fantasies benign that I was beginning to have about my new boss, G.R. "Zeeke, you have to go. Now!"

I finished the sketch, turned off the lights downstairs and went up to my bedroom. I did not go to bed right away but made an entry in my journal. G.R. was now an official candidate for my fantasies. In my mind, I was able to visualize endless acts of pure gratification with that man. My fantasies would have to sustain me for now, since he was a married man. I made no entry about Zeeke in my diary. I closed the padded book and my eyes as the sun crept up onto the desert.

"Three tomatoes, the pear shaped ones, three ears of corn, bacon, do you have bacon?" asked Marlene.

"Yes."

"Okay. And a can of evaporated milk."

"Anything else?" I asked.

"No. I have all the seasonings you'll need."

I had been after Marlene for a long time to show me how to prepare her tasty southern dish of smothered corn. I had barely closed my eyes that morning when Marlene called and woke me up. She offered to give a cooking lesson later that day. All I remembered about the early morning call was that 3 p.m. in at her place in the afternoon was a good time.

The new condo Marlene purchased in Inglewood suited her perfectly. She decided not to move into one of her rental units she owned. She used the questionable location in the South Central neighborhood as the reason. Marlene bought all new furniture and plants and sent the bills to Dennis. He was shocked by all of the expensive items she bought, imported crystal and china, numerous wood carved art pieces she ordered from a catalogue she got in the Caymans. We were about to begin cutting up the vegetables for the corn dish when Dennis called to express his displeasure.

"I don't care!" Marlene screamed through the receiver of the telephone. She held the receiver in one hand and a knife in the other. All of sudden she said. "Screw you!" then very calmly put the phone down on the kitchen counter. She didn't have to explain a thing to me. I already knew what was going on.

Watching Marlene cut vegetables was always a visual treat. With a small cleaver in hand she stripped each ear of corn of its fruit. Next she used a paring knife to slice and dice the oddly shaped tomatoes until they resembled tiny cubes. For another dish she sliced a zucchini lengthwise, carefully carved out the center then chopped up what remained. She did this quickly, filling the small glass bowls she had set close by.

"How do you do that?" I asked, with a bewildered look on my face.

"It's simple. All you need are the proper tools." Marlene went through each step with me and guaranteed delight when I tried it at home. "Did I tell you about my new job?"

"What new job?"

"The one I begin next week. I'll tell you about it later. Right now I've got to jump in the shower because Gil's on his way over."

Marlene was getting her life back in order and I was glad. I thanked Marlene for the cooking lesson and wished her a sensual evening. I went home to get Teddy and we went to see a film.

The more time I spent with the horses at the ranch made it clear to me that I loved the animals and actually craved their company. Although intimidating in size and weight, I figured a horse was more willing to become a partner. If trained and properly cared for, a horse could give its owner many years of pleasure. I was no expert on horses but sensed that they understood me. So, as I went through all steps of grooming, I talked to each horse constantly. I loved the bonding because I rambled about things that were personal to me, things I didn't necessarily want or need a response to. The horses just listened. They never argued. And whenever I rode they responded to the subtle commands as if originated within the horse's own head. Occasionally a horse would protest, but after readjusting to the notion of who the boss was, they made progress. Why don't more people have horse sense?

One afternoon G.R. took time to observe me riding. He slowed his Mercedes as he drove up the road from the street. Jennifer and I were in a practice arena next to the road where G.R. stopped his car. We were exercising Shiloh, a three year old stallion that G.R. had recently purchased. G.R. got out of his car and stepped up to the fence. I began to perspire when I trotted past G.R. I smiled while keeping Shiloh close to the railing of the fence.

"That's great, Sasha! Keep your heels down, just like that! Keep him on the rail! When you get halfway around the arena, ask him to cantor, using your legs." Jennifer walked from the center of the arena to join G.R. where they talked for a few moments, while I rode. I circled the arena several times before turning around and going in the opposite direction. Maximum toning and conditioning of the horse was achieved this way, not to mention what it did for my thighs. When I passed them again, G.R. said, "Hey, you look like a champ up there!"

I moved too fast to respond, I smiled, passed them and prayed that I wouldn't lose my balance and fall. I was lucky that day.

I rode a feisty gelding called Nashun a week later. I rode him bareback, lost my grip and balance, and slipped off doing a nose dive in the sandy surface of the arena. I lay there a moment, then checked my hands to see if I had broken a nail. Nashun came to a complete halt and just stood there, looking at me. He was probably wondering what the hell I was doing on the ground instead of on top of him. I got up, dusted myself off and climbed back on

Nashun. We ended our training session on a good note, but I paid for the fall with much discomfort.

The hot steamy bath I took in the morning felt so good. I used an entire box of Epsom Salt and added rubbing alcohol to that. I didn't bother using bubble bath soap because I knew the bubbles couldn't survive in the concoction for my aches. I lay there immersing herself until every trace of soreness vanished. About an hour. I lifted my head from the shell shaped air pillow to get out of the bathtub when I heard Teddy's knock on the bathroom door.
"Mom!"
"Yes," I answered, as I reached for a towel.
"Aunt Pam just called. She wants you to call her back as soon as you get out of the tub. She said it's very important. Will you pick me up from school today?"
"Sure, and have a good day."
As soon as I dried myself off, I put on a peach terry bathrobe and sat on the edge of my bed so I could call Pam. I picked up the telephone receiver and dialed Pam's number. I hoped Pam had not gone to work yet. She answered the phone during the first ring.
"Hello."
"Good morning. Did I catch you on your way out?" I asked.
"Oh, hi girl. No. I'm just sitting here, having my coffee. Teddy told you I called?"
"Yes, and he told me it was an emergency so please don't keep me in suspense. What was so important?"
"Girl, you will never believe what I did."

"Probably not, but tell me anyway."

"I married Pookie."

"Excuse me, you did what?"

"I said I married Pookie. We did it last weekend in Las Vegas."

I was speechless. I did not comment at first, then I said, "Pam, if you're happy, then I'm happy. Best Wishes. Where's Pookie so I can congratulate him, too?"

"He's not here. He didn't come home last night."

"Pam, what the fuck is going on?"

"Sasha I know I did a stupid thing when I married him. Please don't make me feel worse than I already do."

"I couldn't possibly do that, Pam." I wasn't really interested in Pookie's whereabouts. I secretly hoped he would never return. "So now what? Are you going to put up with his foolishness?"

"No, I'm not." Pam began to sniffle. I could feel my friend was about to fall apart on the other end of the line.

"Pam, get dressed and come out here today. Please come spend some time with me. I won't go to the ranch today, my body's sore anyway from yesterday. We can talk and you can figure out what to do. Okay? Will you come?"

"But I want to be here when he comes home."

"Pam, the place he calls home may not be *your* place. Has he called at all? Just come, please."

Pam was at my house in an hour. I knew right away that Pam was a wreck. She walked in the house, sat down at the dining room table, put her purse down on the floor after taking something from it, and asked me for an ashtray. Next she asked for a cup of coffee, then lit a joint.

"Sasha, who does that sonofabitch think he is?"

I put the ashtray down on the table in front of Pam.

"You know, Pam. I believe in nipping things in the bud." We looked at each other and burst into laughter.

"You're right again, Sasha. I don't know what I could have been thinking when I married Pookie. I never should have gone to Las Vegas with him."

"Now look, Pam. Don't you dare get on the pity pot today. The situation is not really as bad as it appears. You just need to decide what you want. Do you want harmony or disruption in your home? Which is it?" I put Pam's coffee mug on the table next to the ashtray, "would you like cream with that?"

"Yes, thanks." Pam pulled a stick of incense from her purse and lit it. She stuck it in the pot of a nearby ficus plant.

"Pam, this is ridiculous. Look at yourself. Did you sit in front of a mirror and say 'fuck you' for thirty minutes? We are going to get rid of Pookie once and for all. We just have to figure out how to do it in a nice way." But I knew there was no nice way.

We smoked cigarettes and drank coffee most of the day. At 2:30 we picked Teddy up from school and went back to my place. Pam called her house several times throughout the day hoping Pookie would answer, but she got the answering machine instead. Poor judgment in her decision to marry Pookie wrecked sensible thoughts Pam had that day. She even blamed herself for his absence and had no prescription to make her own self feel better.

"Pam, check your messages. Maybe he's called by now." I said.

Pam dialed a combination of numbers giving her access to recorded messages on her phone. She had one. It was from someone named Kadedra. Pam was shocked at what it said:

Pookie is wit me, Pam. I am his woman an' I got hiz baby. I don't know why he didn't tell you 'bout me. I jus' got out of C.I.W. and we' goin' to try ta make it now. Pookie say he hope you understand. Bye.

I followed Pam home and we changed locks on her apartment door. Pam finally realized she was not dealing with someone she knew. What other secrets did he have? We quickly gathered up Pookie's things and put them in a cardboard box. After loading the box into the trunk of Pam's car, we drove to a liquor store around the corner from Pam's apartment to purchase a can of lighter fluid and a pint of vodka. We got back in the car and drove around until Pam spotted a vacant lot behind a boarded up gas station. Pam stopped the car on the street beside the lot. We removed Pookie's box of belongings from the trunk of the car and carried it fifty feet into the lot. Pam squirted the entire can of lighter fluid inside the box. I struck the match and tossed it inside. Pam had planned the execution of the beautiful bon fire at dusk. We toasted. It was her final farewell to Pookie. She would have the mistake marriage annulled immediately.

22

Three months later

Talk of the prestigious dressage show spread rapidly. According to G.R., the horse show would top all shows hosted by local ranchers in recent months. The announcement of the horse show came when I began to reevaluate my commitment to designing. My career in fashion seemed to be fading. I was spending less time designing, more time with horses. Grooming horses was no replacement for the joy I got from designing costumes, but for the time being it was satisfying. I looked forward to going to the ranch and offered to help out with special events on weekends. "Can you help out this weekend with team penning?" Jennifer's huge brown eyes were hoping for a 'yes' answer. She hoped I would not mind saddling up to help settle cattle between runs at the team penning competition on Sunday.

"Sure, if I can ride the Duchess. And I'll bring Teddy. He likes coming out here." I adjusted the nozzle on the water hose and began to spray the feet and legs of the Duchess. She loved her baths.

I was fond of G.R.'s favorite mare. I aimed the water hose at the belly and underside of the horse, gradually wetting her for the application of horse shampoo. I walked around to the other side of the Duchess to finish wetting her body.

"Would you pass me the soap, please?" I extended my hand in the large plastic container Jennifer held and scooped a handful of creamy solution. I soak sprayed the top of the horse and its mane. I rubbed shampoo into the body and mane and worked up a good lather by adding warm water and used circular movements with the wooden brush I was using. I dug for more soap in the large container and applied it to the horse's tail. When I dampened the tail and hind side with the running water, I used the tail as a scrub rag for its rump and back of the hind legs.

"Sasha, you look like you're enjoying this," Jennifer said.

"I am." I used a brush and continued to work shampoo into the coat. Using circular motions and small amounts of water, I distributed cleaning solution over the remaining parts of the body. I squatted down beside the Duchess, using a different brush to scrub each hoof, soaping each one thoroughly. Jennifer stood there in silence, as if she were learning something new. "People tell me I'm to short to be a groom. Actually, I hate doing this," she finally said.

I finished scrubbing the Duchess and began rinsing her off. I realized I may have used to much shampoo that time because it took forever to rinse the soap out. What should have only taken fifteen minutes took much longer. Jennifer had warned me many times about using too much soap.

When there were no more bubbles on the Duchess or in the puddle of water we stood in, I put the water hose down.

"Has the date been set for the show?"

After waiting a few moments for a response, I realized I was talking to myself. Jennifer was nowhere around. Vanished. I figured she had gone to the office to use the telephone to make a call to her boyfriend, Shane. He was home waiting to hear from his sister who had buried her husband recently, and who had decided to stay with their parents in Missouri.

I shrugged my shoulders. I hoped she would hurry back so we could finish. I reached for the scraper and used it to remove excess water from the Duchess'. When I was satisfied with the horse's overall appearance, I sprayed the mane and tail with a show sheen conditioner that beautified and strengthened the hair on its body.

"You look so elegant, Duchess, but I think you need to be braided." I lightly brushed and combed her mane hair. I started at the top of the head, parted small sections of mane hair and began to braid. I put tiny rubber bands at the end of each braid. By the time I completed everything, Jennifer reappeared.

"You're fast!" Jennifer said as she walked up to me.

"What happened to you?"

"I called Shane. His sister hadn't called yet."

"Are they pretty close?" I asked her.

"Yes, but he only found out about her ten years ago."

"What?"

"It's a long story, with a happy ending, really." Jennifer said, with a smile.

"Okay. The Duchess is ready for the hot walker. You can take her now."

Jennifer led the Duchess out of the bathing bay and into the nearby exercise arena. She attached the Duchess to an awaiting chain that hung from the exercise carousel. As soon as the Duchess was connected, I flipped the switch on that put the huge apparatus in motion, like a merry-go-round. With her head held high, the Duchess pranced with the movement of the machine.

"Did you find out who sent the roses?" Marlene asked.

"No," I was frustrated about receiving flowers without a note and it was getting to me "the roses that came today are pink."

"Sasha, you have no idea who sent them?"

"You know, I have my own idea but, no, it couldn't be."

"What? Who?"

"Maybe Eddie's sending them from the grave."

"Sasha, I think you're getting to much sun at the ranch. Have you been drinking lately?"

"You know I don't drink. I could use one though." I thought about the drink I had the night before. How I had gone to the liquor store just before it closed and bought myself a pint of Remy Martin. I wanted to eliminate thoughts of G.R. The fast talking ranch owner who had a wife. I couldn't understand why I liked him so much. Maybe it was the fact that he was nice to me. I knew nothing would materialize simply because I had thoughts about him. Having to drink over a man I couldn't have made me angry. I had broken my sobriety. Through the telephone receiver I could hear the sound of clanging ice cubes in the drink Marlene was having. The noise made me wince.

"I have to go," I said.

"Wait a minute! Before you hang up I have something to tell you."

"What?"

"Dennis called me."

"He did?"

"Yes."

"Were you civil to him?"

"That depends upon what you mean. I didn't hang up on him."

"That's good, Marlene. Is he still griping about his money?"

"No, not this time. The ugly subject didn't even come up. We actually had a decent conversation. No yelling. I was amazed."

"You mean he didn't read last month's loss statement to you?"

"No, he was actually quite calm. We talked about the twins and he mentioned a new woman he's dating now."

"What?"

"She is someone Lou's girlfriend introduced him to."

"What does she look like?" I wanted to know.

"Sasha, I didn't ask him all that. I'm a little pissed off at Lou right now."

"Why?"

"Lou is stabbing me in the back."

"What for?"

"It's pretty complicated."

"I've got a minute. What's this about?"

"Do you remember, a year and a half ago, when Dennis and I started having problems?"

"Very much so. When Dennis and Lou were working late all the time."

"Yes, around the same time we went to the Caymans. Actually, before then."

"Marlene, I'm dying here. Talk to me."

"I'm still trying to put this shit together in my mind. I don't like Lou's girlfriend. She's money hungry."

"Damn. Really?"

"Yes, and I get the impression she doesn't like me at all."

"What does *she* have to do with anything?"

"She made a comment once about her good friend who had just gotten divorced. When she was talking about her friend, she thought I was out of earshot. I heard what she said, though. She wanted her friend to meet Dennis."

"Where were you guys?"

"At my house."

"Really." I calculated all the events and people that had in some way affected Marlene's mental state and how I almost lost my dear friend. "Marlene, I know its painful to think about, let alone talk about. Have you talked to Lou?"

"I called him last week and left a message on his machine. He never called me back."

"Why did you call him in the first place?"

"I don't know. I guess I wanted to know what Dennis was doing. For some reason, the twins are not telling me much these days."

"Have they found an apartment yet?"

"No. Still looking. They're both working and are finding it difficult to get together to look."

"Why do they want to move out anyway? They have everything at home. Separate rooms, weekly maid service. I don't get it."

"I think they just want to have their own apartment."

"There's nothing wrong with that but it would be nice to have spies in the big house." I teeheed at the thought.

"Jasmine said Dennis has late night parties with Lou and some of their business associates.

"Did Jasmine say who these people were? Or what they looked like?

"No. Just two of them were women. Lou's girlfriend and another woman."

"Did you ask Dennis about the other woman?"

"Well, kinda."

"Marlene, what exactly did you ask him?"

"If he was making love to her."

"What did he say?"

"He refused to answer me. Then he said he wouldn't ask me a question like that. Sasha, he asked me if I was jealous."

"What did you tell him?"

"I told him no."

"Are you a little jealous?"

"No, I have Gil."

I had a hard time digesting what I was hearing. Did she really think Gil was all hers? He wasn't even a match. "For how long, Marlene?"

There was silence on the phone. Marlene did not respond.

"Marlene, do you still love your husband?"

"Hold on a minute Sasha. I need to get more ice."

Marlene returned to the phone with a fresh drink. I could hear the fizz sound of 7-Up she poured over the double shot of vodka in her glass. Marlene didn't bother to get ice this time.

"Sasha, I love Dennis," her voice was beginning to slur. "Sasha, he wants to take me to dinner."

"Oh, really? When?"

"Anytime I want."

"That's good Marlene. Maybe this is a sign that he wants you back."

"To hell with Dennis! I don't want him back!"

"Are you working tomorrow?"

"Yep."

"Me too. I have horses to groom. I'll talk to you tomorrow." Poor Marlene. She'll sleep good tonight though. She had two stiff drinks while we talked. She was still in love with Dennis, but liked being with Gil. I prayed hard that night Marlene would continue to talk civilly to Dennis. I thought she *should* let him take her out to dinner. And listen to what he had to say. And even if she didn't like what he had to say, just listen to him anyway. And not mention who she thought he was sleeping with because that was not really important, yet. And for God's sake, don't bring up or discuss Gil. After all, he was married and chances were he would never leave his wife. Marlene was cozy in the condo but I knew she missed the extreme home Dennis bought for her. I knew Marlene would go crazy again if Dennis put another woman in her house. Marlene had a lot to think about.

I tried to put myself in Marlene's shoes to understand what my friend was going through. On the one hand, she had a loving husband, who, unlike so many men, took care of his family.

Dennis' family consisted of Marlene, the twins, and a niece of Dennis' whose mother was living and working somewhere in Europe. His sister felt it would have been impractical to take the child away from her friends since she only had a year of high school left. Dennis told her he would keep his niece and make sure she graduated. So far, Dennis had paid most of her senior class expenses and never complained about it. Dennis made sure both twins graduated from college and had the same hopes for his niece.

They had always taken annual vacations. He didn't mind going to the theater with Marlene. In the early years of their marriage, they continued to go to concerts to see their favorite recording groups that were popular in their youth. Just last year they attended a Patti LaBelle concert in San Diego. Marlene still talks about the wonderful weekend they spent together at the Embassy Suites Hotel in La Jolla. I couldn't think of any spouse of my friends who had been so generous. Neither one of my husbands had been so giving. Nah. Dennis had everything in a man most women look for, including great hair.

On the other hand of the goodness lay doubt in his ability to remain truly hers. She needed him. After standing in Marlene's shoes for a moment, I wanted to scream and pull out my hair. There was something going on that I didn't get. Like with Pam, I refused to make a judgment. I never lived in the house with Dennis and Marlene so how would I know what was right for them?

G.R. was satisfied with the outcome of the dressage show. His 200 acre ranch was chosen for the location because of the picturesque setting and knowledgeable training staff. He was even more pleased when his own Arabian herd received high scores in a variety of competitions. Following the show, he started making preparations to enter his horses in an even larger showing of Arabian and half-Arabian breeds. The extravaganza was held every year in Scottsdale, Arizona.

G.R.'s wife, Dora was away, visiting her family in Indonesia. She missed her homeland and enjoyed going there at least twice a year. The marital problems intensified between she and G.R. and went beyond her capacity to deal with them. She chose to take her trip early, even though it was just a week before his birthday. She was not getting her way with him. She had a deflated spirit and loss of patience.

She tried many times to communicate troubled feelings to G.R., but he was always busy working, exhausting innovative schemes to make money. The fact was that Dora, who was creative, wanted to market her own ceramic and oil art work. G.R. showed little interest in what she did in her spare time, which she had plenty of.

Dora was always in her studio, outside adjacent to the patio, creating something unusual. G.R. had no idea she was serious about what she was doing. Frustrated, she wanted to pack up her art work, put it in temporary storage and return to her aristocratic family. Her aging father hated the idea of his oldest daughter being emotionally deprived, so he suggested she come to Java to relax and be with her own kind. His political ties were still strong and if necessary, he could arrange for her permanent return to the country.

G.R. had no idea what forces worked against him when Dora boarded the airplane taking her to her father. He had contemplated what his life would be like without Dora. He was not crazy about being alone, or without Dora.

"When is she coming back?" asked Deon, who took another sip from the can of diet soda he was drinking. Dressed in a pin-striped suit, he wore his shirt open at the neck. He had just put a paisley print tie in his outside coat pocket.

"Soon I hope. I'm tired of eating out every night." G.R. took another bite of his cold ham sandwich.

"You should learn how to broil a steak, man. Then I wouldn't have to drive so far to make sure you eat." Deon came to the ranch to see his friend G.R. after having lunch with a city councilman from San Bernardino.

"Well, how did the meeting go?" asked G.R.

"It was all right but those people are determined to spray malathion all over Southern California just because they found one single pregnant medfly in Corona. They don't realize how hazardous that stuff is to people and livestock. The ag people continue to deny its effects. There is still a lot of work to be done. You're lucky to be living out here where you don't have to worry about it."

"What about the homeless people? Didn't they consider what it would do to them?" G.R. said.

"The people making the final decision about this affair don't live there or are they homeless. So why should they care?" Deon looked through the big window in G.R.'s office to see Jennifer and I walking up the road from the barn. "Who is that with Jennifer?"

"That's Sasha."

"Does she work here?"

"Yep. She's our new groom."

"Is she married?"

"No, she is single. And happy to be that way, she says. Why, do you like what you see? I might be able to fix you up."

"She is fine." Deon smiled. He unbuttoned his coat.

"Yeah, I feel the same way. My devilish side wants to jump her bones," G.R. said. "God, I wish Dora was here. Do you feel like riding this afternoon? I just carved out a new trail a few days ago and I want to check it to make sure its safe. Do you have some jeans with you? I have a T-shirt."

"Yeah. I'm taking the rest of the day off anyway."

Jennifer and I walked past the office and continued up the steep driveway that led to the racetrack. Just beyond the entrance of the racetrack sat a small observation booth. It overlooked the track and provided one of the best vantage points for viewing the entire ranch. I discovered the special location late one afternoon shortly after I started working there. I liked the spot because I was able to sit on a wooden bench inside the tiny structure and absorb the panoramic vistas, alone.

Whenever I went there and sat on the highest elevation on the property, I experienced a new sense of hope and determination. I felt in control of my destiny. Jennifer and I both liked the spot. We stepped in the booth and sat down.

"What do you usually think about when you come up here?" I said to her.

"Oh, I don't know. Different things," said Jennifer, as she looked around at green hilltops, shaded by rays of sunlight peeking through irregular cloud formations. "Do you believe in spirits, like the ones that live in animals?" Jennifer asked.

Spirits, I thought, are very real. "Yes, in a strange way I do. Maybe that's why I talk to horses. I actually think they understand me." I laughed at what I said, not thinking Jennifer took me seriously.

"People who don't understand nature don't know how profound the connection is. My grandfather used to tell me about a bald eagle that would sit in a tree in his yard. The bird would fly in from the wilderness and just sit there, for hours, every day. Around that time, I was born. I was the first grandchild in our family, and my grandfather had hoped my mother's first born would be a girl. My grandfather said after I was born, the eagle disappeared for a couple of years. When my mother got pregnant with my brother three years later, the eagle returned and sat in the same spot in the tree. The bird came back every day, including the day my brother was born. The next day the bird was gone. A few months later my grandfather sold the farm and moved to Tennessee where he lives now."

"Umph."

"Grandfather said it was a good omen for a wild bird, especially something as magnificent as a bald eagle, to want to get that close to humans. Do you believe in reincarnation?"

"I sure do. I'm going to tell you something. Please don't laugh at what I'm about to say, Jennifer."

"Okay, I promise."

"Okay, I have always felt that I had a former life, and in that life, I was a wealthy white woman. Extremely wealthy. I had servants, a personal maid, and a very greedy husband. We owned a lot of land and had livestock, mainly horses. And from what I recall of the experience, I was extremely mean to the people who worked for me."

"Wow."

"And because of my own arrogance and shortsightedness I was sentenced to relive my life as a struggling abused black woman, who just happened to have a little talent to keep me frustrated."

"Sasha, that's really amazing. I don't find anything strange about that."

"And my daughter Eileen, bless her heart, wonders every morning when she wakes up, when her nightmare is going to end. She goes through this every day." We both laughed hard, leaning forward in unison.

"Is Eileen still thinking about getting married?"

"I don't know what she's going to do. She recently broke an engagement. Now she's dating a man who seems to be much more suited for her, and I'm glad. I just want her to be sure about who she commits to."

"Oh, look who's riding with G.R. He took off his business suit." Jennifer said. "Have you met Deon?"

"No."

Jennifer and I looked in the direction of the gravel path we had walked up. Deon, like his friend G.R. was extremely handsome. His rich mahogany skin exaggerated powerful features in his face and body. His dark eyes were fixed on me as they came closer on horseback.

"Is that Deon?"

"Yeah, he's a real nice guy." Jennifer said.

G.R. and Deon trotted up to where we sat and stopped. Knowing that I had never met Deon, G.R. said, "Do you two know each other?" Why, just because he's black too?

After the formal introduction, they continued to follow the new trail into the mountains behind the ranch.

I reeled from the smile Deon greeted me with. I was afraid to ask if he was married for fear of the wrong answer. I just pretended he wasn't. I knew enough about him to qualify him as a suitable acquaintance, though. He had a job. A black man with a job. That was great for starters.

"Eileen, you should have seen him! And he's into horses, too!"

"Mom, did you guys have a chance to get acquainted?"

"Well, not really. I think we just gawked at each other. G.R. never told me his best friend was black."

"Well Mom, I guess he figured it wasn't important."

"Guess so. How is J.T?" There was a heavy click sound on the telephone line that signaled Eileen of a waiting call.

"Hold on, Mom."

About ten seconds later Eileen returned to the phone.

"Guess who that was."

"Who?"

"My dad."

"Were was he calling from?"

"He didn't say. I told him I was talking to you and for him to call me back."

"Do you want to hang up now?"

"Of course not. He can wait. I want to tell you about J.T."

"Oh, what's going on with J.T.?"

"I had to help him overcome his fear of heights."

"Say, what?"

"Yeah. Mama, he didn't want me to know about it."

"How did you find out?"

"Do you remember when I went to his parents' house for dinner?"

"Yes, I remember."

"Well, they have this shed in their backyard his father used for storing yard equipment and junk. The aluminum building is not that tall and it had a slanted roof. When J.T. was small he and his friends would throw things on the roof of it just to see if they would slide off. One day J.T. tossed a pair of his father's shorts on the roof of the shed and waited for them to slide off, but they didn't. J.T. had been warned repeatedly by his father not to do this."

"Uh, oh. What happened next?"

"J.T. knew if his father saw his shorts on the shed, he would get a whipping. So he and his friend got the ladder from the garage so one of them could climb up and get the shorts. His father and mother were inside taking a nap, so they had to work fast. J.T. wasn't even comfortable about climbing a simple tree, so he paid his friend to go up and get the shorts."

"Did his parents ever find out about it?"

"No, but they know about it now, years later. The evening we had dinner with his parents, his father mentioned a problem leak in the roof needing fixing before it rained. He asked J.T. if he had time to look at it after dinner. Mama, when his father asked him that, J.T.'s eyes got *so* big. He looked horrified."

"What did he do?"

"That's when he confessed about the shorts. He said he couldn't go up on the roof. It was a full moon that night and his father even offered to turn the bright lights on outside. But J.T. still refused to go. Mama, I was sitting there listening, in my blue jeans and Georgetown sweatshirt, wondering if there was a ladder outside.

So I excused myself from the dinner table and went into the kitchen. I peeked out the kitchen window and spotted a ladder lying on its side in the backyard, next to the fence. Just about that time J.T. came into the kitchen and I grabbed him by the hand and pulled him to the back door."

"Eileen, what did you do?"

"Mama, please don't get mad. But told him there was a surprise for him if went up to the roof with me."

"Did he go?"

"You bet he did."

"What was the surprise?"

Eileen paused, then giggled.

"Eileen, no you didn't. On the roof of the house?"

"In the light of the silvery moon. He's not afraid of heights anymore. He wants to marry me now. He asked me last night."

I couldn't stop laughing at what Eileen told me. I thought at least my daughter found someone who was as adventurous as she was. But I wondered if they ever found the leak in the roof.

23

The east side neighborhood close to where and I grew up continued to survive over the years. Little was lost when the freeway came through the old neighborhood. Certain shortcuts we took to school were eliminated by the freeway, and it took a lot longer to cross Imperial Highway. It was amazing how some families managed to maintain the essence of the neighborhood in spite of all the changes around them.

The vacant lot on 116th and Wadsworth Avenue was gone, its diagonal path was part of the freeway now. At dusk, scattered pebbles of broken glass glistened on the sidewalk near the new expressway. He was not used to the different route he had to take to the alley behind the house he grew up in. He kept walking until he reached the sidewalk that took him to its entrance.

Barry walked into the alley and brushed past a dusty pink oleander bush growing wildly there. His movement past the vegetation sent flower petals precariously to the ground. Graffiti covered most of the aging garage doors that securely hung from their hinges. Barry remembered how as a kid he used to get into trouble for doing the same thing with chalk. Now permanent spray was used and no one was punished for the vandalism. He stepped over empty, rusted aerosol paint cans and walked through overgrown grass that lined the alley. He kicked a flattened beer can as he approached the faded old car with no wheels he now called home.

Barry reached for the rusted chrome handle on the door with his free hand. In his other hand he held the plastic garbage bag he had carried for blocks. When he opened the car door he looked inside to make sure no unwanted creature or person had invaded his domicile.

Mrs. Jones still lived next door to his mother's house and said it was okay for Barry to sleep in the old car next to the fence, if he wanted to. He was still a favorite neighbor child. She didn't care what the neighbors said.

Barry placed the plastic bag on the passenger side of the wide front seat, being careful not to crush the potato chips he bought at the neighborhood market when he went to the telephone to call Eileen.

He would call her later. That would mean having to go out again, which he needed to do in order to get something for dinner. And possibly find Ira so they could go get a drink, and after that, maybe find some smoke. He would call Eileen later, after he had done everything he needed to do, first. Not knowing what to do first engaged Barry in a mental battle, not satisfied easily.

He made sure all his things were safely hidden in the old car. He put the bag of chips under a blanket on the floor of the back seat. He never thought he would find himself without a place to lay his head. Betty refused to take him back. She would not let him in the house to get what he didn't have time to pack when he left. When he tried to see his son, she called the police. They took him in for causing a disturbance. When he was at Norwalk, his car was repossessed and he lost everything he stuffed in the trunk when he left Tucson. He had no idea he would return to a shit storm at his former residence.

With the sun securely set and street lights fully functioning, Barry reached in the back seat and felt around for the acid washed denim jacket he had on when his lost his sanity. Besides what he was wearing, it was the only decent piece of clothing he owned. Barry pulled the jacket on his body then opened the car door and stepped into the alley. As he looked in the direction of Wadsworth Avenue, the bright headlights of an oncoming car temporarily blinded him. The car sped past him, going at high speed. Mrs. Jones, in her nineties now, turned on her backyard light when she heard the skidding sound of the car and Barry disappeared into the early evening.

He thought about the rush he got the night before with his friend Ira. It was not the first time they had done drugs together. Ira was the single kid in the neighborhood who could always get the drugs. Twenty years later, still the supplier. Barry crossed Imperial Highway and began the search for him. He decided to eat later, if at all. He would call Eileen at some point that night but he wanted to get high first.

Being cut off from familiar things that make up a home made Barry feel like an outcast. Having no place where he belonged, the pain and fear caused by not having a place to eat regularly, a place for true rest, decent conversation, and companionship was unbearable. He had expected to live a long life and die a peaceful death at home in comfort. Barry had once envisioned himself sound as a tree whose roots always had water, and whose branches were wet with dew people praised.

They had failed to see he was hurting and dying physically and mentally. In better times he gave advice and people were silent, listening carefully to what he said. having nothing to say when he finished. He knew his words had the effect of raindrops everyone welcomed. He smiled on people who had lost confidence in themselves, and encouraged them. Even though he knew he was in a temporary predicament he still had his dignity.

Barry understood that God brought him down to teach him humility, respect and kindness. At times he was terrified of the mean streets, often overcome with horror. He wished he had wings like a dove so he could fly away and find rest. He would fly far away and make his home in the desert to find shelter from the raging storm of humanity. Barry prayed constantly as he reached Central Avenue and headed south, in search of the dope man, Ira.

"Sasha?"
"Hi girl!" How are you doing?"
"Fine. What 'cha been up too?" asked Marlene.
"Oh, not very much. Just the usual. I bathed some horses today."
"You went to the ranch today?"
"Sure did. After that I went shopping. I needed jeans."
"Did you find any?"

"I bought four pair. At the Gap. And I bought a shirt for Teddy."

"Oh, you've been busy today."

"I had fun. What's going on with you?"

"A lot. Dennis and I have been talking."

"What?" That's great, Marlene."

"We went out to dinner. Sasha, he's so sorry."

"Oh, yeah?"

"Yeah, real sorry. He wants us back together. He wants to talk about reaching some kind of agreement."

"Agreement to do what?"

"First of all, Dennis and I need to agree that he's stupid because he thinks I'm stupid."

"Marlene!"

"I'm tired of playing games with Dennis, Sasha. He thinks I'm going to come back home with things the way they are. He still stays out late with Lou most nights."

"How do you know that?"

"Because Kai told me."

"Oh, you have your spies watching things? Ha, ha, ha."

"Sasha, its impossible for them to miss anything. The twins live there."

"But, having them report to you isn't fair if Dennis can't spy on you. Marlene, do you really want to work it out with Dennis? What's happening with Gil?"

"I don't want to talk about Gil. I almost bumped into his wife." It was a close call. Gil and his business friends met at their favorite hangout. Marlene told Gil she would meet him there for drinks after work. She walked past a dark loudly dressed plump woman in the parking lot of the restaurant. She nearly collided with the staggering woman, not knowing it was Gil's wife. Marlene walked into the café and found Gil, who looked shocked when he saw her, even though he was expecting her. Gil had no idea his wife decided to have a few drinks after work, at his favorite spot. By the time Gil got there that day, she had tied one on and wanted to talk to him about their crumbling marriage. He was not pleased by her presence there but bought her more drinks anyway, knowing Marlene could show up anytime. When his wife finished speaking her mind she got up and whizzed on out the door. And Marlene walked in right after that. That explained the look on Gil's face.

"He almost got busted." Marlene said. "I was so mad at him. I didn't want to meet him there anyway. He wanted me to hang out with he and his friends."

"Well, did you guys get to have drinks?"

"We stayed there for a little while. Then we left together and went to the Snooty Cat. We argued some about what happened. Then we got busy."

"Oh."

"And when he makes love to me I forget what I'm mad about."

Why in the hell was I listening to that shit? I was so sick of hearing about that dangerous, scary game she'd been playing with that married man. What the fuck was wrong with Marlene? She had to be losing her mind. I couldn't believe she was not able to decide what was best for her. Did I have to decide everything?

"Marlene. You need to remember what happened. You damn near bumped into the wife."

"Yeah, I'll never forget that hot pink lipstick she was wearing. It was loud."

"Was she tacky?"

"No, not really tacky. Just loud colors."

"Marlene, what about Dennis? I know I sound like a broken record, but what are you going to do?"

I was getting myself ready for a luxurious bubble bath. I turned the faucet on in my bathtub to run water when the phone rang. It was Pam.

"Hi, Sasha. How are you?"

"Pam? Where have you been? I've been trying to call you for days."

"Oh, I've been working hard. I just took on a new patient. I think I want to do private duty nursing for a while, you know, get out of the hospital."

"Really?"

"Yeah, but that's not why I called. You will never guess what came in the mail today", Pam said.

"No, I can't guess. What?"

"You know how superstitious I am. My left hand has been itching all week. Do you know what that means?"

"Yep. Money."

"A letter came today from an attorney representing the estate of Needa Stream. I am invited to the reading of her will."

"What?!"

"You heard me. I couldn't believe it. Sasha, should I go?"

"What on earth do you mean? Is there any reason why you shouldn't go?"

"I don't know. I don't even know these people. What should I wear?"

Year round school was the smartest creation ever developed by the public school system. I liked the fact that Teddy was out of school three weeks at a time, and if he wanted, he could spend that time with his father. It was a great arrangement for me, especially when I had a nonstop project requiring my undivided attention. I needed time alone to reflect on current activities, both personal and professional, and try to decide which direction my life would take.

The horses continued to dominate most of my time and interest, leaving less and less free time for sketching and sample making. Teddy wanted to spend time with his friends since he was going to be with his father three weeks.

"Mom, if you just take me to the mall, you can pick me up later, when you finish with team penning at the ranch."

"Okay, okay. Who's going with you, anyone?"

"Rock and Chris are going to meet me there. We're going to meet at the arcade then go to the movies."

"Do you have money for that?"

"Yep. The money my dad sent me. Mom, can we go by the cycle shop on the way to the mall? I want to show you what I can buy if I turn in this tagger I know about."

"You know someone who does that?...tags?"

"Yeah. Lots of people."

"Are they friends of yours? " I remembered how unpopular snitches were when I was growing up. What was this child up to?

"No, Mom. You know I don't hang out with those types. We can get at least a thousand."

I had seen a public service announcement about the nagging problem of vandalism in the growing Antelope Valley and like most people, resented its annoying presence. I felt parents should be held responsible when their minor children are involved.

"Let's go." I said.

I drove my car onto the small parking lot of the Honda dealership. The shiny new cycles that sat out front fascinated my curious son. Before I could turn the engine off, he jumped out of the car.

"This is the one, Mom."

I got out of the car and walked up to the blue metallic speed machine that, if improperly handled, could cause permanent physical damage to my son. "It's pretty nice, son. Can we go now?" I was clearly not interested in shopping for motorcycles. Shit. Shopping for a man would be more satisfying. "Can I take you to the mall now?"

When Eileen walked past the coffee table she kicked it hard enough to send an artificial potted plant crashing to the floor. She turned around to look at the black cordless phone that had carried her father's voice. She then slowly bent her upper body over so she could pick up the plant that was knocked over. Why in the hell did this happen? She set the arrangement back on the coffee table.

All her life, she had to listen to her friends brag about their fathers. How much money they made. The trips her friends took with their fathers. How daddy would pay for their nails to be done. Eileen's nails would be done too, but I paid for the service, as well as everything else.

She wished her father had acted like a father, and treated her better. Instead, he chose to ignore us. His pitiful phone call to her confirmed what she suspected. Barry was homeless.

He finally lost everything. Leaving Betty was one of his most recent hair-brained ideas. She knew her father was drinking heavily because he called her when he was drunk one night, after his return from Arizona. She remembered not being able to go back to sleep that night.

That night he called her at two hour intervals, all night, asking for money and eventually showing up at her door at 7 a.m. He had walked all night, he said, leaving his personal items stashed in different places along the route he took down Imperial Highway. The only way he could have done that much walking in one night was if he had been smoking a crack pipe.

Naw. Not my daddy. The dog, she was thinking. Why couldn't he have been a decent father so I wouldn't be so happy right now? He deserved to be in the street, living in the alley behind the house he grew up in. What goes around comes around. I wonder why he called me anyway. Did he want sympathy? Wait until Mama hears about this. My daddy is a homeless drug addict, Eileen said to herself.

I entered the second set of glass doors that opened into the mall. Teddy was not where he said he would be. Where was he? I was late, he should have been there. So I decided to sit on a bench and enjoy the sights.

All these people. Damn! Ooh, look at *those* people. They look like hillbillies, they're probably lost too. I wonder if this is their first taste of civilization. I'll bet their covered wagon is parked out back. Oh, now they're going to sit on the damn bench. I wish those other people would hurry up so I can have the bench they're on. Where is Teddy? I wish he would come on so we can go home.

Finally. Thank God. I thought they would never move. Sigh. Let me sit down. Where is that boy? I'm glad I brought my book. Yeah, I'll just sit here and read until he shows up.

God, I need a woman. Today, Lord. You know how Francine ripped my heart out. She hurt me and I don't want to be alone anymore. I've suffered long enough. I don't like jacking off. It's not good for me. I want the real thing. A real woman. Why did I come to this mall today? I'm so lonely. If I could get a good woman, I'd giver her everything. Everything I have. Oh, my God! There she is! And she's by herself. And I know she's not married. She sure looks good today, with that nice body of hers. Hmm..., I like the way she carries herself. She likes to read, good. So do I. I wonder where she's going? Nice walk. Yes, she has confidence. I'm going to watch her to see if a man shows up. The bench she was sitting on is empty, so I'm going to sit right down and wait for her to come out of the coffee shop.

This is entirely too much money to spend on coffee. I don't care if it is cappuccino. I should have just ordered a latté. This is mall robbery.

"Can I get you anything else?" asked the teenage boy behind the counter.

Hell no. "No, thank you very much", I said, as I paid for the large cup of cap. I grabbed a few napkins and put a lid on the cup then walked out of the coffee shop hoping my seat on the bench was still there.

Oh, my goodness. Will you look at this? That's the same hunk I saw a few minutes ago! And now he's sitting on my bench. I bet he's waiting for his wife. She's a lucky woman, if he's married. Who *is* he? He looks like a football player. Big ol' fine black man. I'm glad he chose my bench to sit on. Shoot, I hope my lipstick is still on. But I'm going to sit on this end of the bench since he's sitting in my spot. Ooh, yeah, he gets a smile from me if he looks this way. Teddy, please take your time.

Here she comes. She's smiling, so I'll smile. Did I brush my teeth? Yeah baby, you sit right down.

"Hi." he said.
"Hello," I answered.
"Are you waiting for someone?"
"Well, yes. My son. What about you?"
"No, no. I just had a drink with an old friend. What's your name?"
"Sasha. Sasha Friend. And yours?"
"Maurice Benjamin." She's not wearing a wedding ring, he noticed. "Are you married?"
"No, I'm not. And you?" If he's married, I'm not interested.
"No, I'm divorced. I have two children."
"Oh? Girls or boys?"
"One of each." said Maurice. "And they're smart, too."
"Really? Who's raising them, their mother?"
"Yes she is."
"Oh, is that why they're smart?"

Maurice looked at me with an eye of skepticism and hoped his facial expression had not delivered his thoughts. "Yeah, that's part of the reason," he smiled.

"At least you give her credit. Unlike most men."

"Oh, I agree with you. Women are much smarter than men."

I began to smile. I liked what I was hearing. He thinks women are smart.

"Do you have children?" He knew the answer to that question.

"Yes I have children. I have one of each also. I'm waiting for one of them now."

"Your daughter?"

"No, my son. I dropped him off earlier. I was running a bit late this afternoon and he's probably wondering what happened to me."

"Oh, did you have to work today?"

"Well, no. I went to the ranch today. I don't call what I did today work."

"The ranch? Oh, do you ride?"

"Horses, yes. I also groom them."

"You groom horses?"

"Yes I do, in my spare time." Next he'll ask me what I do for a living. I knew the line of questioning.

"So, you're a groom? That's what you do?"

"Just in my spare time." Is that Teddy I see? Yep. Good. He sees me now. Here he comes. "There's my son." Teddy walked up.

"Hi, Mom. I've been looking all around for you."

"I know. I was at the ranch longer than expected. I'm sorry."

"Oh, that's okay. I just went back to the arcade when I couldn't find you. Do you want to go now?" He gave Maurice a look of approval.

"Oh, I'm sorry. This is my son, Teddy. Teddy, this is Maurice."

"What's up, man." Maurice extended his hand for a shake, then winked at Teddy.

"Hi. Mom, do you have any quarters?"

"Why?"

"I want to go back to the arcade so I can play this game. Can I have a dollar?"

If I had had twenty dollars I would have given it to him just so I could have kept talking to Maurice.

"I don't know. Let me check my wallet."

"I have some quarters, I think." Maurice said when he stood up and jammed a hand in his pocket of the designer jeans he was wearing. He made eye contact with Teddy while slowly pulling his hand from his pocket. Then he opened his hand to reveal a pile of change. He winked again and smiled at Teddy indicating he had permission to help himself. I felt a bit lickerish when he did that.

He's generous. Maurice was handsome up close with perfect teeth, long dimples, a football player body plus he used correct grammar. He got points. I hoped he would ask for my number. Teddy better take his time at the arcade.

Maurice sat back down, placing himself closer to me on the wooden bench we shared.

"Come on, let's walk." I jumped up and tossed my empty coffee cup in a nearby trash can. We joined the slow steady flow of shoppers that had been moving steadily past us.

"I'm also a Costume Designer. What do you do for a living?"

"I'm a Sales Manager, for a large soft drink company."

Great! He's got a job. He's wearing crisp new looking tennis shoes. Hmm, perfectly trimmed mustache. No razor bumps. Neat appearance. He knows how to match his colors.

"I've been with my company seventeen years."

"That's a long time." I said.

"Well, you know, its been good to me, so I couldn't leave it."

"Does he have a girlfriend?" asked Pam.

"My goodness Pam. I barely got his name. I gave him my business card. He gave me his. And yes, he does have a job."

"Sasha. I know what I'm wearing."

"Wearing where?"

"To the reading of the will. My white suit. The one you like."

"Good choice. Guess what?"

"What?"

"G.R. asked me today if I could go with the ranch to the horse show in Scottsdale, Arizona."

"Oh really? Are you going?"

"I want to go. He is paying for everything. Even the car I'm going to rent. All I have to do is groom a few horses while I'm there."

"Sasha, when are you going back to designing full time? Aren't you tired of those horses yet?"

"That's a good question. I've thought about it. I love what I'm doing right now. When I go back to designing, I want to be totally committed to it because I want my own company next time. I almost died while I was making Yoshi rich. Then he lost it all. The stupid idiot let his insurance expire and ended up loosing everything I worked so hard for, doing it for him. Pam, if I had had had a business like that I would have made sure my insurance was paid on time.

"What was he thinking? You have to have insurance in this country." Pam said.

"I don't know. But I sure learned a lesson from him. I am a designer. I can do what Yoshi did. All I need is money."

"What's your new friend's name?"

"The guy I met today?"

"Yep."

"Maurice."

"Nice name."

"I think so."

"Got a body?"

"Nice one."

"You go girl."

No Teddy for three weeks. What would I do with myself? I had to find something to do with my time. I thought about cutting out the Palazzo pants. I had put it off for weeks. Or, I could decide how to design the western shirts I planned to take to Scotsdale but that could wait. I needed to finish Eileen's dressing robe first. It had been sitting on the table, all cut out, for days. Every time I walked past the sewing machine and saw it sitting there and I felt guilty. It should have been finished. Okay. I decided to do that first.

I hope Teddy remembered to pack his toothbrush. Well, if he didn't, his daddy would buy him another one. Every time he visits, they buy him a new toothbrush. I hoped Teddy would ask his dad for new Nikes this time. I forgot to mention new shoes to Big Ted. Teddy's feet were growing so fast. A size eleven shoe and he was only thirteen! I wondered if he made up his bed before I took him to the airport.

I wondered what fine Maurice was doing. I should have had my babies by his good looking ass. He sure had pretty brown eyes. And nice, thick wavy black hair. No. I have to stop thinking about breeding among humans. I have cute kids anyway. I'm grateful they turned out as beautiful as they did. It would have been nice to hear from Maurice that week. Well, I started thinking. Jennifer wanted me to help her with team penning that night so I would have to cancel dinner with Marlene. I was hoping to get the latest scoop on Dennis.

Marlene was beginning to soften and see the light, but she said one apology did not clean the slate. She was going to make him pay, especially if she decided to go back to him. She'd be giving up the good lovin' she got from Gil, even though he had been a real asshole lately. The near-miss incident with Gil's wife still upset Marlene whenever she thought about it.

I needed to call Jennifer so she wouldn't freak out about tonight. I'd help out but she'd see very little of me in the next couple of weeks. I had to catch up on my sketching and sewing.

I persuaded Jennifer to take special care of the Duchess while I was away, in exchange for a night of partying in Scottsdale. She said 'no problem' and she didn't need my help for team penning after all. That was a relief so I decided to finish the robe for Eileen. Afterward I took a long, hot steamy bubble bath and thought about the conversation I had with Eileen earlier that day.

Eileen told me she had heard from her father who finally confessed to being on drugs. His hopelessness was no accident. In some way it seemed like appropriate punishment for his past infractions. She gave woeful details of her father's declining state of humanity. I couldn't believe my ears but knew Eileen was telling the truth. I vibrated with anger at the terrible news my daughter sobbed to me over the misfortune of her father. Barry couldn't sink any lower.

"Mama, why did this have to happen to *my* father?"

"Baby, I don't know." I knew, but would not say. I also knew there were worse things that could have happened to him. I reasoned the tragedy was the result of divine retribution. I understood punishment for going against righteousness.

"Mama, he's a smart man. He's too intelligent to be homeless." Eileen continued to cry.

"That's not his only problem, though. We won't talk about the unfaithfulness in his marriages. Yes he is a smart man. He should have been a millionaire. But from what I remember, his major problem had to do with alcohol and drugs. I walked down that road with him once. It's a problem for all of us, especially for our men. I know deep down inside of him there's a good man who wants to do the right thing. But there's a beast of some kind he fights with, whose winning all the time. So don't give up on him. Maybe you can help.

"Help?"

"You want to, don't you?"

"Mama, I don't know what to do. I want him to give me away at my wedding."

"What wedding?"

I stepped into the bathtub and immediately rested my head against the soft air pillow that awaited me, then closed my eyes...Lord, if only you knew how important Barry was to us you would help him, I know you would. He's done some pretty fucked up things in the past but this is the nineties Lord, and I have forgiven him. He's old, Lord. Please show him some mercy. I'll finish this prayer at bedtime. Right now I have to figure out how I'm going to pay for another wedding that might not take place. Lord, would she actually put me through that again? I really don't want to think about a wedding right now. It'll take a miracle for Barry to walk Eileen down the isle anyway.

Three days passed before I realized what day it was. My steady flow of energy and focus was directed at designing the classy western shirts I wanted to take to Scottsdale. I waned them to be different. That called for total concentration, and with Teddy gone nothing kept me from working. Except the phone call I got from Maurice.

"Yes, this is Sasha."
"Hi. This is Maurice. The man you met at the mall."
"Oh, hello, Maurice. I remember who you are."
"What are you doing? No, that's the wrong question. How are you doing?"
"Just fine." I was not going to get excited about the one phone call, yet. "What about yourself?" I asked him.
"Oh, I've been hardly working. I've only put in forty hours this week, and its just Wednesday."
"Do you work that many hours all the time? How many days do you work?"
"I usually end up working more hours and more days than I actually get paid for. But heck, I like what I do."
He enjoyed his work. He was generous with his time. I was thrilled. I could levitate at any time. I was not going to ask about a girlfriend. "Do you like jazz?" I said.
"Jazz? I'm crazy about it. Do you?"
"I like jazz, classical music, R & B and most rap. I guess you could say that I like all kinds of music," I answered with a velvety tone.
"Do you know of any jazz clubs out here? I've only lived in the Antelope Valley a year and I haven't found a place to relax and enjoy good music."
"There are a couple of places out here. One is in Lake Los Angeles, and the other club is not far from where I live."
"Would you like to go out for jazz sometime? And dinner too?"

I didn't mean to set him up. "Well, yes I would like that. It might be nice."

I hoped he did not detect my eagerness to go out with him. He seemed too good to be true. He had most of the qualities important to me, but so did Rod and Zeeke, in the beginning. And there was Eddie, poor Eddie. I made the mistake of falling in love with him, and he hurt me anyway. Just like Barry, who, after twenty plus years, was still capable of inflicting pain. I didn't want to spend any more time working on what could turn out to be another disaster.

Relationships have never worked for me and its probably my fault. My psychotic assignations have brought me no closer to happiness. Why did I give the impression that I might accept an invitation for dinner with Maurice?

I worked on the design of the western shirts until I was completely satisfied. A veil of cigarette smoke filled the room as I finished the single Newport 100 I bought earlier at the liquor store. I refused to buy an entire pack because I knew it would only lead to chain smoking again. A few months ago my doctor warned me against tempting the fate of my delicate recovery from Valley Fever, so I took his advice and quit. One cigarette alone could not kill me, besides, I felt I earned it.

I lazily crushed the smoldering cigarette butt into the ceramic ashtray and it began to quiver. I stabilized the ashtray with my free hand keeping it from dropping to the floor. Exhausted from working all night long, I realized at approximately 4:30 a.m. in the early morning, I was feeling a major earthquake. And I was home alone.

A thundering explosion of glass startled me and I braced myself against the dining room table. The marble statute I had temporarily placed on top of the china cabinet had fallen down and crashed through a glass top table previously holding a potted plant. I wanted to move about the room so I could catch any falling items but became alarmed when my movement was completely uncoordinated. I remembered the earthquake drills I regularly gave my students and immediately dove under the glass top dining room table.

What the heck was I doing under there? I tried to crawl toward the bathroom. The floor shook my knees. When is it going to stop? What was that? Ohhh, Mama's crystal pitcher. Shit. I looked at all the fruit punch and glass I had to clean up. It felt like a six-pointer. O-kay. The shaking and vibrating stopped. And the power was still on. Lord have mercy. Where was the remote? I wondered which channel got the story first. Then I spotted the remote, under the plant.

The initial earthquake lasted about a minute and a half followed by constant after shocks throughout the day. By mid morning all networks had live remote coverage of the ongoing drama that unfolded as a result of the natural catastrophe. I glued myself to the television after several unsuccessful attempts to reach Eileen and Big Teddy. I was unable to make long distance calls from my home.

Eileen finally called before noon with Teddy calling shortly after. I exhaled and finally underwent the task of cleaning up the minor earthquake damage done to the condo.

"Girl, the earthquake threw me out of bed. I was on the floor during most of it."

"I had been up all night sewing and had just poured myself a glass of fruit punch. And I was about to turn the lights out and go to bed. What are we going to order?" I asked Pam.

We had lunch at the Black Angus that had remained open since the quake. It was apparent the action of the quake two days prior had little effect on business at the location we chose to dine at.

"I'll have the shrimp salad."

"Me too," said Pam.

"Did you see what happened to the Santa Monica Freeway? And the 14? Did you come around the back way?"

"The Angeles Crest Highway. Oh, I got a letter from Needa Stream's lawyer. It's going to be another month before her estate goes into probate. They have to wait for a relative whose out of the country right now. They can't do anything without him."

"Oh well, I hope for your sake he brings himself back. Soon."

"Me too! I still wonder why the old 'bag' wanted me there. Oh, guess what! I went to a deaf school with a friend from work last week. Her little brother is deaf and goes to school there. But anyway, I saw the cutest little girl. Sasha, she was sitting at a table with her teacher learning a lesson when she looked up at me with the brightest brown eyes. She gave me the biggest smile you ever wanted to see. She signed 'hello' to me, just like she was waiting for me to come. Sasha, all I could do was smile back at her and somehow I remembered how to wave my hand. Sasha, she was so cute." Pam looked somber as she talked about the little girl.

"Why the look? Was there more?" I knew Pam had more to say.

"That little girl had been abused. Her parents were crack addicts. The mother is white and the father is black. The little angel had these huge shiny natural Shirley Temple curls around her tiny face. They told me she was four years old, but she looked younger than that. She's in foster care now."

"Oh."

"Sasha, I want to help her."

"Pam. Are you ready for something like that? Are you thinking what I think you're thinking?"

"Sasha, I've watched you and Marlene raise your children and quite frankly, I've always been a little jealous."

"Pam, I never knew that."

"An on Mother's Day, no one calls to wish me a happy day."

"I'm sorry. Would you consider adopting a child with special needs?"

"From what I could see, it was not a situation that I *couldn't* handle. She was born deaf with other problems associated with crack baby syndrome, but at the school they say she's made remarkable progress. She was frail and withdrawn when she first started at the school. Protective services removed her from her parent's home when a neighbor reported the child had been left unattended while the mother was out getting high. The baby was screaming her head off all day long until the neighbor finally realized no one was home with the baby. The child's mother had gone out the night before, like she had done so many times before, and left the child unsupervised, with no food. When the welfare workers arrived to rescue the child, its feces had spilled out of the diaper she was wearing and into the crib."

"Where are the parents now? Getting professional help I hope."

"Sasha, I didn't find out all that. But they need to be locked up. So, have you and Maurice gone out yet?"

"Nope. Not yet. This weekend, maybe."

"No more coffee, thank you," Pam smiled at the waitress.

"Have you talked to Teddy since he's been with his dad?"

"Yes, once. He's having a good time. This breather from motherhood has been nice."

"You can invite Maurice over and entertain in peace."

"Yeah, but I want him to take me out first. He wants to take me out this weekend. We want to listen to some jazz together."

"I want you to meet my new friend." Pam said.

"Oh yeah?" Pam I'm happy for you. I mean it. I'm glad you finally allowed someone to speak to you. I was beginning to worry about you."

"Well, you know, Pookie made me lose my confidence in relationships with his bullshit. Sasha, at this point I'd much rather have a dog. They are a lot less trouble and I would not have to worry about it being loyal. I don't mind working on a relationship but I can't do it alone. It's been like playing a game of tennis all by myself. I need a real man who can work with me. When I was with Pookie it felt like I was alone because he was locked up most of the time. I have a vision of myself being comfortable, but there's no man in the picture. Did you like your salad?"

"Yes, it was great. You know, I don't really know if I will ever be patient enough to work on a relationship either."

"Well, Sasha, let's go. Do we have time to go to the mall?"

24

The postcard Paulette mailed me from Greece came was a complete surprise. She was on 'holiday' with her new lover and was enjoying topless sunbathing and other nefarious delights. An airline stewardess by profession, Paulette's new love spent much of her time on the golf course 'chasing those little white balls.' They were due to return home in a few days after stopping in London to see Big Ben. I hoped Paulette would be able to come and spend a weekend with the children when I go to the horse show in Scottsdale.

Eileen had been talking constantly about J.T. and how she was in love again. Hints about a wedding kept coming up in conversations I had with her, so I began to take the comments seriously. I knew I would need help with things, and Paulette would be there if I needed her.

I moved mountains while Teddy was away, but the three weeks flew by so fast. In that time there had been a major earthquake that city officials were unprepared for, and there was the question of whether or not I wanted to begin another relationship, this time with a Maurice. So far, he met minimum standards. He appeared to be a decent man with a secure job that he liked. One thing I failed to do when Teddy was away was to go out with Maurice. I made excuses not to see him. I knew he thought I was crazy. The first excuse I gave him was that I was sewing and couldn't get away.

That was Friday. My excuse for Saturday night was flaky too. Actually, it was an outright lie. The revival I told him I was going to left town two weeks before. And after lying to him I felt like scum. Teddy came home, which *was* the truth, and I had promised Maurice I would go out with him to Mr. B's to listen to a jazz band. How was I to know Teddy would be back sooner instead of the original date? I couldn't just go out, and leave my son on his first night back. But I really *did* want to go out with him. My excuse sounded so lame. Maurice got quiet. He sat on the other end of the phone and said nothing. The icy jolt I felt and his muteness made me shudder. Then he very calmly said, "Call me when you have time."

When Maurice said that to me he pressed the 'off' button on his cordless phone to disconnect the call. He placed the receiver in an upright position on his nightstand. He took in a long deep breath of air and blew it out, disturbing the hair in his moustache. He ran his fingers through his thick hair then fell back on the pillows he had neatly arranged on his king-sized waterbed.

Why is she acting like this? I thought she wanted to go out with me. Shit, man, what next? Things are not going well. What did I say to her? I didn't say anything about my ex-wife, except that I had just sent her some money for my kids. I didn't brag about my kids even though I wanted to. I let her brag about her own kids. I even told her I would like to meet her son. I casually mentioned that my '64 Mustang was in the shop. She didn't need to know that it's a classic that's probably worth more than the car she drove. She doesn't know that my other car is a late model Volvo. Did I mention that I play golf? Maybe she thinks I'm boring. This is so crazy. I've never missed a child support payment. Never been late, not even once. I bought this condo so she could keep my house for the kids. I wish I knew what women wanted. Shit, they don't know what they want. I thought they liked roses. I thought she liked roses. Well, that's what her son told me. He said that if I gave her roses, she would like me. I can't let her know that I've been sending the roses. It would spoil the surprise. I'll see Teddy at the Community Center this week. I swore him to secrecy about his mom. She's so beautiful. Teddy was so cool when I saw them at the mall. She had no idea I already knew who they were. She doesn't even know I'm her neighbor. I feel like a rouge. Fuck it. She gets more roses. Tomorrow.

"Deon asked me about you," Jennifer said.
"Deon? What did he want to know about me?" I asked.
"If you had a boyfriend and if you were going to Scottsdale. He was out here last week when you were off."

"Oh. Well, my plate's kind of full right now. He waited too long to ask about me. I met someone new. His name is Maurice."

"Have you been out with him?"

"Nope. Not yet."

"Why not, Sasha? You need a boyfriend. I told Deon I'd put in a good word for him, but if you like someone else I'll just keep my mouth shut."

"Deon is good looking and all, but I think he might be a little arrogant. He's a lawyer. No. Let me restate that. He's a black lawyer. I don't trust legal men to begin with. I hate to say it, but an educated black man with a job is hard to hold on to sometimes. My first husband was well educated, but he wasn't smart enough to hold on to his family."

"Hmm."

"When I was eighteen and went away to a black college, there were all those guys who were full of themselves, just waiting to take advantage of someone immature like me."

"Well, I think Deon is a nice black man."

"Of course you do."

"I'll be right back. I'm going to the office to get a soda. You want one?"

"Sure do. Thanks."

She's a very sweet girl, I thought, but she doesn't know black men at all. She's probably never seen a black man in action, and I'm not giving her the opportunity either. Just because they look benign and present a fine image, black men don't always choose to go through the really tough times with a sister. Jett was there for me, though. He was an exceptionally good man. And he didn't find it necessary to be arrogant, either. He stuck by me when I was having problems with my mother, God rest her soul. Then he died. Why did he have to die? I might have been happy today instead of feeling so confused all the time. Jennifer must have run up to that office.

"I hope a root beer is all right. G.R. took the last Coke. He wants to know when we're leaving for Scottsdale. He and Dora and José are leaving this weekend."

"Dora's back?"

"Yep. She got back last night."

"I'm glad. G.R. needs to get laid. He had that needy look in his eye when I saw him last," I laughed after the comment. "What did you tell him?"

"About what?"

"Didn't you just tell me he wanted to know when we are leaving for the horse show?"

"Oh, I'm sorry. I was thinking about something else. I told him next weekend. Was that all right?"

"Oh yes, that was all right. Come on, let's finish cleaning these saddles." I handed Jennifer a saddle brush.

"Sasha, don't you miss your real work? I mean, you're a designer, for Christ's sake! Why are you doing this crap?"

"Crap this is not, my dear. Caring for horses has been therapeutic for me. I was a workaholic in the design business and it nearly killed me. I do miss it though."

"Sasha, I have a feeling that you will go back to it. And you'll get more out of it next time. Did I tell you I saw that eagle again?"

"No. And you know what Jennifer? I had the strangest feeling last night. I had a brush with Cindy, my friend from design school. It felt like she was close by, and I wanted to talk to her, but for some reason, I couldn't say anything. My mouth wouldn't move."

"Was it a dream?"

"Well, not quite. I was just laying there in my bed, on my way to sleep when I felt something touch me. I opened my eyes for a second or two and when I closed them, Cindy was walking away, looking back at me. I couldn't move my lips at all."

"I don't know. That's pretty strange. When did you talk to her last?"

"It's been over twenty years. I have no idea where she is. I would love to find her. Just to say 'hello'.

When I walked into my kitchen and put my keys down on the counter, I could smell the scent of freshly cut flowers. I followed the heavy essence of fragrant herbs through the kitchen and into the dining room where I found a stunning bouquet of roses, this time pink with baby's breath. The flowers were sitting on the dining room table. I lifted the small white envelope carefully perched in the arrangement and opened it to reveal a note that read 'To Sasha with love from your secret admirer'.

"Paulette, Teddy said they were on the doorstep when he came home from school. He put them in the dining room where he puts all the flowers that come. It's so eerie. It's like being stalked."

"Well, at least the stalker had good taste."

"That's not funny but they are lovely, like all the others. So, are you coming this weekend?"

"Yes, I'll be there. Teddy and I will have a great time while you're in Scottsdale. Eileen and I can work on a guest list in case she decides to go ahead and jump the broom. I'll be there before you leave."

"Thanks, girl. There's a dance at the community center this weekend and Teddy wants to go. I told him you would take him. Would you?"

"Yeah, it will be fun. Sasha, I've got some pictures we took on a nude beach in France." Paulette started giggling.

"You're so scandalous!"

"I know."

"But you know I love you anyway."

"I know."

"I'll see you this weekend. I gotta go now so I can call Eileen. She called me today when I was at the ranch. I listened to my messages just before you called."

"Is she really serious about getting married?"

"Yes, and I can't stop her. I wish she would wait."

"Sasha, you've wanted her to wait forever. She probably doesn't know why she should wait. Wait for what?"

"How the hell should I know?"

"Tell Teddy I have something for him. I bought him some Legos."

"O-kay, o-kay. I gotta go. Shit! I forgot to pick Teddy up. He's at the community center. See ya!"

Teddy stood in front of the brand new community center contemplating, wondering if I had forgotten to pick him up. Maurice had already gone, having volunteered his time and services for the evening. Teddy wondered if he should tell me the secret he had kept for months. That

Maurice was not the stranger I thought he was. That he was actually Teddy's basketball coach, who for months, had wanted to take me out on a date. He was torn between the loyalty to me and the friendship he had with Maurice. He wanted to tell me where the ardent flow of roses was coming from since lately I had been in fear of being ambushed by the sender. He did not want me to feel frightened any longer. Maurice's unwavering interest in me was beginning to make him feel uneasy as well.

Teddy looked up to see me swerve into the partially full parking lot. I stopped the car right in front of Teddy, then rolled my window down.

"Have you been waiting long?"

"No, just a few minutes." Teddy walked around to the passenger side of the car. As he climbed into the car he once again thought about the secret. "Did you like the flowers that came today?"

"Yes, they were gorgeous. Were you home when they came?"

"No, they were on the front porch when I got home from school. So I just took them inside and put them in the dining room. Mom, can we go to Taco Bell? I'm hungry."

"Sure. I don't feel like cooking anyway. And I have to call Eileen back. Baby, I'm sorry I was late. I was on the phone with Paulette. She'll be here in a few days and she's going to take you to the dance this weekend."

Since Teddy noticed I didn't seem too upset about receiving the flowers, he decided not to tell me who was sending them. He silently hoped he would never be as shy as Maurice was. It just didn't seem right to him.

I was relieved to be off the hook for dinner. Teddy ordered two tacos and two burritos from Taco Bell. I gave a five dollar bill to the teenage Hispanic girl in the drive-thru window and thanked her when I got my change and food. I was eager to get home to call Eileen and take my bubble bath. After the phone call to her, I just wanted to relax.

"When are you leaving for the horse show?" asked Eileen.
"Friday. Paulette's going to be here before I leave town. Are you coming up this weekend?"
"I don't know yet. J.T. is supposed to get my ring this weekend and I kind of want to be around. Mom, I've decided to move in with him."
"Oh, you have?"
"Yep. He wants me to be with him now, before we get married. After I graduate this semester, we want to get married."
"This summer?" I was surprised. At least they had plans.
"I think so, but we don't have a date set."
"Mom, my dad called me today. He's finally getting some help. He's in rehab."
"What?"
"Yes. I guess he decided to get some help after I talked to him last month. I made him feel really bad."
"How long will he be there?"
"As long as it takes, Mom."
"I'm happy."
"Me too. What are you doing tonight?"
"Not much. I'm going to go through my closet and make a final decision about what I'm taking with me this weekend. Then I'm going to run some nice warm water for a

bubbly strawberry bath. I think I'll put some Epsom salt in too. And if I have no more interruptions tonight, I just might be able to enjoy my bath. I think I'll float some petals from the flowers that came today. Yeah, they'll look pretty on the water with the bubbles."

"You got more roses?"

"Yes, and I feel like I'm being stalked. I love the roses but I wish I knew who they were from. I'm confused right now. I really like this man I just met. His name is Maurice."

"Where did you meet him? Have you gone out with him yet?"

"At the mall. No, not yet. I'm not sure if I want to go out with him. I'm tired. When you're in your forties you don't get all excited about a date. You just get up in the morning, do your job for the day, whatever it may be, and you hope you have enough money left after you pay your bills to do something nice for yourself. Like getting your nails done and your hair braided. Like I'm doing tomorrow."

"Mom, is he nice?"

"Yes."

"Does he work?"

"Yes, on a job he's had a very long time. He's divorced."

"Who isn't?"

"I know that's right."

"Mom, he's probably just lonely, like you are sometimes."

"That's the scary part. I'll go out with him eventually, and he'll probably make me feel good and then I'll begin to want to get close and quite frankly, I don't want that right now. I don't want to get hurt again. Or be disappointed. In the last four years I became involved with men I really cared about and it got me nowhere. Where are they now?"

"Well, one's in heaven. Mom just go out with him once. And have fun."

I sank deep into foamy lavender suds I chose over the strawberry bubbles. For a moment, I thought I was in heaven but I came back to the reality of my sometimes unpredictable life. I wondered why in the hell I was going to a horse show when I should be studying the classifieds this weekend and concentrating on a real career as a designer.

I really must be losing my mind. Why can't I just take a simple bath and not worry about this stuff? I'm getting my hair braided tomorrow. Hopefully I'll get a lift from that. I'm going to try this new wrap style. Nine hours in one spot. Gosh, I sure go through a lot to be beautiful. Oh well, it's worth it. This is enough soaking.

I pulled a peach satin chemise on over my head and allowed it to slide onto my body. I misted my neck and collarbone with a spray of Knowing cologne. My thoughts then turned to Maurice as I turned back the covers on my bed. Who was I kidding? It would only be a matter of time.

I realized that even at my age, I was still a very sexual woman fully capable of having feelings of passion for another human being. They were the same feelings most single people have even though they may say they are happy to be living alone. I began to understand the loneliness and desperation Eddie must have felt after his wife died. I felt the same way after my divorce to Big Teddy. He had been my bed warmer for years, then suddenly it was up to me to keep my own bed warm. At one point I bought an electric blanket to keep me warm and realized there was nothing like real flesh.

I felt I had blown it with Maurice whose attitude chilled with our last conversation. I crawled between the red percale sheets on my bed and pulled the matching comforter up to my chin. When I felt secure I turned off the Tiffany lamp on my night stand and fell asleep.

"Paulette, these are some scandalous pictures. Was everybody naked? I asked as my mouth dropped open.

"It's a nude beach Sasha. They have those on the Mediterranean. So what time are you guys leaving?"

"Jennifer is supposed to be here by 7 a.m. If she's on time, we'll be there way before dark. Paulette, I'm so glad you're here. I don't know what I'm doing these days. I feel like I'm stuck and running in place most days."

"I'm glad I'm here too. Who were the roses from?"

"I don't know. That's one of the problems. They keep coming with a note signed by a 'secret admirer'. And then there's Maurice.

"Who's he?"

"Someone I like, but he doesn't know. Paulette, these are some great pictures. Your friend is not bad looking." I gave the pictures back to Paulette.

"She's real sweet, Sasha."

"Well, I hope you two are happy."

"What are you and Jennifer planning to do in Scottsdale after you show the horses?"

25

Scottsdale, Arizona, known as mecca for Arabian horses is home to the most celebrated champions in the world. Although I had heard about the horse show from G.R. I was surprised by the large number of Arabian horse enthusiasts assembled at Westworld from over forty states and five nations. It was the place where horses, riders and trainers competed for ribbons and championships from Scottsdale, that meant so much to their collections. Thousands of people, commercial exhibitors, their families and friends, support crews and spectators made the annual trek to the Arabian horse show.

"My God, Jennifer, look at all these people! I had no idea it was like this!" Some of those cowboys actually looked good.

"I told you it was *big*. Shaun was upset he couldn't get off this weekend so he could come. We both came last year. I'm kinda glad to have this weekend to myself. I needed some space."

We worked our way through a tightly packed crowd only to realize the event we hoped to see had concluded its afternoon session. We got close enough to put both hands on the railing that encircled the huge outside arena. I looked at Jennifer who stood beside me.

"Well, we didn't miss that much. There's a whole lot more to see tonight and tomorrow. It's a good thing we checked into the hotel first," said Jennifer, above the noise of the crowd.

We looked for the show barn G.R. had reserved for his horses. We worked our way back through the crowd of people leaving an event. The rental car we traveled in was parked illegally, next to the show office, where we left it in a hurry. Jennifer said it was all right to leave it there as long as we displayed our exhibitor's pass on the windshield. The car was where we parked it. I gave Jennifer the car keys. "You drive. Can you find the G.R.'s barn?"

"Yes. I think I can find it from here."

"That's good, because the directions G.R. gave me are on a much smaller scale than this place actually is."

"I know, it's confusing."

Jennifer unlocked the Tempo and we got into the car. I leaned back in the passenger side. Jennifer started the engine and slowly backed out of the parking space. I was taken by the steady action and rich looking people. Pam should have been there.

I sure hoped Jennifer knew where she was going. The place was like a maze. Just plain crazy. I saw a woman in a full length ranch mink. Shit! You can still buy those?

Her reptile boots let me know she had money. A man walked up behind her in a fur-lined suede jacket. He grabbed her waist, and kissed her. Yes, they were together. A red Mercedes came our way. Were there any black people here?

"Is that Ty?" Jennifer asked. "It sure is."
"In this red car? You know him?"
"Yes."

Jennifer waved at the car and pressed the button that lowered her car window. She put her arm through the window and began waving at the oncoming car. The red Mercedes stopped. The middle-aged gentleman with silver hair was an old family friend. He showed his Arabians every year at Scottsdale.

Ty was on his way to his barn to get one of his horses ready for the evening class and competition. For two consecutive years Ty Koons' Arabians had placed first in the Native Costume Class. He hoped to do it again.

Ty had carefully selected the fine silk and brocade fabrics, tassels and jewels that were used to create unforgettable costumes for the occasion. He beamed with pride and excitement as he talked about the benefits of owning Arabian show horses. He finally stopped talking long enough to acknowledge me. I was looking around, admiring the sights.

"I sure like that hairdo, young lady."
"Oh, thank you," I said, and I smiled at him.
"Ty, this is Sasha Friend, a very good friend of mine. I'm sorry for not introducing you. Sasha, meet Ty," Jennifer said. I felt some relief.

"Did that hairdo take long to do? It's sure pretty," Ty said to me in his Texas drawl.

"About half a day. You have to be very patient." I knew my outrageous western shirts might turn some heads, but I hadn't thought about the reactions my hair style would generate. I loved it.

"When the classes are over tonight, why don't y'all come over to my barn? We're having a little get-together."

We found G.R. at the barn and told him what our plans were for the evening. He offered to buy us dinner nevertheless, but we declined, knowing we wouldn't have time. An event was about to begin and we did not want to miss it. Jennifer said if Ty was having a get-together of any kind, it would be a spread the size of Texas. G.R. would be there too.

The Equidome had its maximum capacity of curious spectators waiting to see the grand parade of beautiful native costumes. One by one the elegantly dressed riders and horses streamed onto the arena floor. I had never seen anything like it, was convinced that the spectacle could never be replicated. Ty was nervous as he sat in the front row next to the arena floor in the section he reserved for his ranch members.

The crowd shrieked as his horse and rider outshined the competition. Once again, he placed first. The performance and win from Ty's barn gave him more reason to want to celebrate.

"Jennifer. Look at your friend Ty. He's fired up!"

"I know. And he'll be drunk tonight."

In addition to the Native Costume display, the Purebred Arabian Pleasure Driving Championship presented showcased the high-stepping flashy elegance of horses pulling customized carriages. I wished the "Duchess' had been part of the formal competition. I thought about my commitment in Scottsdale and why I was involved with horses in the first place. I sat back and enjoyed the remainder of the show.

It was late when we got back to the hotel. Ty kept insisting we stay 'just a while longer' every time we tried to say good-night. Finally he allowed us to leave and we thanked him once more for inviting us to his party.

"Boy, did he get drunk or what!" I wanted to slap him once.

"I told you. He's that way. And he loves to spend his money. He was trying to flirt with you tonight."

"Oh, you noticed. He kept trying to touch my hair. He said the braids made me look like an African queen. I guess he was just being friendly, with his drunk ass. I wouldn't care how much money he had. I can't stand a drunk. I want to take time tomorrow to see what the vendors have for sale. I have to buy souvenirs for the kids. A T-shirt for Teddy, maybe a mug for Eileen. I'm spending *big* this weekend." Jennifer and I laughed.

"Sasha, you won't believe all the stuff you can buy. Those huge tents you asked me about are full of shops. Actually, it looks like a bazaar inside."

"I'm sleepy. It's been a long day. What time does G.R. need us tomorrow?"

"6 a.m."

"Goodnight."

The breaking dawn illuminated the bronze sculpture of three Arabian horses outside the main entrance of Westworld. Once inside the gate, I drove down the long curvy driveway I had driven down the night before. I went past the same row of diesel powered horse trailers parked along the path. It was too dark last night to estimate the grandeur of the customized trailers horse owners used to transport their valued horses to Scottsdale. The horses traveled in comfort. We rode another fifty yards past the horse trailers to the park designated for recreational vehicles. Most owners preferred their mobile homes because they could be close to their horses and minimize the stress on the road.

Behind the RV camp was an open field. Polo matches could be observed from the edge of the field by patrons of the Tavern Restaurant. Early risers were going into the restaurant for their first cup of coffee before heading to show stables. The road took us to a spot where it made a sharp hairpin curve turning us in the opposite direction taking us to a guarded gate. The gray-haired security guard leaned out the door of the small building he was in.

I showed him our exhibitor's pass and he let us enter the highly secured section of the park. We drove past the information center where we had parked last night, just a few hours ago. Ty's party kept us out much later than we planned.

We stayed on the twisting road that took us past beautifully decorated stables. The facade of each barn had its own theme of attraction, and proudly displayed winning ribbons from previous shows. The curious were allowed inquiry within each barn. The daylight showed a well organized chaos I couldn't grasp the night before. We drove slowly past several grooms leading their horses to a centrally located bathing rack. I spotted G.R.'s barn, sitting directly in front of a bathing area, as he requested.

I parked the rental car near the show barn leaving ample room on either side of the car for easy access with horses. "Is this okay?" I asked. I knew it was.

"Yep, this is fine. There's plenty of room on both sides. G.R.'s not even here yet. Let's go get some coffee. We have time," said Jennifer.

"Yeah, I could sure use a cup. I wonder if they make lattés here?"

"There's coffee and pastries at the information center," Jennifer said. "But I don't know about lattés."

I backed the car away from the barn, just enough to make a U-turn. I drove the car backward in the direction of the Information Center, where we parked, in front of the small white building. In desperate need of caffeine, we quickly walked inside.

"Good morning! You gals are up early! Grooming this morning?" The plump blonde middle aged receptionist in the compact headquarters was wide awake and knew why Jennifer and I were there. It was too damn early to be that cheerful.

"Hello." Jennifer forced a smile with the greeting. She was thinking about the all day drive the day before, the party the night before and the fact that we were up at dawn to groom G.R.'s horses, with only four hours of sleep. Oh, what the hell. The woman who greeted us was wearing a brightly colored vest with an unusual desert landscape pattern. I liked the intricate labor that went into the construction of the garment. Each saguaro cactus on the fabric was outlined with hand sewn jewels that sparkled subtly with every move she made with her full body.

"What a fabulous vest!" I was wide awake now. Something was familiar about it.

"Oh, thank you so much. I bought it last night. It was so pretty, I felt I had to wear it right away!"

I leaned toward the woman to get a closer look, reached out to touch the lower front edge to feel the texture of the fabric. She allowed me to inspect it more closely.

"I bought it at the bazaar," she said. This girl had some pretty things she made herself. Her booth is in the tent that's on the other side of the indoor arena. You have to go up the stairs and come down on the other side. Then you can get in. The pastries just arrived so you gals help yourself. I have CAF or decaf coffee over there." She pointed to a small table behind me.

"Jennifer, when we finish working this morning, I want to shop."

"Well, Sasha, you know Dora wants to cook lunch for us today in the RV."

"Well, after lunch, for sure." I can't wait to see all they have.

We actually ate lunch around 2 p.m. because Dora insisted on cooking a major feast. She had been cooped up in the RV for two weeks and wanted to entertain. She cooked Indonesian curried chicken and coconut yams. Jennifer and I debated having second helpings for fear of total collapse due to lack of sleep but ended up yielding to

Dora's delectable cuisine a second time. After lunch, it was back to the stable where more horses were waiting to be groomed.

As the day progressed, I started to think about home, my children, and Maurice. I wished they were with me so they could see what I would tell them about. I wanted to call Paulette to ask if Maurice had called. When we returned to the hotel Saturday evening after the halter class competition, we stretched out on our hotel beds and fell asleep, not waking up until Sunday morning. We slept very soundly, fully clothed.

At 9:30 a.m. Sunday morning the hotel phone pierced a chilling ring into my ear. I immediately opened my eyes to see the phone vibrate with a second ring. I grabbed the receiver of the telephone and answered, in a barely audible growl, "Hello."

"Hi, Mom." It was Teddy.

"Oh, hi baby. Geez, it's early. What time is it?"

"9:30. When are you coming home?"

"Oh, tonight probably. But I won't know exactly what time. I won't know until I see G.R. later on."

"Did you buy me something?"

The souvenirs! Shit! I haven't even had a chance to shop yet. I've barely gotten any sleep.. "No, baby, not yet, but I'll do it today. promise. Where's Eileen and Paulette?"

"They went to the store. Aunt Paulette wants to make enchiladas today. Mom, she thinks her enchiladas are better than yours. Ha, ha, ha!"

"Be nice."

"Okay."

"Did anyone call me this weekend?"

"Yep."

"Who?"

"Maurice."

I grinned from ear to ear when Teddy said Maurice's name. He had not forgotten about me. Maybe we have a date with destiny. "I'll see you later ."

I stood at the bottom of the loading ramp, firmly holding the lead line that was attached to the 'Duchess'. She was the last horse to be loaded onto the diesel drawn trailer. G.R. motioned for me to walk the horse up the ramp.

"Easy," I said to the 'Duchess'. I stepped on the ramp and the Duchess walked with me. Once the Duchess was in the bay of the trailer, G.R. backed her into an empty stall. It was then secured shut.

"Good girl," I said, then patted the Duchess on her head. "I'm going shopping. It's now or never." If I didn't go to the huge tent now, there would be hell to pay. I had to buy Teddy's souvenir. "Jennifer, are you coming?"

"Of course I'm coming."

We walked down the last flight of stairs that led to the entrance of the huge vendor tent. With Jennifer close behind, I eased into the herd of last minute shoppers. Everyone knew it was the last opportunity to get gifts and mementos of the two week horse show. I stopped at a counter where I spotted beautifully hand crafted gold jewelry. The one of a kind creations drew me closer to the display. I knew I couldn't afford anything but inquired anyway.

"May I see that one, please?" I pointed to a 24 carat gold bracelet made of connecting Arabian horse heads.

"Of course you may." The dark haired young woman behind the glass counter smiled as she reached to her wrist for a dangling key that opened the case. I extended an arm so she could put the bracelet on me.

"Jennifer, have you ever seen anything so beautiful?" I tried to sound rich.

"Yes. Look at that ring!"

"Would you like to see it?" the clerk asked.

"Yes, I would. Thank you," said Jennifer.

I noticed the $1,100.00 price tag on the amethyst and diamond ring Jennifer was trying on. I checked the price of the horse bracelet.

"Oh, that's *all*?" It was $1,275.00. "Thanks for sharing." We gave her the jewelry back and moved on.

"Look, Jennifer. There are the tee-shirts! I have to get Teddy a tee-shirt." I know I can afford that.

A few booths down the counter was a merchant who sold Scottsdale sweats, sweatshirts and tee-shirts. I was happy to see there was much to choose from, in my price range. I fumbled through piles of sweat shirts on a table in the center of the Tee shop. I could not find the size I wanted so I moved to a shelf where tees were stuffed into labeled cubicles. At that moment a red headed clerk in a cowboy hat appeared wearing tight-fitting jeans, a long-sleeved white silk blouse, and a striking vest that resembled the one I had seen on the show clerk the day before. I made my selections and took the shirts to the smiling cashier.

"Will that be all for you today?" she asked.

"Yes, and where did you find that vest?" I knew the question was rude, but I stood behind the intuition that made me ask it. Shaquita. Just when the clerk said 'next door', I made eye contact with a woman in the booth next door. Our eyes locked.

She looked like Cindy. No, it couldn't be. Vests. That's the *vest* shop. Next to a T-shirt shop. Made them herself. Blond girl. Used to live in California. I replayed the voice of the show office clerk over and over. She's beginning to smile. My God. Is that Cindy?. She's staring back at me. Does she know who I am?

"Sasha, what's the matter?" Jennifer nudged my arm with her elbow.

It *was* Cindy, and we lunged to each other. We held on tightly until a customer interrupted the euphoric reunion. There was pure joy in the small booth where fancy vests were sold. Where had she been all these years?

Cindy confessed that if it were not for my unforgettable smile, she might not have recognized me. She stroked my hair and said she wanted to wear her hair the same way, for years now. She's white though. and knew it would cause problems.

Vendors all around us were closing their temporary shops and preparing to go home. For Cindy, home was in Missouri for the moment. Her husband passed away five years ago and she had been with her family ever since. It was impossible for us to visit like we wanted to so we exchanged telephone numbers and promised to stay in touch.

26

Maurice was not the only person who called when I was in Arizona. I sifted through phone messages to find notes from Marlene and Pam. Paulette and Eileen managed to put together a tentative guest list for a medium sized wedding. Eileen was just going to mail out seventy five invitations this time. Paulette agreed to stay a few days longer to finish the list. Her new lover was at her house in Oakland and she promised Paulette she would water the plants while she was away.

"Sasha, I talked to this Maurice guy. You know, he's real nice. At least, he sounds that way on the phone," Paulette plopped down on my bed.
"Yeah, and I thought about him the whole time I was in Scottsdale."
"Why don't you call him?"
"Call him? I just got back. I'll return his call tomorrow."
"Return his call. Return his call. You sound so formal!"

"Do I really?"
"Yes you do. Sasha, lighten up some. Call the man."
"Okay. Tomorrow."

I stared at the telephone while talking to Marlene. She decided to go home to Dennis. The news of it was a complete surprise, although anticipated.

I was glad Marlene made her decision to take her ass home to Dennis. I didn't trust that Jamaican, anyway. I guess Dennis decided it would cost him less if he forgave and took her back. He's smarter than I thought. Even though there was no proof, he probably had an affair, too. Marlene said he was willing to forget the past, but I know damn well that won't be the case. People don't always find it easy to forget. And Marlene knew she missed the luxury associated with being Dennis' wife. She hadn't shopped as much lately and all of a sudden, the Jamaican got cheap. She said she would rent the condo out for now, but eventually sell it. Or she would let one of the twins have it. Oh well, I can stop worrying about Marlene now. That makes me happy.

Paulette went home three days after I returned from Scottsdale. Before she left town though, she made me call Maurice. And when I called, his answering machine was on. Caught off guard, I left a jumbled message sounding silly in nature. I was feeling stupid when I hung up the phone.

"Pam, have you ever thought about adoption? I mean, seriously thought about it?"

"No, I haven't. Boy, you've been thinking about this a lot lately." I said to Pam, in a worrisome tone.

"I know. All I've been thinking about is that sweet child I met a few weeks ago."

"Have you seen her again?"

"Yeah. Yesterday I went to the Deaf School. I saw her, again."

"Did she see you?"

"Yes she did. And she ran to me and hugged my legs when she saw me."

"Oh, Pam." I sensed a change of tone in Pam's voice.

"Pookie called me."

"From where?"

"Sasha, he's locked up again."

"Oh, well. Well, where's the bitch he was with?"

"She's locked up too."

"What? To hell with *her*. What's *he* in for?"

"A violation of parole." Pam started crying. "Sasha, I still love him."

"I know, I know." I couldn't think of anything warmer to say to my friend.

"Sasha, what's wrong with me? Why do I fall for men that are always no good for me?"

"You're not the only one." A picture of Eddie's face flashed before my eyes, as well as Barry's. I didn't want to think about all the other faces in between. "I don't think anything's wrong with you. It's always hard to tell what a man's going to be like after you meet him. In the beginning things always seem great, Pam. Then there's the bombshell, but it's usually too late because you're already hooked. It's *not* you. Any remember this. The men we want, you know, the ones our age who have good jobs?

Well, they don't always want women like us who are independent. Pam, are you still there?"

"Yes. I'm still here."

"Sorry about the lecture. You and I both have fallen in love with men who were different. Why we continue to take the abuse is beyond comprehension. It's okay to acknowledge the fact that Pookie still loves you but as long as he's locked up he can do nothing about his love. I don't think he would call you if he didn't care about you. You can't let him hurt you from inside."

"Hold on, Sasha."

I could hear Pam blowing her nose in the background.

"I'm sorry. Did you find a billionaire when you were in Scottsdale?" Between tears, Pam managed to chuckle.

"Everybody looked rich, but I did run into someone. Do you remember Cindy, from fashion design school? I used to talk about her a lot, remember?"

"That white girl you were friends with?"

"Yes."

"Does she still live on a boat?"

"I don't think so. She said she lost her husband years ago and now she's living in Missouri. I sure was happy to see her. In a way, seeing her gave me hope. Is still want to manufacture but I don't have the money it takes."

"Oh, you'll do it someday. And I want to be a mom, and someday I will."

"I know you will. Oh, have you talked to your lawyer about the will?"

"He said he was going to call me next week. It's taking forever, but I know what I want to do with my life. When is Eileen getting married?"

"Your guess is as good as mine. Sometime this Spring, I think."

2 months later

How am I going to pay for all this shit? Two graduations and a wedding. I'm afraid to put the stamps on these invitations. If I do, I know I'll mail them. But I know I can't wait forever. Yoshi said my royalty check was in the mail, but where is it? I'm glad Eileen's coworkers at the station are planning a bridal shower for her. But those are people from her job. Pam and I will have to give her some kind of party so I can invite my friends. It can be a lingerie bridal party. A girl can never have too much lingerie. Yeah. That's what I'll do.

It felt like everything was going to work out after all. I added up the cost of everything involved in having a decent wedding. I was painfully happy to know I would be able to pay my portion of the expenses. The C.D.'s I purchased years ago when I had money finally matured and were ready to be used. My dad had money I didn't know about and offered to pay for the honeymoon in Can Cun, for his granddaughter and her new husband. J.T.'s parents offered to pay for everything associated with the reception and the rehearsal dinner. Their close friends owned a catering business with a reputation for having the finest Cajun cuisine in the Southland. I had prayed that everyone would do as they promised and be in place on time. That included Eileen, the star of the show.

"What time are you guys going to be here? I still need to go to the fabric store."

"Kai is on her way now. I'll call you when we're about to leave." Eileen said.

I wanted to go to the fabric store before Kai and Eileen arrived. It was the final fitting for the bridesmaid gown Kai was wearing in the wedding. Kai wanted the bronze off the shoulder chiffon evening dress to fit her the same way Jasmine's fit. The length of the above the knee bouffant dress was fine but I needed to alter the waist in the dress. Since the last fitting, Kai had lost some weight. Her new exercise routine had finally worked and begun to pay off. Jasmine's dress fit fine. There was no need to make further changes on it. Making dresses for the twins was a relatively simple chore since both dresses were made exactly the same way.

"Marlene, is Jasmine with you?" I had just finished the fittings.

"She sure is. You should see her. She's dressed like a hootchie. I'm wearing a suit. The aqua suit you designed for me."

"Eileen and Kai look like hootchies too. They must have planned it. Don't worry. Pam and I are going to be conservative, like you. The girls are still young. They can walk on the wild side, besides, they will be with us."

"The black dress Jasmine is wearing looks like it was painted on. And those spiked heels! She looks cute, though."

"Well, Eileen told me they wanted to dress that way tonight, since it was just the girls."

"Do they know where we're going?" asked Marlene.

"No. I told them we were going to meet you and Jasmine, then go have dinner and drinks. It will be girl's night out before the wedding next week. Pam's already here."

"Girl, Eileen's going to die. I can't wait to see the expression on her face."

"Hey, the pizza delivery man is here. As soon as I pay for Teddy's pizza, we'll be on our way."

"Okay, we'll see you at 'Harold and Belle's', in about an hour."

I looked at my watch at 11 p.m. Eileen reluctantly agreed to wear the blindfold when we left the restaurant, riding with Kai and I to the next location. Marlene and Jasmine followed us in the Jag. I led the two car caravan on a quiet route to the night club we had only heard about. I spotted the well-known marquee.

"There it is," I said, pointing ahead.

"Can I take this blindfold off? It's beginning to itch." Eileen pinched the long piece of soft black fabric covering her eyes and tried to adjust it.

"No, you have to wait. Just a few more minutes."

"Mom!" Eileen whined.

Still blindfolded, Jasmine and Kai escorted Eileen into the nightclub. She removed the blindfold.

"Surprise!" Jasmine and Kai uniformly hailed.

"Where am I?" asked Eileen, fully surprised. The loud music gave her a hint.

"You'll see. In about five minutes," and Jasmine.

Thankfully, it did not take long for our party to be seated. Tiger's was packed, but Marlene saw two small empty tables close to an elevated platform, the stage.

There was no band or disc jockey on the platform. Just a bathtub, filled with milk. This was male entertainment at its finest.

A strong beam of white light filtered through smoky air hanging over the stage. Suddenly, the beam of light focused on a tall buff black man wearing a white terry cloth bathrobe. The long belt on the robe was tightly pulled around his slim waist and revealed a bulge underneath, the focal point of his routine. He held a crystal bowl full of Oreo cookies he placed on a small pedestal which sat next to the bathtub. As the beat and volume of the music increased, he began a slow, seductive stripping of his attire.

The stripper untied his robe belt and slowly pulled it through booth belt loops. When the belt was free, he picked up the other end of it with his free hand, holding it like a jump rope. He then stepped down from the stage and walked directly to the second row of tables where a boisterous twentyish woman had been screaming her head off since he first appeared. I wondered what the woman planned to do when he removed his robe.

Pam and I watched intensely as the man draped the belt around the neck of the young woman and allowed it to fall in her lap. The woman's body vibrated when he extended his arms outward. He allowed her a peek at his covered bulge and sculptured six-pack stomach underneath his robe. He closed his robe quickly then turned his body around and went back to the stage. The howling crowd went berserk when he finally removed the bathrobe. The females in the club roared. He posed for the audience for a brief moment, then turned his back to the screeching crowd and revealed a tight perfectly shaped buttock divided by a chocolate colored g-string. He looked naked. I wished for five minutes alone with the beautiful man.

He motioned for the woman to bring him the belt. She stumbled on to the stage, weary from excitement. The stripper performed an air-back flip, and took the belt then offered her an Oreo cookie. He bumped and grinded his luscious body and stepped into the milk filled bathtub. He sat down in the tub, submerged his body to his chin then quickly stood up, allowing milk streams to cascade down his magnificent onyx body. He reached for a cookie, dipped it in the milk bath and shoved it in his mouth. The exalted woman did the same thing, then put dollar bills in his front pouch. After that, one by one, women from all categories approached the stage. Pam and I sat in amazement when all three girls left our table and joined in the fun. Marlene laughed, and took another sip of her drink. The girls helped themselves to cookies and gave the stripper a tip.

Freak Daddy provided the ultimate kick start entertainment for the evening. His bizarre characterization of a freak on a picnic brought the house down.

Clad in leather with chains and handcuffs dangling from his clothes, he came onto the stage with a gingham checked blanket that he immediately spread on the floor. He brought his picnic basket and his date, an inflated doll.

His body moved erotically with each beat of the music as he began to peel off his clothes. Partially clad in skin tight black leather pants, he caressed and fondled the doll, as if it were a real person. He laid the life-sized doll on the blanket and stroked it's body repeatedly. Marlene had been pretty quiet until now, but sat up straight when

Freak Daddy kissed the inflated doll between its legs. He opened the straw picnic basket and removed a small tub of whipped cream. He used his hand to scoop up the sweet creamy contents then rubbed it all over the body part he had just kissed. The women in the crowd rose to their feet shouting fervent squeals of approval as he used his tongue to lavishly lick away all traces of the whipping cream. By the time he finished his act, Marlene was on the stage, putting money in the strap of the g-string Freak Daddy was wearing. No one could stop Marlene once she had two drinks in her. Pam and I cheered her on.

"Is this what you have to look forward to in the nineties when you get married?" I said to Pam.

"Sasha, I don't know. But it is pretty hilarious."

"J.T. would be very upset with me if he knew I brought Eileen here."

"He'll never hear it from me. Eileen is having a great time," Pam replied.

"Yeah, yea. Too good. Let's get these hootchies out of here."

Keeping Maurice at bay was becoming a game to me. I continued to make excuses not to see him, knowing I had no real interest in him any more, but still believed in miracles. And would probably develop a new interest in him.

Teddy decided one day that he was not going to keep silent about the unsolicited flowers that had been coming. The flowers had stopped coming, and Teddy noticed that I was much calmer than I had been in months.

"Mom."

"What, honey."

"There's something I have to tell you."

"Oh, yeah?"

"Yeah. Something has been going on for a long time. Do you still talk to Maurice?"

I wondered what Maurice had to do with the conversation. Teddy looked dead serious and did not change his facial expression.

"You never figured out who the roses came from, right?"

"Right. You know, I haven't gotten any lately."

"Mom, I know who sent them."

"What! You knew and you didn't tell me?"

"No, because you liked flowers. I like it when you're happy."

"Who sent the flowers?"

"You're not going to believe me."

"Who?" I demanded in a nice way to know.

"Maurice." Teddy lowered his head after saying Maurice's name.

I dropped a fork in my lap when I heard the shocking revelation. I thought my son was playing a silly game with me.

"You're joking, right?"

"No, Mom. But you're really not going to believe me."

"Try me, honey." But that explained Maurice's strange behavior lately. And the flowers not coming anymore. Maurice had not called as much. He actually stopped calling, but I didn't notice because I had been busy with other things. I was so disturbed I could barely eat another bite of lasagna. I placed my fork on the table. I looked at Teddy. "Is there more?"

Teddy nodded his head slightly while chewing his last mouthful of food pointing to his bulging closed mouth, indicating his inability to speak. After a hefty swallow he wiped lasagna sauce from the corner of his mouth with a folded paper towel.

"No, that's all." Teddy was not ready to tell me that Maurice had replaced his original basketball coach and the he'd known him for months. Finding out about the flowers was enough shock for the evening.

I began to change my feelings about Maurice, now that I knew he was the one sending the flowers. I decided not to ignore him. He would have to wait until after Eileen's wedding if he should choose to wait that long for me.

"Sasha, when are you coming back to the ranch? I miss you. People ask about you all the time," Jennifer nearly choked when she spoke.

"Well, I don't know for sure. So many things have been going on lately. How is the Duchess?"

"She's doing fine. She was shod yesterday, and I think she likes her new shoes. G.R. took her out and worked her this morning. She looks great!"

"I guess she's happy to have new shoes. How are G.R. and Dora?"

"Well, Dora's on vacation again. This time she went to Florida. I don't know about those two."

"Are you coming to the wedding?"

"I think so. I'll be there."

Teddy was not thrilled about the color of his tuxedo. He wanted to wear a white tux, but I had explained numerous times that Eileen and J.T. decided on colors they wanted to use in their wedding. They had that right.

The dress rehearsal went without any major catastrophe. The pastor arrived late however, because he had attended a funeral and was held over for dinner afterward. There was a one hour delay, he unlocked the church when he arrived and rehearsal began.

Eileen had been talking to Barry, who was now out of recovery. He said he was going to attend the rehearsal. When he did not show up for the rehearsal Eileen did not get upset. She only reiterated what she had said before. That her grandfather, my father, was going to give her away. After the rehearsal, the wedding party met at Marlene's home in Ladera Heights for dinner.

Marlene prepared gumbo, steamed rice and blackberry cobbler for desert. I insisted on preparing a mixed green salad. I wanted to do something to help.

"Marlene, let me finish this salad. You go ahead and change your clothes. The kids should be on their way."

"No, no. I'm going to help. Pass me those radishes, Sasha. They're on the island, next to the cucumbers."

My girlfriend was so lucky. I looked at the kitchen. Brand new. If I had a husband who wanted me to live this way, he would get head every night.

"Okay, and I'll do the greens." I walked to the turquoise tiled work island in the recently remodeled kitchen. Redoing the kitchen was part of the deal Marlene made with Dennis before she went back to him. An no more business transactions requiring his presence after 8 p.m. during the week. No late night meetings at the house with Lou or anyone else. Marlene agreed to forgive all of Dennis' indiscretions. She would give up the Jamaican and he would forget unwise choices she had made . They began remodeling the kitchen a week before Marlene moved back and two months later it was finished.

"Did you see the trash compactor? Next to the dishwasher. Girl, I got all new appliances."

"I see. You sure made him pay..."

"He's not through paying, either. My bedroom is next. Did Paulette make it down yet? And what about Barry's sister Liz?"

"Yes, everyone is here. They got in this morning. Everyone is at the same hotel by the airport. And Paulette's not alone."

"Who's she with?"

"Her girlfriend."

"No kidding?"

"Yes, I'll see them tomorrow, before the wedding. Where are those kids?"

"I don't know. They're probably running a little late. Use the crystal salad bowl, the one at the end of the counter.

I walked around the work island. Then paused for a moment. Visualizing my tiny kitchen compared to this one. I gently shook my head and continued the long walk to the far end of the continuous kitchen counter. I picked up the heavy salad bowl and took it back to the work island. Together we finished assembling the leafy green salad.

"Well, Sasha. Everything is ready. We can relax now."

"Can we? You still have to get dressed. Where are the kids?"

Barry gave Eileen away at her wedding. She was surprised to see him in the foyer of the church. He first appeared after all the wedding party members had assembled outside the church. He slipped past everyone and went inside, as guests were being seated. Pam and I had just been escorted down the isle by Teddy. We joined Marlene, Dennis, Paulette and her friend, and Liz.

J.T. had been nervously pacing outside. The grass in the church lawn was flat from his walking on it. When he looked up and saw the decorated white Lincoln limousine turn the corner, he smiled with relief.

"She's here, she's here!" J.T. exclaimed with excitement.

"Don't you think it's time to go inside now?" my father said to J.T. He escorted him inside. "Eileen is going to be happy today."

Eileen was a radiant bride. And the simple phenomenon of her father walking her down the isle, his actually being there, made it a totally fulfilled day for her. Barry danced with his daughter so much that J.T. appeared to have to pry her away from him. When she danced with her father, she gazed up at his clear dark brown eyes, a smoother complexion and a neatly trimmed mustache. Barry wore a more confident smile, unlike the one Eileen had seen months before, when he went into rehab. He had just started a new job. He was so elated that he danced with just about every woman at the reception. Barry even did the two-step with Jennifer. What a pimp.

27

The honeymoon was delayed one week because of Eileen's graduation from U.C.L.A. It was four days after the wedding. Teddy's graduation from middle school was the day after that. I was exhausted from all the activities in June, but I searched for and found time to reflect on all the chaos that had just ensued. I decided that were it not for my family and close friends, I might not have accomplished my goals.

I thought about Maurice and was determined to get to know him better. He had not called for weeks. The last time I spoke to him he told me he would be out of town in June and could not attend Eileen's wedding. I was disappointed. He traveled with his kids to Seattle for two weeks, an annual trip they made, but he apologized for not being able to attend the wedding. Our last conversation occurred on the eve of the bridal shower for Eileen. At that time, I didn't tell him I knew about the roses.

He sent Eileen a box of chocolates in a gesture of kindness for no apparent reason which I though was sweet. It was late but I dialed his number anyway, hoping he was back from Seattle.

"Hello," he answered in a groggy voice.
"Maurice?" I sounded cheerful even though it was 11 p.m.
"Who's this?"
"This is Sasha."
"Oh, hello stranger."
"Hi. Were you sleeping?"
"No, but I was laying here, about to go to sleep. Let me call you tomorrow."
"All right. Goodnight."

Maurice called me early the following morning and invited me to lunch. I accepted the same day invitation because I had the free time. He suggested we go to a quaint little restaurant he knew of in Venice Beach. There was something very important he wanted to talk to me about. I hoped he wanted to talk about a commitment.

I wondered what could be so important that we could not talk about it over the phone. At first I thought maybe he wanted to confess about the flowers. Or possibly, he might be interested in having a permanent relationship with me. I wished for a happy chat.

During lunch, Maurice bit and chewed on his gourmet fish sandwich as if there were bones in the meat. He acted as though he was afraid to swallow the food. He ate just a few French fries and I wondered what his damn problem was. He was not that talkative and insisted he had probably eaten too much breakfast that morning.

Instead of returning to the Antelope Valley right away, I wanted to explore the canaled neighborhood in Venice. I thought it would be a nice diversion before going back to the desert. Maurice drove his car toward the beach then made a U-turn. I told him where to park his car on the street, next to the entrance of the one-of-a-kind district.

"There's the entrance. We can go in here." I pointed to the clearly marked sign. "Have you ever been here?"

"No, I haven't. But I've heard about it."

"Come on. Let's go for a walk." I was hoping the walk through the canals would bring some peace to Maurice. He seemed terribly troubled. And quiet.

We took the flight of steps down that took us onto the main walkway of the Grande Canal, casually strolling on the narrow concrete sidewalk, past custom built homes so close to the walkway the landscape vegetation could be touched by passers-by. Brilliant purple and red bougainvillea vines overwhelmed many low chain link fences that surrounded each property.

We soon approached an arched bridge, one of many, that made the other side of the main canal accessible to strollers. I stepped onto the bridge and when I was halfway across, I stopped, placing both palms on the wooden railing. I peered down at the surprisingly clear water as if concentrating on a particular thought, before making a silent wish.

"You know, this is really nice," Maurice said as he came closer to where I was standing. "I didn't know this place actually existed."

"Yeah, peaceful, isn't it? I don't know where this water comes from, but it's cleaner than the ocean water."

"It is pretty clean for canal water." Maurice said. "It's amazing."

We continued to walk across the bowed bridge, taking in the natural beauty all around us. Just as we stepped off the bridge we saw a mother duck and her goslings leap from the water's edge and into the canal. Maurice saw a vacant wooden park bench in the corner of someone's yard, sitting under a shady willow tree.

"Why don't we sit here and rest for a moment. We can talk."

At that moment I felt a flutter in the pit of my stomach. I followed him to the nearby bench and sat down.

"Sasha, I really feel bad."

"Yeah, I know. You don't look very well. What's bothering you?" I asked. He looked horrible. I was not prepared for the answer I was about to get.

"I'm still married. My wife moved back home."

28

"When I count to five, you will wake up. One...,two..., three...,four...,five."

I suddenly opened my eyes and rapidly moved my eyeballs from side to side. I closed my eyelids for a brief moment then reopened them.

"How do you feel?" my therapist asked. She looked forward to her retirement in a year.
"I feel like I've been dragged by a locomotive. But I couldn't possibly know what that's like. Why can't I move?" I tried to lift a finger but found it difficult. I remained in the frozen state I had been in for hours. With all of my strength I forced my body to cooperate and managed to sit up. The leather sofa I was laying on was moist with perspiration from my bare legs. The case on

the pillow my head rested on was soaked. "What did I tell you today?"

"Everything, I think. We had a great session. I think we're finally getting to the bottom of things."

"I hope so. But I can't remember anything I told you."

"Well, I was able to put you in a deep trance today. At one point I was going to bring you out of it but you kept on talking. As your psychologist, I thought it best just to let you continue."

"Oh."

"I think you deserve to be waited on hand and foot tonight. I'll tell your son how important that will be to you. See you next week?"

As we walked to the car, my therapist said "I never had a chance to catch Otis Redding…"

Teddy had been patient about the extra long therapy session. After waiting for hours, he was ready to do some long awaited shopping.

"Mom, can we go to the cycle shop now?"

"Yes, Teddy. Do you know which motor bike you're going to buy?"

"Yep. The one I showed you. I'm going to buy it today. And I'll even cook up some spaghetti tonight so you can rest."

"Thanks, hun. Mommy is exhausted."

Still drained from the session, all I had strength enough to do was climb the torturous staircase that took me upstairs to my bedroom. Before going to bed I wanted to take a bath. My clothes were still damp from the therapy session. I checked to see if I had any phone messages before running my bath water. And I did. There were two.

An extremely elated Pam screamed the most joyful and uplifting message into the phone I would ever hear in my life; 'That bitch left me some money, and I'm splitting it with you! I'm purchasing the deaf school and by the end of this year, I'm going to adopt that little girl I told you about. I'll be a mom! Sasha, we'll never have to worry about anything ever again! Call me.'

Through tears of joy, Sasha listened to the second message; 'Sasha, this is Cindy. I'm coming home. I'll be in Los Angeles next week. I'm ready to ride that Zebra with you now, if you still want to. Call me.'

CPSIA information can be obtained
at www.ICGtesting.com
Printed in the USA
FSOW02n2046080118
43200FS